TO HAVE AND TO HOLD

Solange didn't know what to make of Nicholas Campion. She watched his back as he retreated, the sound of his footsteps echoing in the emptiness of the large area around the pool.

With each step she felt more relieved. She didn't care how much he said he'd changed.

He still unnerved her, and probably always would.

He was almost at the exit when he turned suddenly. "The man you're going to marry?" he asked. "What's he like?"

Okay, Solange thought, *now this is getting creepy.*

She was about to tell him where to get off when she heard the door opening and glanced up at someone entering the pool area.

She was excited and relieved at once, if that's possible. *Rupert.*

"He's like that guy over there," she told Nicholas, pointing to Rupert.

She began running toward Rupert, who was coming to meet her with his arms open wide and a huge grin on his face.

Nicholas spun around, his brows creased in a frown. "Who?" He stopped short when he caught sight of the lip-lock Solange was in with the tall, dark-skinned stranger.

A scene like that did more to crush any illusions he might have had about a second chance with Solange than hours of her telling him there was no hope for them.

Other books by Janice Sims

Published by BET/Arabesque Books

To HAVE AND TO HOLD

Janice Sims

ARABESQUE
★BET
BOOKS™

BET Publications, LLC
http://www.bet.com
http://www.arabesquebooks.com

ARABESQUE BOOKS are published by

BET Publications, LLC
c/o BET BOOKS
One BET Plaza
1900 W Place NE
Washington, DC 20018-1211

All Kensington Titles, Imprints, and Distributed Lines are available at special quantity discounts for bulk purchases for sales
promotions, premiums, fund-raising, and educational or insti-
tutional use. Special book excerpts or customized printings can
also be created to fit specific needs. For details, write or phone
the office of the Kensington special sales manager: Kensington
Publishing Corp., 850 Third Avenue, New York, NY 10022,
attn: Special Sales Department, Phone: 1-800-221-2647.

First Printing: April 2004
10 9 8 7 6 5 4 3 2 1

Printed in the United States of America

Unbreakable . . .

Unending
Nuances
Becoming
Real
Existential
Allowing
Kisses
Arousing
Bliss
Loving
Eternally

Unbreakable

The Book of Counted Joys

To have and to hold,
from this day forward.
To love and to cherish,
till death do us part.

To make what's impossible
possible. To share the past,
present, and the future.
Making inroads in my heart.

To envision a future in which
the two of us become the three
of us, the four of us, the five of us.
How to get there? Love is a start.

The Book of Counted Joys

One

Solange DuPree closed her eyes and breathed deeply. There was a chill in the air. That was to be expected when you were wearing a paper gown, your feet were in stirrups, and a male gynecologist was probing your nether regions. The room had to be cold, his hands colder, and the instruments he was using felt like they'd just come out of the freezer.

Okay, maybe she was exaggerating a little. Darrell Van Ness, ob-gyn, was one of the kindest brothers she'd ever met. He looked like a movie star, had a voice like Barry White's and the demeanor of St. Francis of Assisi. She couldn't fault the doctor for the mood she was in. That could only be attributed to her fears.

"I don't detect anything out of the ordinary," Darrell said after giving her a routine pelvic examination. "I assume this is the first time you've had the bleeding?"

"No," Solange answered. "This is the third month."

"And you're just mentioning it to me?" Darrell was irritated. He always was whenever she failed to inform him of any changes to her health. The doctor-patient relationship is a partnership, he'd often told her. "Solange, you know better than most women that unusual bleeding can signal problems," he said, sighing. "Because of your underdeveloped ovaries, you've never had a normal period, just spotting every now and then. So, tell me, how long did the bleeding last the previous two months?"

"Five days," Solange replied with a hint of regret at not telling him before now.

"That's not an unusual length of time. How about pain?"

"Minor cramping. Nothing intolerable," she replied.

"Good, good. It doesn't sound like endometriosis." Darrell moved to the left and picked up an endoscope. It was a flexible tubelike instrument with a camera inside.

A light on the tip allowed him to see inside his patients' bodies.

Solange squinted at the endoscope in Darrell's hand. "No sonogram today, huh?"

"No," Darrell said. "The endoscope will let me see everything in living color."

He gestured to the computer monitor with a nod of his head. "You can watch my progress on the screen. Try not to tense up."

Solange laughed. "Don't I get dinner and a movie before you do that to me?"

Darrell's assistant, a young nurse who hadn't been with his office long, gasped, her cheeks turning pink with embarrassment.

"Remember, we have someone new with us today," Darrell said, barely able to contain a guffaw. "Yolanda isn't used to your unique brand of humor."

"Who's joking?" Solange said. "I deserve a lobster dinner, and later some salsa dancing at a club I know in South Beach. That's the least you can do, doctor." Yolanda laughed along with them this time.

Solange relaxed, and Darrell gently slipped the flexible probe into place.

"Hmm," he said contemplatively after a minute or so.

"Hmm, good, or hmm, bad?" Solange asked. Her eyes were trained on the monitor.

"This is interesting," Darrell commented. "Your ovaries look plumper than usual."

"They still look like two wrinkly walnuts to me," Solange disagreed.

"That's normal," Darrell said. "Everybody's look wrinkly. The difference is, yours were shrunken before. Now they look healthy. The color's good, too. Those babies seem to be on the job."

"On the job?" Solange asked, hoping Darrell would just spell it out for her. Was she dying of some rare form of cancer? Why had she, at age thirty-five, suddenly gotten her period?

"Have you ever heard of spontaneous healing?" Darrell asked. His tone had suddenly turned reflective. "Be perfectly still. I'm going to remove the endoscope."

Solange heard a slight sucking sound when the probe came out.

She sighed, glad to have the exam over with. "Spontaneous healing? Do you mean my body just decided to repair something that's been wrong with it for years? As in, I now have brand-new ovaries?"

"Not new ovaries. You still have the same ovaries. They've become viable, that's all; which means, if I'm not mistaken, you can get pregnant just like any other healthy woman."

Darrell helped Solange remove her feet from the stirrups. She sat up and faced him. Darrell's dark brown eyes were sparkling with delight. He had been her doctor for the past ten years. He never thought he'd be giving her this kind of good news. He had sympathized with her, had agonized over her case, and had burned the midnight oil trying to come up with a solution to her sterility. Now, for this to happen—he felt like he was in the presence of a miracle!

Solange was stunned.

While Darrell stood gazing at her, probably waiting for her to say something, she was searching her memory, counting the months since she'd touched the fertility goddess the old African woman had given her in Burundi more than a year and a half ago. "Do not touch the goddess if it isn't your desire to bear a child," the woman had warned her. Then, she'd died the very night she'd entrusted Solange with the wooden idol, which had further spooked her.

Solange wasn't superstitious. But for some reason, she heeded the woman's warning and had not touched the little wooden fertility goddess. Not until she'd met Rupert. She wondered why she'd chosen that time to hold the goddess in her arms and dare it to work its magic. Had something been directing her actions? Gently leading her to this moment? Did she really believe in fate?

She wasn't prepared to put her faith in a wooden fertility goddess hand carved by a long-dead African artisan. There was no way the goddess had healed her!

She hadn't noticed she was laughing until Darrell asked, "What's so funny?"

Solange had tears in her eyes. "Doctor, you don't want to know."

"Of course, I do. Is it, perhaps, the hysterical laughter of someone who is relieved that she may someday have the child she's wanted for years?"

"No, it's the hysterical laughter of someone who thinks she might have come in contact with the supernatural." Solange discreetly glanced in Yolanda's direction.

"Yolanda, how about taking Solange's chart to the front desk for me? Tell them to charge her double."

Yolanda took the chart from him. "Sure, Dr. Van Ness."

"I was just joking about the double charge," Darrell said to her as she retreated.

"I know, doctor, you meant triple," said Yolanda as she pulled the door closed.

Darrell laughed. "She's gonna fit in nicely around here." Then he turned to Solange.

"Okay, tell me everything. What's on that brilliant mind of yours?"

Solange told him about the goddess: how the old woman had given it to her, and how convincing the woman's spiel about not touching it had been.

"But you touched it anyway," Darrell said, and then hummed the tune to *The Twilight Zone*. He laughed. "I'll buy it from you. If it works for everyone who touches it, I'll be the most famous fertility specialist in the state, the country, the entire world!" He had a crazed look in his eyes, as if he'd suddenly been possessed with the desire to rule the world—or at least the baby-making part of it.

He took her by the shoulders, shaking her. "Sell it to me, Solange!"

Solange's brown eyes stretched. She'd never seen Darrell so excited. Then, he threw his head back and laughed heartily and deeply, infusing her with the desire to join in. When he lowered his head and met her gaze, she saw that he had been pulling her leg all along, the big dope!

Calmer now, he said, "My dear Solange, this has nothing to do with the supernatural. Science doesn't know enough about the human body. That's all. Other physicians have told me stories similar to yours. I've read about spontaneous healing in countless medical journals, but this is the first time I've ever been lucky enough to witness it firsthand. I'm a Christian; therefore I'm going to call it a miracle. But, I assure you, your wooden fertility goddess had nothing to do with it."

Solange was so relieved to hear exactly what she was thinking from someone else, someone she trusted implicitly, that she threw her arms around the six-foot-one Dr. Van Ness and hugged him firmly.

"Now, go home and start working on that baby."

Solange smiled up at him. "That may prove difficult, with Rupert in London."

As Solange drove her late-model white Mustang across town, sunglasses on and with the air-conditioning blasting cool air in her warm face, she was still tingling from hearing the good news. She had to tell somebody. But who first? Her mother, Marie?

Marie would be ecstatic, of course. They were closer today than they had ever been. Marie had had to live through a cancer scare before she'd loosened up and confided in her daughter about the reason why she'd been distant toward her all her life.

Solange still had a hard time wrapping her mind around her mother being a killer. But a member of the Tonton Macoute, ousted Haitian dictator Francois Duvalier's secret police, had murdered Marie's mother and was caught red-handed by a then-teenage Marie. He certainly had had it coming to him.

Having that burden off her chest had psychologically freed Marie. And after the biopsy on her breast proved that the lump was benign, she considered herself twice blessed. She began making up for lost time where Solange was concerned.

A successful interior decorator in the greater Miami area, Marie had Solange's entire bungalow redone as a thirty-fifth birthday present. Then she suggested taking

Solange on a shopping spree for new clothes. Solange, however, refused to allow her mother to spend any more money on her. "I feel like you're trying to buy my love when you already have it. I've always loved you, Maman, I just never understood you. Now, I love you and I understand you."

Solange briefly glanced at her reflection in the rearview mirror. It would take a truckload of dynamite to blast that grin off her face.

Everything was falling into place.

The five-carat diamond on her ring finger was evidence of Rupert Giles's love for her, and her love for him. She had put the poor man off for six months before finally accepting his proposal, citing the need for him to be certain he wanted to spend the rest of his life with a woman who could never give him children. She loved him enough to give him up if he wasn't sure of his feelings. She loved herself enough not to want to be in a one-sided marriage. And she knew she loved him with all her heart. It was easy to love a man who was willing to bare his soul to you, to hell with the consequences. She had not been as forthcoming about her weaknesses in the beginning, though. It had taken almost losing him before she'd confessed that she was incapable of conceiving a child.

Rupert told her it didn't matter. They were going to adopt Desta, the Ethiopian orphan they'd both fallen in love with on their adventure in northeastern Africa. If they wanted more children, there were plenty of black children who needed good homes. They could adopt a house full.

Still, she'd insisted on a six-month moratorium on marriage proposals. During that time, Solange had hired an attorney to get started on Desta's adoption. She'd been told that the process could take a year or more. Desta was devastated. She had not been looking

forward to spending a year in another orphanage.
However, through the connections of Rupert's father,
millionaire businessman Theophilus Gault, they'd been
able to secure a place for Desta in a well-run orphanage
in Addis Ababa. She and Solange communicated nearly
every day now by e-mail, and once a week they spoke
over the telephone.

As for Rupert, he was liable to surprise her at any time.
His job as an insurance investigator for a prestigious
firm, well known for insuring the valuables of the world's
wealthiest people, allowed him to pick and choose his
cases. He'd simply begun requesting cases that would
bring him to the United States more often.

Last month, he'd shown up at her office at the University
of Miami, where she was a professor of archaeology,
with a large bouquet of red roses in one hand and a gift
box under his other arm. She'd opened the box to see it
contained a diaphanous negligee he'd picked up in a
shop in Cairo. She took the afternoon off from work, and
it wasn't until the next morning that they emerged from
her bedroom.

Such was life with her British guy.

Could life get any better? Obviously, it could.

They'd both been prepared to never welcome children
who looked like them into their lives. As it turned out,
they'd now been given a gift. Being a pragmatist, Solange
wondered what the ramifications of such a gift would
be. Rupert loved her now, but what if that love had been
born out of sympathy for her more than genuine emo-
tion? Their meeting and their courtship had been one
adventure after another. Danger and intrigue followed
them at every turn. How would Rupert, who had lived a
hectic, fast-paced lifestyle for most of his adult years, adjust to being a husband and an instant father to Desta?
All of these things ran through Solange's mind.

Of the two of them, Solange was the more settled. She'd lived in the same house for nearly ten years, ever since her move to Miami from Key West, her hometown. In contrast, Rupert traveled extensively. He felt perfectly at home anywhere in the world.

Then, too, there was his background as a former spy for the British government. He had not been able to fill her in on every detail of his life as an agent, but to Solange, that wasn't the point. She didn't want the details. All she wanted was the assurance that Rupert truly meant it when he'd told her he was finished with that part of his past.

She sighed as she cruised down Ponce de Leon Boulevard in her Mustang, heading to Stanford Drive. She had a class to teach in half an hour. Unable to resist, she picked up the cell phone, and said, "Gaea."

She had to tell someone, and her lifelong best friend was the safest person she could talk to. Should Darrell be mistaken—God knows she hoped he wasn't—about her condition, she didn't want to break the news to everyone in her life, and then months later not be able to conceive. No, the thing to do was keep the news under wraps for a while longer. Of course telling Gaea didn't count. Gaea Maxwell Cavanaugh had seen her through every crisis since they were both knobby-kneed seven-year-olds.

The phone rang three times. "Hi, Pudge. What's up, girl?" Gaea said cheerfully.

"I hope I didn't catch you in the middle of something."

There was a time difference between them. Gaea was a marine biologist working on an undersea station in French Polynesia. After the station was built, it would house a crew of twenty scientists, who would be able to study the ocean more thoroughly than ever before, she'd told Solange. A fully equipped laboratory and various submersibles, capable of diving to the ocean floor without those on board having to suffer from the bends or decompression sickness, would be at their disposal.

Since Gaea would be on board the research vessel, *Poseidon,* for several months, she'd brought along her four-year-old son, Micah Jr., called Mikey by everyone. Her husband, Micah, a corporate attorney, was at home in New York City. He visited every chance he got.

"I just got into bed," Gaea said. "Mikey's already asleep."

"How is he coping out there, with no other children to play with?"

"Oh, we go to Bora Bora every weekend. He's made friends with some very sweet Polynesian children. This place is so beautiful, Pudge. You've got to come for a visit."

"You know I avoid the ocean. I'll stick to the pool, thank you," Solange said.

"Yeah, that's why you went into a field where you dig in the earth, and I went into a field where I have to spend most of my time in the sea. But you don't have to come onto the *Poseidon* if you don't want to. I'll get you a great hotel room. Bora Bora is known for catering to tourists. Hey, how is that fine man of yours?"

"He's doing well. Working in London. I miss him like crazy."

"Have you two set a date yet?"

"No."

"What are you waiting for?"

Solange paused. "I'm afraid as soon as we set a date, my mother will turn into the mother of the bride from hell and try to monopolize the situation. You should have seen her when I allowed her to redo my house. She was General Patton ordering the troops. She made a big, brawny carpenter cry."

Gaea laughed. "Mama Marie can be forceful when she wants to be."

"The woman is a menace," Solange corrected her. "I have to admit, though, she is easier to live with since we had that long talk."

Gaea sighed on her end. Though the ship was very stable, she could hear the lapping of the water on the sides. It had a calming effect on her. "I'm so glad that you two are appreciating each other more these days."

In Miami, Solange stopped the Mustang at a traffic light. A young, handsome Cubano was behind the wheel of a black Jaguar in the left lane. He flashed white teeth at her.

Solange smiled back, then returned her attention to her conversation with Gaea. "I'm glad, too. Listen, the reason I phoned is because I've got to tell someone my news before I burst. I've just returned from an appointment with my gynecologist. He says it looks as if my ovaries have healed themselves!"

"What!" Gaea could not contain her excitement. "Say again . . ."

"He says it looks like I will be able to conceive a child after all!"

Gaea stifled a scream, mindful of her sleeping son a few feet away. "Oh, Pudge, I'm so happy for you and Rupert. Desta, too. From what you told me about her it sounds like she misses her older brother, Tesfaye, a lot. Now, she can be the big sister."

Solange hadn't thought about how the possibility of having a child might affect Desta. Desta might feel threatened by another child. Perhaps she would think that since the child would be Solange and Rupert's natural child, they would love him or her more than they could ever love her. "You've given me food for thought," Solange told Gaea. "What if Desta believes there won't be enough love to go around?"

"There you go, worrying ahead of time," Gaea

complained. "Have you ever thought that maybe Desta would love to have a brother or a sister? Someone she can be a role model for? Someone she can be close to besides you and Rupert? I can't tell you how many times I wished I had a brother or a sister when I was growing up," Gaea, who had been an only child, said.

"Me, too," Solange agreed with a contented sigh. She noticed the guy in the black Jaguar was keeping pace with her, still giving her that sparkling grin at every opportunity.

They stopped at another traffic light at a busy intersection where there was an eatery on every corner. She saw him point at a popular bistro, then give her a questioning look.

"Oh, Lord," she said into the cellular phone. "Some guy is trying to pick me up, and I'm driving down Ponce de Leon Boulevard."

"Show him your ring," Gaea suggested.

Solange did.

The guy shrugged, obviously disappointed. The light changed to green, and he sped off. Apparently he'd been driving slowly just to flirt with her.

"That did the trick," Solange said.

Gaea laughed. "Good. Now, when are you going to tell Rupert the good news?"

"Whenever I see him again. I don't want to tell him over the phone."

"I wouldn't want to tell Micah something that important over the phone, either. So, when are you going to see him again, and what are you two going to do about the fact that he lives in London and you live in Miami? I've heard of bicoastal marriages, but that's ridiculous!"

"I'll move to London if I have to," Solange said. "And he said he should be back in town some time next month.

Most of the time he simply turns up unexpectedly. His sudden appearances keep me on my toes."

"You're loving your courtship period," Gaea said. She could tell by the sound of Solange's voice when her best friend was truly happy. Rupert Giles made Solange a very happy girl.

"I'm loving it," Solange confirmed, grinning.

"You deserve all the happiness life can throw at you. Enjoy yourself," Gaea said. "Don't take anything for granted."

"I won't," Solange promised. Then, "Goodbye. Love you much."

"Love you, too," Gaea said. "Set the date for the wedding so that I can rearrange my schedule. I'm not going to miss your big day."

"You'd better not. I was there crying my eyes out on yours."

"Nothing could keep me away," Gaea assured her. "Later, Pudge."

They rang off and Solange hung up the phone, then returned both hands to the steering wheel. She glanced at her reflection in the rearview mirror. The grin hadn't lessened one iota. "Life has something really good in store for you, girl," she told herself.

Rupert knew he wasn't being paranoid. Although in his former line of work, it paid to be a little paranoid. No, he had seen Jason Thorne, his old partner. Jason was unmistakable with his shock of white-blond hair; his five-eleven frame, which was extremely fit and muscular; and his blue eyes, which didn't reveal his emotions unless they were perusing a beautiful woman. Then they could be deceptively open and welcoming. Women had always found Jason terribly appealing. However, they'd invariably fared badly in his hands. Jason was a company man, and nothing took precedence over the company.

That's why he and Rupert hadn't spoken since Rupert walked away from the agency more than five years ago. Which was enough of a reason for Rupert to be on his guard.

What was an agent doing tailing him along a busy London street?

It was a little after eight P.M., and Rupert had just left a posh restaurant where he'd had dinner with his boss. It was sort of a farewell because Rupert had resigned from the agency. He hadn't even told Solange about his decision. He wanted to surprise her. He had his bags packed. He'd sold his flat. Tomorrow morning he was flying to Miami, and by tomorrow night he hoped to be in bed with the woman he loved.

It hadn't been hard for him to say goodbye to his life in London. Not when Solange was a world away in Miami. He could not bear to be away from her any longer. That had been reason enough. Rupert was the sort of man who put a greater value on people than on material things. He was confident he could work at anything and be successful at it. Due to his military background, and his training in the martial arts and in security, he could get on board any major security firm in the world and swiftly rise within the ranks. If he wanted to, he could open his own security firm. Or simply live off of his assets, which were substantial. What mattered most to him now was Solange. He was forty, and he'd waited a lifetime for a woman like her to fall into his arms, and he wasn't going to lose her over anything as trivial as being separated by several countries. He would be perfectly happy in Miami as long as she was there with him.

Rupert could have hailed a cab. There were plenty on the street. He preferred to walk tonight. It was a lovely

April evening. The air was bracing. Besides, he wanted to find out how long Thorne would tail him without making contact. Perhaps the agency had sent Thorne with a message for him. He couldn't see Thorne doing this on his own. Rupert hoped they weren't going to try to press him into service again. He couldn't imagine why they would need him. There were plenty of young agents who were eager to serve their country, no matter the nature of the orders they would have to follow. Although the world climate was slowly changing with respect to world leaders invading less advanced countries without sufficient cause, there would always be work for those who didn't have consciences. Men and women like Jason Thorne.

Another reason, Rupert thought, Jason Thorne could be following him was to carry out orders to eliminate him. Perhaps the company had come to the conclusion that he was a security risk after five years of being in the private sector. In that case, he might have to fight for his life tonight, a notion that he found surprisingly inviting.

He glanced down at his wing tips. He'd recently bought them at James Taylor & Son on 4 Paddington Street, a store that has been making quality shoes since 1857. Too bad they were about to get scuffed. Rupert prided himself on his appearance. He felt clothes were a extension of the man, and one had to put one's best foot forward at all times. Tonight his six-foot-four-inch frame was clothed in a dark gray double-breasted Armani suit. Instead of a button-down dress shirt and a tie, he wore a black polo shirt underneath.

Seeing the lighted sign of a popular pub ahead, Rupert decided to step inside and see if Thorne would take the bait. The familiar sounds of voices raised in lively conversation and contemporary rock music coming over the sound system welcomed him. The smell of robust ale assailed his nostrils, along with cigarette smoke. Unlike many American bars, smoking was not banned in most British bars. Rupert seriously doubted that the pubs would have many customers left if the opposite were the case. He didn't smoke, but most of his friends and acquaintances did. He strode up to the counter and sat down.

The bartender, a tall, gangly fellow sporting a blond buzz cut and an earring in his nose, eyed him with a singular lack of enthusiasm. After all, the product he was selling was a perennial favorite that required very little salesmanship to move off the shelves.

"What'll it be, mate?"

"Ale," Rupert said.

From the corner of his eye, Rupert spotted Thorne purposefully moving toward him.

Thorne sat down on his right. "Guinness," he told the bartender.

Rupert slowly turned his head to look at Thorne. "Where'd you get that scar?"

Thorne smiled and trailed his index finger along the raised scar that ran the length of his left cheek. "The girlfriend of a drug dealer, who slept with a switchblade under her pillow, didn't like being awakened in the middle of the night. She was quick as lightning and twice as deadly. We recruited her after we put her boyfriend in prison."

The bartender came with their drinks.

After he'd gone, Rupert said, "What do you want?"

Thorne took a swig of his beer, closed his eyes, savoring it before answering. "I hear congratulations are in order."

"For?"

"Your upcoming nuptials, of course."

Rupert's expression showed no surprise. He knew the agency had been keeping tabs on him. How else would they know if he'd kept his oath to never divulge anything he'd ever done while in Her Majesty's Secret Service?

"Thank you, I'm sure," he said coolly.

"She's quite a looker, your archaeology professor," Thorne said nonchalantly. He went into his inside coat pocket and removed a snapshot. Handing it to Rupert, he said, "And she swims like a fish."

Rupert glanced down at the photograph. It was of Solange at the pool on the campus of the University of Miami where she did laps practically every day. Wearing a black tank suit, she was standing near the pool's edge in conversation with another woman whom Rupert didn't recognize, probably one of her colleagues.

Rupert put the photo in his inside jacket pocket. "Thank you. I'll treasure this."

Thorne laughed. "There're plenty more where that came from. Listen, Giles, they've got me acting like an errand boy. I'm supposed to ask you to do one last job for us. Upon the conclusion of this assignment, we'll generously compensate you and take all eyes off of you and your little family. Desta is such a sweet child, overcoming her life as a pickpocket on the streets of Addis Ababa the way she has and snagging parents such as Solange and yourself. I'm sure you don't want anything to happen to her. She's come so far!"

Rupert bit the inside of his lower lip to keep from smashing Thorne's face in. His outward appearance remained calm and collected. Tasting blood, he said evenly, "I've been out of service for five years. Why would they need to bring me back in?"

"I'm sure you remember Aziz?"

"Who is rotting in a Senegalese prison," Rupert said, recalling the vicious general who had ordered the murders of nearly twenty thousand of his countrymen before he had been brought down.

"Someone helped him escape forty-eight hours ago. We don't know where he is. Since you infiltrated his

Janice Sims

inner circle and were never identified as an agent, we think you would be the man for the job. We're watching those who were closest to him before he went to prison. Should he contact any of them, we'll know it right away."

"He would be a fool to remain in Senegal once he's free. If they could bust him out of prison, they would also have resources to spirit him out of the country. He could be anywhere by now."

"This is what we think," Thorne said. "Aziz's wife, Ashante, divorced him and remarried after he was jailed. Aziz was wild about her, and he was devastated when she divorced him. Ashante's new husband is a wealthy businessman from across the border in Mauritania. We think Aziz will try to exact some form of revenge on Ashante for her disloyalty."

"Then why don't you stake out her place of residence in Mauritania and pick him up when he shows his face? Why is he so important to the agency, anyway? He's small time compared to the terrorists on the world scene nowadays. He's a petty ex-dictator."

"With connections to Obed Bedele."

Now Thorne was speaking in a language Rupert understood. Obed Bedele was behind the bombings of several British government offices that had resulted in the deaths of sixty-seven people. The agency wanted him as badly as President Bush wanted Saddam Hussein. Bedele wasn't wanted solely in Britain, though. There were warrants out on him in at least six other countries.

"Then you think Bedele is behind Aziz's escape from prison," Rupert concluded.

"Who else would be interested enough in him, plus have the means to bring it about?" Thorne asked reasonably. He paused, assessing Rupert. "Do I detect some of that old spark, Giles? Do you miss the action?"

"Hell, no," said Rupert. "I don't miss anything about your world, Thorne."

"But you'll do it," Thorne guessed.

"What kind of assurances do I have that the agency will keep its end of the bargain if I do accept?" Rupert wanted to know. "That this will be a one-time thing?"

"You've kept your word over the past five years, so the agency hasn't seen fit to terminate you. If we didn't think you were uniquely suited for this job, we wouldn't have come to you. I was told to make subtle threats concerning the safety of Solange and Desta, but the agency would not actually carry them out even if you refused, Giles. This is simply an opportunity for you to do us a favor. A favor for which we would be grateful. There are worse things to have on your side than a grateful intelligence agency."

Rupert drank some of his ale, thinking.

Thorne drank, too, his steely blue eyes squinting in amusement. Putting down his mug, he said, "I was completely surprised when you quit the agency, Giles. You were one of the best. You seemed to relish each assignment. Took pleasure in bringing down the bad guys."

"It was when the line began to blur that I lost my taste for intrigue," Rupert said.

Thorne's amused look faded. "Yes, well, that comes with the territory. We just have to wear blinders and follow orders. That's the only way to survive."

Rupert thought it best to change the subject. No use getting into an argument about ethics with Thorne. "I want to sleep on it. How do I contact you if I should decide to go through with it?"

"You don't need to contact me," Thorne said. "Just show up at Heathrow tomorrow morning, and someone will be waiting for you with your travel packet."

Two

Solange was wiping down the blackboard in her auditorium-sized classroom when she heard someone clear his throat. She paused midstroke with the eraser in her hand and turned to peer in the direction of the main entrance. Solange thought the stranger standing in the open doorway looked familiar.

He was tall, dark skinned, and in his late thirties. He wore a light-colored suit. His natural black hair was twisted into fledgling dreadlocks, only about two inches in length. He was smiling at her with a hopeful expression on his good-looking face.

"May I help you?" Solange asked, figuring he must be in the wrong place or had shown up at the wrong time. Other instructors held their classes in this room. He laughed. When he did, his golden-brown eyes lit up his dark brown face. "That's not the first response I expected from you after three years. But I'll take it." His tone was contrite, with a hint of laughter beneath the surface.

Upon recognizing his voice, Solange dropped the eraser on her foot. A mini cloud of chalk dust rose. Her mind racing, she bent and picked up the eraser. Looking at him, she marveled at the change in him. Gone was the ultraconservative manner of dress, which consisted of a very short haircut, rimless glasses, and the three-piece suits he preferred. Now his jacket hung open, revealing a turquoise T-shirt underneath. His slacks were slightly wrinkled, and he wore sandals.

Solange was certain she'd never seen him in sandals the entire time they'd dated.

"What, what do you want?" she managed to say after her throat opened enough for her to squeeze words out. She didn't care if she sounded unhappy to see him.

She *was* unhappy to see him! What did he expect after the way he'd treated her?

He watched her from across the room, not moving closer for fear she'd bolt. She looked ready to. How could he blame her? There was a time when she would have flung herself into his open arms, but not anymore. Now, he was someone to be feared, someone under suspicion. He took a deep breath, preparing to tell her why he was there.

But first, he simply wanted to take her in a moment longer.

Her silky black hair was cut shorter than he remembered. She wore it in a layered style that accentuated her lovely medium-brown face. Her dark chocolate-hued eyes held mistrust in their depths. Still, he took his time. He would satisfy her curiosity soon enough.

He lowered his eyes to her full mouth. How he'd missed those lips. He could admit it now. In fact, he'd been admitting it for months. He'd loved this woman with all his being. Then why had he turned into someone he didn't know when she'd made her confession? It was the sort of thing that should have brought them closer. She couldn't conceive. Now he knew that wasn't the end of the world. But then, he'd been selfish and had worried about what others would think when they found out. Would he be deemed less of a man if he couldn't get his wife pregnant? Did it make her less of woman? Now, he knew the answer was no. But then, all he saw was betrayal.

He felt he'd wasted his time dating her when at the end of their courtship there would be no marriage and no children. The natural order of things. Whose natural order of things?

If he had been stronger, they would be married now. Perhaps they would have adopted a child. There were thousands of children who needed good homes.

Solange pursed her lips in consternation. "If you don't say something soon, I'm leaving," she said. "I don't care if you did move out of state, the restraining order is still in effect."

"My mother died the day before yesterday. I came back to say goodbye to her."

Solange breathed in and exhaled. His mother had always been kind to her. She met his intense gaze. "I'm sorry about your mother. She was a nice lady."

"Much nicer than her only son," Nicholas Campion said with regret. He smiled sadly. "I won't keep you, Solange. I simply wanted to apologize for my behavior three years ago. I was cruel. I'm appalled by how cruel I was. When I look back on it, I think I must have lost my mind. I didn't recognize the man I became when you told me you couldn't marry me, that you were afraid my abusive behavior would only get worse after marriage."

He sighed. "And, in retrospect, you were probably right. I was so full of myself, I never considered your feelings. I didn't respect you, especially after you told me you were infertile. I saw you as inferior. I thought you should be grateful to have a man who still wanted to marry you after that revelation, when the opposite was true: I didn't deserve you. I railed at you for keeping secrets. Well, I had a secret of my own. I was an alcoholic." He smiled again when he saw the surprised expression on her face.

"I know you didn't know. I successfully hid it from

everybody in my life. I couldn't hide it from myself, even though I tried my best." He laughed. "I've been sober for eight months. I have a lifetime membership in AA. As you probably know, one of the things we're advised to do is to apologize to the people we've hurt with our drinking. You were at the top of my list. So here I am. I know it's hard for you to accept that I'm sincere, but I am. I wish I could take back the words I said to you, words meant to demean and make you feel like nothing when, inside, I was the one who felt like nothing. I wish I could take back my mean and spiteful actions. But I know I can't erase any of it from your memory."

Solange stood there, gazing at him, with her mouth slightly agape. She would have laughed if someone had told her yesterday that Nicholas Campion would be asking her to forgive him before day's end. She never would have imagined the arrogant, mean-spirited man who had once made her life a living hell could change. Nor would she ever have thought that some part of her would actually want to grant his request.

Mostly, she remained unconvinced of his miraculous metamorphosis. She could not chance leaving herself open to being hurt by him again. With no visible crack in her resolve, she eyed him. "What you say is all well and good, Nicholas. But a drinking problem doesn't excuse your behavior. You reveled in your cruelty. You took every opportunity to hurt me, no, to punish me for my body's failings. I will never be able to forget what you put me through. It affected my self-esteem, even though I was fully aware of what you were trying to do to me. That's the insidious thing about verbal abuse: you can tear down with words without even lifting a finger.

"So, don't ask me for forgiveness. It will be a long time before I can forgive you, if ever!"

A male student who'd heard their raised voices stuck

his head in the classroom. "Hey, Professor DuPree. How is it going?"

"Hello, Charlie," Solange said, smiling at him. "Everything's great. How're you?"

Smiling at Solange, then checking out Nicholas, Charlie said, "Everything's cool. Later, Professor DuPree."

He sauntered on down the corridor.

Nicholas stepped further into the room and closed the door behind him. "I see you're still much loved around here. Go ahead, Solange. You deserve your say."

Realizing she was still clutching the eraser in her right hand, Solange sat it on the narrow shelf at the base of the blackboard and brushed the palms of her hands together.

Meeting Nicholas's eyes, she said, "Yes, I do deserve my say. For three years I've wondered what I'd say to you if I ever saw you again. Well, here it is. You didn't break me, Nicholas. Your actions only made me stronger. No, I may never have a child, but that doesn't make me any less valuable as a human being than anyone else.

"I know you were angry when I broke up with you, but there was no way I was going to marry a man who didn't cherish me. And you proved time and time again that you did not! Is it any wonder that I wanted to get as far away from you as I possibly could?"

Nicholas exhaled slowly. His eyes narrowed. "You have every right to hate me, Solange. But know this. I loved you as much as I could love any woman back then. Admittedly, it was a twisted kind of love. If I'd continued on the path I was on, and you had married me, I would have tried to control every aspect of your life. I know that about myself now. I felt out of control; therefore, I wanted to exact control somewhere in my life. After counseling, I realize that's the main desire of men who abuse the women in their lives. It's all about control. You were wise to leave me when you did."

Solange nervously shifted her weight from one side to the other. The azure summer skirt suit she was wearing suddenly felt confining. She removed the jacket, revealing a white shell underneath, and laid it on the back of a nearby aisle seat. She bent and pushed the seat down, and sat.

Nicholas, feeling uncomfortable standing above her, followed suit, only he sat down several seats over. Solange crossed her legs, trying to look relaxed even though she was far from it.

"What brought you to your epiphany?" she asked, her voice low but still quite audible in the cavernous room where the acoustics were superb. Her brown eyes bore into his.

Solange felt she was learning something about the human spirit here. If Nicholas Campion could change, then there was hope for anyone.

"You really want to know?" Nicholas asked. He hadn't detected any sarcasm in her tone, but had to make certain she wasn't asking just to hear more evidence of how much of a mess he'd made of his life after she'd thrown him out. He had his pride.

"Yes, I really want to know," Solange said, sincerely.

"Okay," Nicholas began with a sigh of resignation. "About a year ago I woke up in the bed of a coed who was failing my class with a hangover the size of Texas. Wouldn't you know, her boyfriend showed up at that very moment to try to kill me with a baseball bat? We fought, destroying much of the cheap furniture in the place. The police were called, and I wound up in the drunk tank for twenty-four hours. When my lawyer finally came to see me he gave me two options: clean up my act, or never work in my field again. I spent three months at a substance abuse center in Arizona. After that, I started going to AA every week. Every day is a struggle. You never lose the taste for the stuff. Never. You always believe that just one drink will dispel the misery in your heart. Make it all better. But it's a farce. Nothing on earth can make you happy if you haven't already made up your mind to be happy."

They sat for several minutes, during which time neither of them spoke. They simply digested what had been said. Then, Solange said, "What do you really want from me, Nicholas?"

She was stunned to see that Nicholas's face was wet with tears when he looked up at her again. "I don't believe I deserve to ask you for anything, Solange. Not your forgiveness, nor your friendship. It's too much to ask."

It was at that point in their conversation that Solange realized she was too happy in her present relationship with Rupert to harbor any ill feelings for Nicholas. She had to let go of all of that to move forward. Hating Nicholas only diminished her. Hating him did him no physical harm. However, it was a poison that might taint her life if she didn't purge it from her system. She couldn't risk it one day raising its ugly head and being directed at either Rupert or an innocent, unsuspecting Desta, whose life it now was Solange's honor to protect at all costs.

"Go and be happy, Nicholas," she said. "I'm in love. I'm in love with a man who would lay down his life for me, and I for him. I'm about to become the mother of a child who, at thirteen years old, already knows what matters most in life. I have no room for hatred in my life anymore. I forgive you."

Nicholas hadn't known how her words of forgiveness would affect him. He had not expected to hear them, so now, as the tears flowed freely and his bottom lip trembled uncontrollably, he did not know what to do with the emotions. Solange got up and went to her desk, where she kept a box of Kleenex. She pulled several from the box and handed them to him.

"I'm sorry," Nicholas said. "I haven't cried since my first night in rehab, and then it was because I was feeling sorry for myself." He met her eyes. "This time it's out of sheer relief. Thank you, Solange." He slowly backed away, blowing his nose and drying his eyes as he did so. "I wish you all kinds of happiness."

Solange didn't say a word. She stood and watched him as he turned and left the room.

When he was gone, she sat back down. The room was so quiet she imagined she could hear the blood pumping through the ventricles of her heart. This was one of those moments you didn't want to miss in life, a defining moment when you never knew what you would do until the time came. She had not known she would be able to forgive Nicholas Campion. She had just known it was the only course of action she felt good about taking.

Her cell phone rang, jolting her out of her introspective mood. She rose and went into the desk, where she kept her purse. Hurrying so as not to miss the call, she grabbed the ringing phone and flipped it open. "Hello, Solange here."

"Darling, I'm at Heathrow, on my way to Mauritania. But after that, I'll be coming home to you," said Rupert's deep British-accented voice.

As always, Solange felt butterflies flutter in the pit of her stomach at the sound of his voice. Her heartbeat instantly quickened. "Good, because I have something to tell you, and I don't want to tell you over the phone."

"Tell me," he coaxed, sounding so sexy Solange was sorely tempted to comply.

"No," she said firmly. "I have to be looking into your eyes when I tell you."

"I'm going to have to invest in a couple of those digital photo phones," Rupert joked.

He sighed heavily. "I miss you so much, it's become a physical pain. I literally ache for you."

Solange's toes were curling. She closed her eyes as she stood with the phone to her ear. "Oh, baby, I miss you, too. My entire body is tingling for you right now."

"I want to smell your skin, taste your mouth, lick the hollow in your back," Rupert intoned. "I want to pick you up and carry you to the bedroom and slowly undress you."

Students began filing into the classroom. "Hold that thought, baby. I have to gather my things and make a mad dash for my car. I'm in my classroom, after class. The next class has started filing in."

"Do you know that spot on the curve of your neck? I want to kiss it until you are putty in my hands," Rupert continued while Solange hastened about the room, collecting her purse, her jacket, and her briefcase. She headed for the door, smiling at students and the instructor, Dr. Poole, who gave her a curious look when she started making smooching noises into the receiver. She didn't care if he thought she was daft. He was known to be a little eccentric himself.

In the corridor now, she laughed. "Sweetie, people are giving me strange looks. Now, tell me, how long are you going to be in Mauritania? Because I'm beginning to forget what it feels like to make love to you." She was lying. She recalled every lovemaking session they'd ever shared, from Miami to Addis Ababa and back again. She'd only said it to bring home the point that they hadn't seen each other in some time now, and she was missing his loving.

"I don't know how long this assignment will take. I'm hoping that I will be in and out of there, but it depends on too many variables to accurately predict how long it will take. I'm sorry, darling."

"Don't be sorry. It's your work. I understand," Solange told him. She was walking down the steps of the building now and heading in the general direction of staff parking.

The day was overcast. Like most weather in Miami in springtime, it could be sunny one minute and gray the next. In the distance, she heard the rumblings of thunder.

"I understand," she said again. "But that doesn't mean I'm not going to complain my butt off. I want you here in my arms."

"I want to be there in your arms."

"I want to wake up beside you in the morning."

"I would die happy if I could wake up beside you every morning," was Rupert's reply.

Solange smiled. "You would definitely die happy if you died in my bed."

"Spent, and happy," Rupert confirmed.

"Okay, you're making me hot now," Solange said. "Shall we change the subject? How is the weather in London?"

"Gray and overcast."

"Same here," she said.

"How is Desta?" Rupert wanted to know. He knew that she and Desta communicated nearly every day through e-mails. Part of Rupert's father's generous donation to the orphanages of Addis Ababa were new computers and connections to the Internet. Desta had taken to the computer like any other self-respecting adolescent.

"I sent her several early Jackson Five CDs, and she's apparently in love with Michael," Solange told him, remembering Desta's enthusiastic e-mail of that morning, in which she'd referred to the then thirteen-year-old Michael Jackson as the handsomest boy in the world. "I want to marry him one day," she'd written.

"Let her down easy," Rupert said. "She's going to be very disappointed when she finds out he's changed somewhat since then."

"She's also quite taken with Philip Pullman's *Dark Materials* trilogy," Solange reported. "She says she may want to be a writer one day."

"I love that trilogy myself," Rupert said, smiling as he remembered those fantasy novels, written for kids but enjoyable for all ages. "I'm sure that whatever our Desta makes up her mind to become she will become. She's one of the most determined people I've ever known. Another two months and she'll be coming to join you in Miami, huh?" He could have said, 'join us,' but he wanted to surprise her later on.

Solange sighed. She'd reached her car and was leaning against the driver's side door, digging in her purse for her keys. "I wish it were sooner. I'm tired of waiting, she's tired of waiting, and my mother has redecorated her room three times already, she's so excited about becoming a grandmother."

Rupert laughed. "Your mother must think I'm a ghost."

"It isn't your fault you haven't met her yet. The last two times I tried to get you two together, she was tied up with something or other."

"At least your dad likes me," Rupert said.

"Anyone who takes to deep sea fishing is tops in his opinion," Solange said with a laugh. Keys in hand, she unlocked the car door, tossed her belongings onto the passenger seat, and slid behind the wheel. Door locked, key in the ignition, she turned the key in order to roll down the windows to let out the warm air, then switched on the air conditioner.

"This assignment in Mauritania, it isn't anything dangerous, is it?"

"Now, baby, don't worry about me. You know what a cautious man I am."

"Yes, but what about the people you're going there to see? Can you vouch for them?"

"No," Rupert answered truthfully.

"Then promise me you will be extra careful. You belong to me now, Giles. I want you to come back to me in the best of health and with all limbs attached."

"Yes, my darling, your wish is my command. I will be ever vigilant. And if anyone wants to play rough, I'll just tell them my fiancée forbids it."

Solange laughed. "You'd better, 'cause if anything happens to you I'm gonna be one mad-as-hell archaeologist, and you don't want to make one of us angry."

"Absolutely not," Rupert said, smiling on his end. "Not when you all are so proficient with dangerous tools like picks and axes."

"That's right, and we wield shovels pretty well, too!" Solange reminded him.

"You're bad," Rupert said with a feigned tremor in his voice.

"I'm bad," Solange said, and meant it.

At the air terminal in London, Rupert spotted Jason Thorne approaching him, with a tall, silver-haired gentleman beside him. "Darling, I've got to go. I'll phone you once I check into the hotel."

"All right, have a safe trip," Solange said gently. She was always sad when they had to say goodbye.

"I love you," said Rupert.

"I love you, too," Solange replied. She broke the connection, closing the cell phone. Sighing, she put the phone in its slot inside her purse and put the car in drive, her foot still firmly on the brakes. She sat for a moment, wondering how their lives—hers, Rupert's, and Desta's—would eventually come together. Was she crazy to have faith that an archaeologist, a former spy, and an ex–street urchin-cum-pickpocket could ever be a family?

She smiled. No, she wasn't crazy. Just optimistic. Somehow, everything would work out, and they would be one happy family, no matter where they ended up living. London, Miami, or somewhere in between, location didn't matter. Heck, she thought, I don't care if we end up in Timbuktu, as long as we're together.

She eased her foot off the brakes and backed out of the parking space.

When Thorne and the silver-haired gentleman got closer, Rupert was astonished to see the director himself had ventured into the field. It was rumored that he never went farther than his desk. Word was he hadn't been in the field since he was a rookie. His subordinates said this was to keep him as far removed from the field agents as possible. The truth was, Edgar Case was somewhat of a legend in the agency. He'd received every medal a war veteran could receive. What's more, he'd come up through the ranks. He hadn't been given a cushy ride to the top. He'd earned his position.

At sixty-five, he was still a fine figure of a man, trim, unbent by his years, and robust.

"Giles, old man," he said, offering Rupert his hand. "I see you've done quite well for yourself since you left us."

"Yes, sir. Thank you, sir," Rupert said. He had always liked Edgar Case. Case had been fair with him, and there had been times when Case had let on to Rupert that he sometimes also had a hard time following orders. But God and country came first.

Being able to sleep at night was a sorry third. Ah, well, he often said, I'll get enough sleep once I'm dead.

"I thought you might like a little more reassurance than Mr. Thorne here could give you," the director said. "We are prepared to wipe your slate clean and consider our association as something that never happened if you complete this assignment for us. Am I making myself clear?"

"No surveillance," Rupert said. "It's as if I and anyone I care about will no longer exist to the agency."

"That's it exactly," Edgar Case said with a smile that reached his gray eyes.

"Then it's a deal," Rupert agreed, giving the director a firm shake to seal the pact.

When he let go of his hand, the director shook the kinks out of it, Rupert had squeezed it so hard.

"What are you bench pressing nowadays, Giles, small cars?" the director joked. He met Rupert's eyes, a steely determination in his own. Commuters walked around them as they stood in the center of the terminal. The hum of human voices, frequent announcements over the loudspeaker, and the sound of pedestrians' footfalls provided sufficient cover for their conversation.

"We want Aziz back, dead or alive, Giles. Any way we can get him. And if Obed Bedele gets caught in the trap, that's a bonus, though we doubt he'll be anywhere near his old friend Aziz. He has other fish to fry in the Middle East right now. Our main objective is to protect Ashante Taya. Her husband, Ahmed Taya, is a reputable businessman who genuinely wants to help his people. The Mauritanians are devout Muslims who only want to live in peace with their neighbors. A wolf like Aziz in the midst of these sheep would not be a pretty sight. He has stored up five years of rage against his ex-wife. I don't think he's planning a reconciliation."

He handed Rupert a thick manila envelope. "Here are your papers. You will assume the identity of the gunrunner Aziz expects you to be. How you explain to him your reason for being in Mauritania is up to you. Just stop him before he can harm the Tayas."

* * *

"What are you doing, standing there staring out at the night?" Ahmed asked as he pulled Ashante into his arms. His strong arms encircled her from behind, bringing her body against his. He kissed the side of her fragrant neck. "Come back to bed."

"The baby is restless tonight," Ashante told him, her voice barely a whisper.

"Come to bed. I'll rub your back for you."

"I feel unsettled," Ashante insisted. "As though something horrible is going to happen."

Ahmed held her more snugly. "The night always finds you fearful, my love. There is nothing out there that can harm you, or the baby. You are safe here. You will always be safe here."

Ashante shivered delicately. She wanted to believe her husband. She loved him more than she loved her own life. As for their child, both their first, she already felt as a mother lioness must feel about her young: fiercely protective. She prayed daily for strength. She prayed to be filled with the kind of joy she was always told pregnant women experienced while awaiting the birth of their children. She wanted to be carefree, but images of the past were burned in her memory. She was marked by those memories as sure as the ink sunk into tattooed skin. Pain and suffering were her tattoos, and they were a permanent part of her makeup.

"I should not have married you," she told her husband. "I fear I will bring bad luck to you. I fear I am cursed, and therefore you are cursed by your association with me."

"How many times do I have to tell you that he is dead to you?" Ahmed said. He was a big man compared to her: six feet tall and broad shouldered. She was five-four and, until she gained twenty pounds during her pregnancy, tipped the scales at one hundred and ten pounds. He still had no trouble lifting her. He did so now, sweeping her up and walking through the big house with her cradled in his arms. "If you won't come to bed, I'll take you. I'll not hear any more of this nonsense about curses. You are my blessing, do you hear me? From the moment I set eyes on you I knew I had been blessed by God."

Ashante wrapped her arms around his neck and smiled through her tears. "I will try to shake this feeling for you."

"Don't try," said Ahmed. "Do it. Your mood can't be healthy for our little one. Do you want a sad baby?"

"No, I want a happy baby."

"Then stop dwelling on calamity, and focus on our love. Believe that you are meant to be happy. It is your destiny. Just like our child is destined to have parents who will love and cherish him all the days of his life."

In the bedroom, he gently lay her on the bed. The lights were dimmed. Overhead, a fan stirred the night-cooled air. He lay beside her and once again drew her into his arms. "I shall cancel my trip and stay here with you. I can't leave you while you're in this state of mind."

"No," Ashante said firmly. "I will be fine. These moods come over me sometimes, but I'm always able to talk myself out of them. You should go to Mali. Your business there is important. The project will bring clean drinking water to thousands of villagers. Please go."

"I will sleep on it," said Ahmed. "If you are much improved in the morning, then maybe I'll go."

Ashante sighed contentedly. "I am already much better with your arms around me like this."

* * *

Once Rupert's plane had taken off and was en route to the northwest African country of Mauritania, he opened the packet the director had given him and withdrew a handheld computer with a monitor no bigger than the palm of his hand. There were also headphones in the packet, which he put on and connected to the computer. Then, he watched the monitor and listened. "Mauritania," the female voice instructed him, "has a population of more than two and a half million. The racial makeup is as follows: forty percent mixed Maur/black; thirty percent Maur; and thirty percent black. The official languages are Hasaniya, Arabic, and Wolof; however, Pular and Soninke are also spoken. The country is one hundred percent Muslim and is an Islamic republic. On the whole, the people are friendly to strangers, though understandably suspicious."

Next came a photograph of Aziz looking puffed up in full military dress. He had liked playing general when he'd ruled Senegal, though he had no military training to speak of. He had been a grassroots politician who came out of nowhere to lead the army. Some journalists had compared his power of persuasion to Adolph Hitler's, and had dubbed him "Little Adolph" in the media. Physically, he wasn't small in stature. He was hard muscled and stood six-feet-five-inches tall. His hands were so big he looked as if he could easily palm a basketball, as well as crush a man's skull with his powerful fingers.

"This is Moustapha Aziz before his incarceration," the voice said. Another photograph took its place. In it Aziz hadn't changed much. He was attired in a pair of green army-issue fatigues and an olive green T-shirt. His head was bald. If anything, he appeared even more muscular than he had before he went to prison.

"Aziz spent much of his time in prison doing push-ups, chin-ups, and sit-ups, and jogging in place," the woman's detached voice reported. "According to the guards, he rarely spoke. He simply read the Koran and exercised. He didn't interact much with the other prisoners."

After Aziz's updated photo, a picture of a very attractive woman flashed on the screen. "Ashante Taya is twenty-seven years old. It is reported that she is approximately five months pregnant with her first child. Her husband, Ahmed Taya, thirty-six, owns a company that manufactures farm equipment and tools. He is a philanthropist who is known for going into remote villages and bringing the means to irrigate and grow crops and for teaching the inhabitants how to maintain the land. He is a devout Muslim, and does not believe in arming himself, so we don't suspect he'll be able to defend himself properly should Aziz invade their home. Good luck, Agent Giles."

The message vanished of its own accord, and Rupert closed the lid of the mini-laptop and returned it to the packet. He sat back in his seat and closed his eyes, wondering what Solange was up to at that moment. It would be nearly nightfall in Miami by now. She was probably preparing a light meal for herself, or perhaps leaving the house to go meet a friend for dinner. He wished he were there with her instead of on the way to the capital of Mauritania, Nouakchott. However, he did not entertain the thought of refusing the assignment for more than five minutes, not when it could mean the difference between being a free man and a watched man. Not when it could mean the difference between a relatively carefree existence, or one in which you were continually looking over your shoulder.

He could never tell Solange about this, but he could live with that. A man had to make sacrifices for the people he loved. If this went well, he could go to her with his past expunged and with less baggage than he would otherwise bring with him to the relationship. The risk was worth it to him. Solange would, undoubtedly, disagree.

She'd already made it perfectly clear that she didn't believe it was only left up to him to decide whether or not to risk his life. He had to consider the effect it would have on her and Desta now. But, the way he reasoned, he was doing this for her and for Desta. As much as he relished the thought of his never having to worry about the agency sending someone to eliminate him, the thought of Solange and Desta never being placed in the line of fire was an even more compelling prospect.

Yes, he was doing the right thing.

Three

At the airport in Nouakchott, Rupert had to present his passport, a visa, and evidence of a yellow-fever vaccination before he was allowed entrance into the country. All of the paperwork was in his travel packet, plus a supply of Lariam, an antimalarial drug. Malaria was a serious health threat in that part of western Africa.

Once he cleared customs, he made his way through the packed air terminal and stepped outside into the dry desert heat. It was midday, and the sun's rays were relentlessly beating down on the earth.

He'd studied his list of contacts while on the plane. After he'd found lodging, which could prove difficult because Mauritania was not a tourist mecca, he was to phone the first contact on his list. This person would be able to provide him with a weapon and ammunition. His second contact would provide suitable transportation and adequate spending money to cover his expenses.

Rupert stood for a couple of minutes, watching the various kinds of automobiles coming and going. It was apparent that Mauritania was a country with a few rich people, and the rest were poor. The rich were very rich, driving luxury cars and big, flashy SUVs. The poor walked or drove rattletraps that sputtered smoke and leaked large amounts of oil.

He gripped his carry-on bag tightly in his right hand

and stepped off the sidewalk onto the street. There didn't seem much point in trying to hail a cab, he decided. He'd take the bus with the other commuters. He climbed onto the air-conditioned bus behind a short, thin man dressed all in white. Rupert wore lightweight cotton slacks and a shortsleeve cotton shirt, both in khaki. Sunglasses shaded his caramel-colored eyes.

On the bus, the languages in the air were French, Arabic, Wolof, and several other local dialects. Rupert spoke French and a little Arabic. He sat down beside the little man who'd preceded him onto the bus. The man smiled at him and said, "Bonjour."

"Bonjour," Rupert said.

"British?" asked the man.

Rupert was reluctant to say he was indeed British. Since the U.S.- and British-led intervention in Iraq in the 1990s, and the subsequent invasion by U.S. and British forces again in 2003, some Muslims had not taken kindly to American and British visitors.

"I lived in England for twenty years," the man said, assuming Rupert understood his thickly-accented English. "I trained to become a tailor there. So, I know by the cut of your clothing and workmanship of your shoes that you at least shop in England."

"You are right," Rupert said. "I shop in London."

"Ah," said the man, delighted. He had a receding hairline and wore round spectacles that made him look like Gandhi. "Is this your first time in Nouakchott?"

"Yes, it is," Rupert gladly told him. "Can you recommend a place to stay?"

"I would be happy to," said his seatmate. "There are several clean places to stay in the city, but you must be careful that you are not overcharged. Hotel proprietors believe they have the right to gouge foreigners because there is a shortage of safe places to stay in the city. Lodging is at a premium. But my brother-in-law and sister own a nice boarding house not far from here. The rooms are clean and cool, and my sister is a wonderful cook."

Solange supposed it was inevitable. She couldn't avoid her mother indefinitely. Not that she was trying to avoid Marie DuPree. Divorced from Solange's father, Georges, for over twenty years now, Marie had never seen fit to resume using her maiden name. Solange loved her mother. It was just that every time they found themselves in the same room, Marie invariably got around to asking, "When are you and Rupert going to set the wedding date?" It was just what her mother was preparing to do now on this Saturday morning when she'd dropped in without phoning first.

Solange resisted the urge to roll her eyes heavenward when her mother began to pry. Instead she closed them momentarily and took a deep breath. She hadn't even had the chance to sample her omelet before the dreaded question had been asked. Her stomach growled as she looked her mother in the eyes. Marie's delicately arched brows were raised questioningly. If it weren't for the eager, woefully expectant expression in her dark brown eyes, a look that told Solange that her mother had her best interests at heart, she might have said something unforgivably rude. But she smiled and said, "You'll be happy to know that I spoke with Rupert yesterday and he will be coming home in a few days, as soon as he completes an assignment in Mauritania."

"Mauritania?" Marie asked, her tone indicating that Mauritania might as well be on the dark side of the moon. "Good Lord, does that man ever stop globe-trotting? I have yet to see him in the flesh."

"Don't worry, Mama, I'm not making him up," Solange

said with a mischievous grin. She cut a big piece of the omelet with the side of her fork and placed it on her tongue, savoring it. She chewed slowly.

"What if I told you I'd spoken with the best wedding planner in the city?" Marie asked. She paused to sip her orange juice and watch Solange's face for her reaction to her statement.

"I'd say you're getting ahead of yourself," Solange said lightly. "Rupert and I don't even know if we want a big wedding. We might not need the services of a wedding planner."

"Darling," Marie said. "The wedding is your father's and my responsibility, not yours. Of course your and Rupert's opinions matter, but you must take into consideration the length of time your father and I have been waiting to give our daughter away to the man of her dreams. You've done your part. You've found the man. Now, we want to be able to do our part and give you a wedding you'll never forget."

"I wouldn't forget my wedding to Rupert if we were married in the living room with a mail-order licensed preacher presiding," Solange told her mother.

Marie's lovely face fell. She was aghast. "I did raise you, didn't I?"

"You did," Solange confirmed with a smile. She turned her attention to her breakfast. For the next few minutes she was sure her mother would entertain her with another one of her speeches on style.

"Sometimes, I think," said Marie. Her dark brown eyes were alight with the enthusiasm she felt for the importance of having style and elegance in one's life. "What separates us from the animals is our ability to make our surroundings more beautiful."

"You borrowed that from somebody," Solange said between bites. "I'm not sure from whom, but I know I've heard that somewhere before."

Undaunted, Marie continued. "It doesn't matter where I got it from, it's true! A sense of style is the best defense against barbarity. And it doesn't have anything to do with wealth. You don't need a lot of money to make your surroundings a feast for the eyes. All it takes is taste and a keen sense of style. I didn't have much money when I started my decorating business."

"Just your unerring sense of style," Solange said. She knew better than to make fun of her mother's life's work. Marie was fiercely proud of what she'd accomplished, as well she should be. She didn't have a college degree. She'd gone to a technical school at night, and with her certificate had built a million-dollar business simply by working hard and relying on her ability to instantly recognize what piece of furniture, what color paint, what kind of floor covering, and what sort of wall treatments would best bring a room to life. Today her clients were among Miami's wealthiest citizens. And she kept learning over the years, sharpening her skills, always ahead of the trends. She was a workaholic, and thrived on it.

"I knew when you and Gaea would traipse all over Key West, barefoot and dressed like rejects from a pirate movie, that you were different from me. I've never enjoyed going without shoes. I was always afraid I'd cut my feet or some other catastrophe would befall me."

"Like your feet would grow so big they'd look like flippers?" Solange said, laughing.

"You're joking, but some cultures do have superstitious beliefs along those lines," Marie told her. "The Chinese bound their little girls' feet for hundreds of years because they thought small feet were the height of femininity. Unfortunately, the practice crippled some of those poor girls." She sighed. "I lost my train of thought. Oh, yeah, how different you and I are. Some mothers would have tried to change you into an exact replica of themselves. But I celebrated your independent spirit. I never felt as free as you seemed to when I was growing up. Then, when you were thirteen and your father and I divorced, you started spending a lot of time at the Maxwells' home.

I never told you this, but I was grateful to them for being there for you when I was an emotional wreck."

Solange put down her fork and gave her mother her undivided attention. "Seriously?"

"Of course, my gratefulness was tempered by a little jealousy. Lara Maxwell seemed unable to do anything wrong as a mother, and I could do nothing right. It broke my heart when you wanted her to do your hair for your first sweetheart dance. Remember?"

"It was just you and I, and you were working so hard as a salesperson back then, that I thought you'd be relieved you wouldn't have to do my hair when you got home from work," Solange told her.

Marie reached across the table and placed a hand atop Solange's. "That was how I relaxed after a long day, spending time with you. I enjoyed doing your hair, listening to what your day had been like. You were my only connection with my emotions. The experience with your father had hardened my heart. I know that now. That's why I still don't have a man in my life. There's nothing left in my heart to give to a man. At least not anything any of them seem to be interested in."

Solange squeezed her mother's hand. "You're a beautiful woman, Maman. If you're willing to let down your guard, I'm sure some man will be brave enough to storm that fortress you've built around your heart."

Marie shook her head sadly. "No, child. I'm okay with that part of my life being over and done with. I'm too set in my ways to welcome a man into my life, my house and, most of all, my bed. I'm happy with trying to be as good a mother to you as I can, and I'm looking forward to being a grandmother to Desta when she gets here."

"You wouldn't have mentioned a man if you truly have given up on ever being with someone special," Solange said softly. She smiled. "I've got an idea. Theophilus Gault is opening a branch of Gault Electronics right here in Miami. He's going to need someone to show him around the city."

Marie was already shaking her head in the negative. "Theophilus Gault is going to be a member of the family once you and Rupert are married. I think your trying to hook us up would create some sticky situations in the future. I would prefer to keep him as an in-law, and nothing more."

"You haven't met him yet," Solange said. "You should hold off on making a final decision until after you two have been introduced."

"When do you suppose that will be?" Marie asked, curious. Not that she was at all interested in Rupert's father as a romantic prospect. She wasn't. She was, however, a social butterfly who enjoyed a good party, and could plan one at the drop of a hat.

"As I said before, if everything goes well for Rupert in Mauritania, I'm expecting him in a few days. Theophilus told me he would be in Miami at the end of the month to inspect his new offices. Samantha will be here, too. It would be a good time to have a dinner party so that you all can meet."

"Including your father?" Marie wanted to know. In recent months, she and Georges had forged a more amicable relationship. She still, however, felt a chill whenever his wife, Elena, was in the same room. Marie had nothing personal against Elena. She suspected that Elena was suspicious of her intentions toward Georges, which secretly pleased Marie, since it had been Elena for whom Georges had left her. In Marie's opinion, Elena was getting a taste of her own medicine. She still knew, realistically, that to hold any animosity for Elena in her heart was unreasonable. If anyone was to blame for breaking up their marriage, it was Georges, not Elena. No matter how much sex appeal Elena had, if Georges had been committed to their marriage, he would not have begun the affair. After her cancer scare, Marie had decided to put it all behind her. She would try to be civil to both Georges and his present wife from now on.

Therefore attending a dinner party at which both of them would be guests did not cause her any stress.

"Because it's all right with me if you want to invite Georges and Elena," she told Solange.

Solange swallowed hard, but didn't comment on her mother's generosity of spirit. It was slowly dawning on her that her mother was recreating herself from the inside out. Soon, nothing much her mother said or did would surprise her anymore.

"Okay, I'll invite them."

The doorbell rang.

Solange slipped her feet into the mules she'd abandoned underneath the table when she'd sat down to breakfast, and rose. "Who could that be this early on a Saturday morning? I'm not expecting anybody."

"There's something I forgot to tell you," Marie began, rising too. But Solange didn't hear her. She was preoccupied with her own thoughts.

Her heart had begun racing when it occurred to her that it might be Rupert. It had only been two days since he'd phoned her from Mauritania. Maybe his business there had fallen through and he'd taken the first plane out of there! It could happen!

She ran her forefinger over her teeth to make certain nothing was stuck in them, and smoothed her bathrobe over her figure. Her hand went to her hair. There wasn't much she could do about it now, at the last minute. Besides, Rupert liked her morning hair.

She was slightly breathless by the time she paused at the door long enough to look through the peephole. "Damn," she uttered disappointedly.

A stranger stood on her porch. An attractive thirty-something black woman with long, straight auburn hair artfully arranged on her head. Solange turned her back to the door.

She was seriously thinking of ignoring the woman. She was probably trying to sell something, or perhaps she was in the neighborhood trying to bring people to Jesus. Solange didn't want to buy anything, and she was already quite familiar with Jesus.

Marie arrived at her side. "I meant to tell you, I asked Danielle to drop by here this morning in order for the two of you to get acquainted."

"Who is Danielle?" Solange asked, feeling cornered like a rat. The woman on the other side of the door was apparently from her mother's school of style. Every hair looked to be in place. She frowned at her mother. Marie stood there, tapping her small Ferragamo-shod foot on the hardwood floor. The sky blue sleeveless wrap pantsuit she had on was the exact same shade as the shoes. Her short black hair, shot through with gray—that looked like highlights on her—was cut in an elegant, modern pageboy.

Solange looked down at her bathrobe resentfully. "You might have warned me that I would be getting company. I could have at least put on some clothes."

"Oh, nonsense," said Marie, her hand on the doorknob. "We're all girls here."

Solange stepped aside and let her mother get the door.

The woman on the porch began talking as soon as she saw the door opening.

"I was beginning to think I had the wrong house," she said, sounding somewhat put-upon. She kissed the air next to Marie's cheek as she entered the room, floating on a cloud of Miracle perfume. She was attired in a tailored red skirt suit. Just as Solange had suspected, she was perfectly put together, from her French-manicured nails to her immaculate feet, which had recently been given a pedicure.

She had a French accent, quite similar to Marie's. Delicately fanning her face with her right hand, she looked at Solange. "Even in that unflattering getup I can see that the apple didn't fall far from the tree."

"It's a pleasure to meet you, too, Miss . . ." Solange's sentence hung in the air.

"Chevalier," the woman said. "Danielle Chevalier. But my friends call me Dani. I hope we're going to be friends." She smiled. Her dark brown eyes reflected genuine pleasure. Stepping further into the house, she looked around. "Charming. I've always thought these older bungalows were very chic. I thought of buying one myself, but with my clothing alone I'd need twice the space."

Her voice was very deep and sexy. If she were a singer, she would be a contralto.

Solange watched her as she strolled about the room, admiring the furnishings and the crystal figurines on a shelf in the corner. There was something about her, something different that Solange couldn't put her finger on. Danielle Chevalier would be unique in anyone's book. A woman as beautiful as she was would be hard to forget. She wore her confidence like a shield. Solange wondered why. When she met Solange's gaze there was a vulnerability there for a split second before the expression once again reflected confidence bordering on haughtiness. She was intriguing. Yes, that's what it was, Solange decided. Solange had always been drawn to people who were mysterious.

"Would you like a cup of coffee?" Solange asked.

Dani seemed to consider her question a moment. Then she beamed and said, "Yes, I believe I would, thank you."

Solange turned and began walking toward the kitchen. "Right this way."

Dani followed, with Marie bringing up the rear, a knowing smile on her face. She'd been certain of Dani's ability to win over Solange.

In the kitchen, Solange went to the cabinet and got an extra cup and saucer that matched the set of white bone china she and her mother were using. She gestured toward the kitchen table, which sat four. "Please sit down. We were having cheese omelets for breakfast. I'd be happy to prepare one for you if you're hungry."

"I never refuse free food," Dani said, smiling. Marie had come into the kitchen and reclaimed her chair. Picking up her fork, she resumed eating.

"You have no objections to onions and peppers, even jalapeno peppers?" Solange asked before going to the refrigerator for the needed ingredients.

"The spicier the better. My people come from Martinique, and we like our food with lots of flavor. Like we like our men."

Solange laughed shortly. "Don't we all?"

"Speaking of men," Dani said. "Miss Marie tells me that yours is British. Where did you two meet?"

"Right here," Solange told her easily. "On the campus of the University of Miami, where I work."

"Now, that's not something that happens every day," said Dani, smiling. When her lips peeled back from her teeth, her smile was disarming. "If it did, I'd be at the registrar's office bright and early Monday morning to enroll in classes."

"I'm sure an attractive woman like you already has her hands full turning down men who'd like to date you," Solange said as she pulled items from the refrigerator.

"Appearances can be deceiving," Dani said. "I meet men all the time, but it can be dangerous to put my trust in them. I have to be very careful about whom I confide in."

"I think that goes for all of us," Solange said. "It isn't easy to find someone you feel you can completely trust."

"But you did," Dani said pleasantly. "That's why you're going to get married." She sighed wistfully, then caught herself as though she were embarrassed by her show of sentimentality. She smiled warmly up at Solange as Solange placed a cup of black coffee in front of her. "Thank you . . . What shall I call you?"

"Oh, call me Solange."

"Solange," Dani began, her eyes trained on Solange's face. "Tell me about yourself and your fiancé. I'd like to get a feel for you both, so that I'll know exactly what sort of wedding would best suit the two of you. You strike me as a person with simple tastes.

"You like beautiful things, but you don't put much value on material things. You're a spiritual person by nature. Am I right?"

"How can you read me so well after only ten minutes?" Solange asked, impressed.

"I'm not reading you, my dear, I'm reading your surroundings. Although I noticed evidence of your mother's decorating skills the moment I stepped into your home, an even stronger presence overpowered her influences. It was your spirit. They say houses retain some of the spiritual residue left behind by the people who have lived in them.

"I tend to think that's true to an extent. If a person's spiritual makeup is chaotic, then her home will reflect that in disorder or, in some cases, in a home that is so orderly and spotless that it becomes sterile. You are comfortable in your own skin, and your home reflects that."

Solange smiled. "My mother didn't coach you?" she asked, suspicious. "I wouldn't put it past her."

Marie laughed. "I didn't tell Dani a thing about you or Rupert except your first names and my relationship to you."

Solange cooked while they talked. "I have to tell you, Dani, that Rupert and I haven't set the date yet. In fact, we haven't talked about what sort of wedding we want. All we know is that we're going to get married. We might fly to Vegas and do it in a chapel there. Or go to the courthouse. I had no idea my mother had asked you to come over."

"Well, if you decide you don't want to hire me, so be it," Dani told her. "I'll at least get breakfast. And hopefully, if you would be so kind, a tour of your home. I adore this bungalow."

Solange poured the whisked eggs into the prepared skillet, swirling the mixture around until it covered the entire bottom of the pan, then added grated cheddar cheese, chopped onions, green and red bell peppers, and jalapenos. "A tour would take all of five minutes," she said. "I'd be happy to give you one after breakfast. In the meantime I'll do as you asked and tell you a little about myself and Rupert."

She expertly folded the omelet over in a semicircle, creating a pocket to hold the melting cheese and vegetables. In a couple of minutes, it was fully cooked. "Would you like toast, Dani?"

"Do you have any wheat bread?"

"Sure."

"Then yes. Thank you."

"I'll prepare your toast," Marie offered, getting to her feet. "I'm finished eating."

After Solange had served Dani, she sat down across from her. "I've waited a long time for the right man to come along. I'm thirty-five. Rupert is forty. What we treasure most about our relationship is the fact that we can tell each other anything and it won't change the way we feel about each other. He knows all of my secrets, and I know all of his."

"Darling, no woman knows everything there is to know about a man. I don't care how perfect he appears to be," said Marie from across the room where she was leaning against the counter waiting for Dani's toast to pop up.

"Seriously," Solange insisted. "Rupert doesn't keep secrets from me. And I don't keep secrets from him. Our relationship is based on truth. We both agreed that that's the only way to be in a relationship. You have to be willing to bare your soul to your partner."

"Baring your soul is one thing," Marie said. "Telling him about your secret bank account is quite another."

The toast popped up and she placed both pieces on a plate and brought them to the table. "Margarine?" she asked Dani.

Dani pursed her lips. "What the hell? And I hope it's not that diet stuff, either."

"It's not. But it does have olive oil in it," Solange said. She looked at her mother whom she had a few choice words for. "Secret bank account? Why would I want to hide money from Rupert? He's the one who's well off, not me."

"How well off?" Marie asked, ever the practical mother.

"I've never asked him, but he says he's made some very good investments. Plus, his father is Theophilus Gault."

"Of Gault Electronics?" Dani asked with a mouthful of cheese omelet. She swallowed and daintily wiped her mouth with a napkin. "He was recently featured in *Black*

Enterprise. What a looker. If I were twenty years older, I'd be after him like Elmer Fudd hunting Bugs Bunny. But I read that he likes more mature women." She gave Marie a meaningful look. Marie saw it, but ignored her.

"What if he asks you to sign a prenuptial agreement?" Marie asked, sounding as if she were horrified by the prospect.

"I don't want his money," Solange said, slightly irritated by the question.

"No one said you wanted his money. But how would it make you feel if he asked you to sign one?" Marie asked again, unwilling to let it go. "You have to consider things like that when you're marrying a man of means."

"Why must I consider it?" Solange cried, putting down her fork, her appetite gone. "Rupert hasn't once brought up a prenuptial agreement. You're gonna make me crazy before we even set the wedding date!"

"She's right," Dani said to Marie.

Marie sat down at the table in a huff. "I was just trying to look out for my daughter's best interests."

"Planning a wedding can be very stressful," Dani said from experience. "It's best not to borrow trouble. There is a possibility that having a prenuptial agreement drawn up will never occur to Rupert. Let's cross that bridge if we ever get to it, shall we?"

Marie sighed. "I suppose you're right."

The wedding planner was growing on Solange more and more. Anyone who could get her mother to acquiesce was all right in her opinion. The three of them fell silent for a few minutes as Dani finished her breakfast with gusto. When she was done, she placed her fork on her plate and smiled at Solange.

"You're a good cook."

"Thank you," said Solange. "You're hired."

Dani held up a hand in protest. "Not so fast. A few

minutes ago, you told me you valued honesty above all else. Well, I need to tell you something about myself before you hire me."

"I can't imagine what you have to tell me that would make me think twice about hiring you," Solange told her.

Dani removed the lovely scarf that had been covering her throat. Solange's eyes stretched when she saw the size of Dani's Adam's apple.

"My real name is Daniel, and I'm a transsexual who is in transition. I have to live as a woman for at least a year before the operation," Dani said.

Solange looked at her mother for elucidation. Marie's face was ashen. It was obvious Marie was just as surprised as she was. Solange returned her gaze to Dani, whom she had liked the instant she'd met her. "Honey, this is Miami! Unless you want to borrow my clothes, you're hired. I don't think I have to worry about your borrowing my shoes because my feet are bigger than yours."

Dani threw her head back in laughter, her Adam's apple bobbing up and down. "Okay, it's a deal, girlfriend."

They shook on it.

Four

He felt like he'd been driving for days, even though it had only been a few hours.

The helicopter had deposited him at a designated spot in the desert last night, where someone was waiting with this Range Rover. He had asked Obed for a driver, but his old friend had told him he couldn't spare a man. Not one. If he wanted to get to Ashante so badly that he would cross the Sahara to do it, then he must do it alone.

Obed had supplied fresh water, food, a change of clothing, a weapon, and ammunition. That was as far as he was willing to stick his neck out. Obed had the nerve to tell him he should be grateful he hadn't let him fester in that Senegalese prison.

I'll show him how grateful I am the next time I see him, Moustapha thought derisively as he drove the Range Rover down a bumpy road on the outskirts of Nouakchott. He had no idea how close he was to his destination. He continually consulted a map given to him by Obed. He'd been promised that the map would show him exactly how to get to the city. So far, the map had him going around in circles. He tossed it out of the window and pulled the Range Rover next to a roadside vegetable stand. An old man stood under a makeshift shed with a watermelon the size of a cantaloupe in the palm of his hand. He offered it to Moustapha as though it were a prize.

"Ripe melon," he said in Wolof, which Moustapha spoke.

"I'm looking for the Taya factory," Moustapha said. "They make farm equipment, I'm told."

"I have never heard of the Taya factory," said the old man. "I am sorry."

Moustapha snatched the melon from his palm and threw it to the ground. It split open, spilling red fruit and juice onto the arid earth. The soil seemed to greedily guzzle the liquid. The old man didn't attempt to reprimand Moustapha. Instead, he bent and picked up the melon parts that hadn't been covered by sand and started eating them.

He smiled and offered Moustapha some of the melon.

Moustapha growled, baring his huge teeth in an angry scowl. "In the old days I would have had you shot, you useless old fool!" With that he turned and stomped back to the Range Rover, got in, and burned rubber, kicking up sand and dust in his wake. The old man stood looking after him, shaking his head, wondering where the world was headed when young people behaved so abominably.

A few miles later, Moustapha had calmed down enough to find his way into the city, where he parked at a rundown hotel. He didn't immediately get out of the car but sat for a while, observing his surroundings. "What a cesspool," he said. "This is not a step up for you, Ashante." He often found himself talking to his ex-wife. He'd held countless conversations with her over the past five years. In them, he would ask her why she'd abandoned him when he'd been captured, tried, and imprisoned. He wanted to know why she had never visited him. Most of all, he needed to hear from her own mouth why she'd broken their marriage vows and slept with a pig like Ahmed Taya. A marriage was sacred in Moustapha's eyes, and no divorce court had the power to sever a bond once a couple was wed. When he found her, he would give her two options: either leave with him, or die where she stood. He was fairly certain she would choose the former rather than the latter. As for Ahmed Taya, Moustapha would kill him before Ashante's eyes. She needed to witness his death in order to get closure. A widow needed closure if she were to get on with her life and give herself fully to the next man who came into her life. It rankled him that he would be the next man in Ashante's life. She had promised to honor and obey him until death parted them. He had made certain the holy man who had married them had remembered to voice those exact words—love and obey. He required obedience.

Ashante had known that when she'd gone into the marriage. Yet she'd willfully broken her wedding vows. Moustapha was almost tempted to simply kill her on sight instead of giving her a way to save her pretty neck. In some places she would be stoned for committing adultery, a fitting punishment. Moustapha was a modern man, though, and didn't condone capital punishment for adultery.

He got out of the Range Rover and locked the doors. Obed had warned him that petty crime was on the rise in the city. Cars were being stolen, or broken into. Better safe than sorry. He had a limited amount of funds on him. It would be a while before he could get his hands on his foreign accounts, and if the car was stolen he'd not have enough money to buy or rent another one. He sighed. He remembered the day when he had a fleet of twenty luxury cars in his garage.

As his wife, Ashante had had her pick of any of them,

plus a driver who had doubled as a bodyguard. She had been treated like royalty, as befitted the wife of the country's ruler. And then she'd chosen to disrespect him like this!

He snapped at the desk clerk when he went to the front desk to register. The man, nervous looking already with extremely protuberant eyes, visibly jumped. "A telephone directory!" Moustapha bellowed. "Is that too much to ask for, or do I have to go elsewhere?"

The clerk hadn't been registering many guests lately, so he did not want to lose this one, no matter how surly he happened to be. "No, sir, I will locate a telephone directory for you and bring it to your room. Just give me a few minutes to track one down for you. Please."

Somewhat placated, Moustapha narrowed his eyes at the clerk and took the key that the clerk was holding out to him. "Ten minutes," he warned. "If I don't have a telephone directory in my hands within ten minutes, I'm leaving." He turned on his heels, still mumbling to himself, "I can't believe this place calls itself a hotel."

The clerk was so relieved to see Moustapha's back that he sank into a nearby chair and let his chin fall to his chest. "He's really going to be upset when he finds out there is no phone in his room."

He rose and began looking frantically for the one telephone directory the hotel had. It wasn't his fault that telephone directories weren't plentiful. Mauritania was a developing country. Even though the population was over two and a half million, there were under eighteen thousand main phone lines. Many Mauritanians had never seen a telephone.

A few minutes later, he was knocking on Moustapha's door with the thin book clutched tightly in his hand. When Moustapha opened the door, he bowed his head deferentially and presented it to him. "Your directory, sir. I am sorry to have to inform you that should you wish to make a telephone connection, you must use the phone at the front desk."

Moustapha took the directory and smiled at the clerk. His smile, though, was lethal.

"I am aware of that since I was unable to find a phone, a TV, or a radio in this square box you so fondly refer to as a room. A prison cell is more comfortable." *And I ought to know!* Then, he slammed the door in the man's face. "Thank you!"

"Finally!" Rupert breathed with satisfaction after looking into Moustapha Aziz's ugly face through binoculars. He'd spent the past two days and nights watching the Taya house for any signs of Aziz. The first day, he'd watched as Ahmed Taya kissed Ashante goodbye at the front door, then gently placed his hand on her round belly and bent his head to kiss it, too. Rupert was relieved to see that the Tayas had a couple of live-in servants who were at the house most of the time. He felt better knowing Ashante wouldn't be alone. Plus, the fact that there were servants about would give Aziz pause once he arrived. He would not be able to simply knock on her door and force his way in. He would have to formulate a plan on how to deal with multiple people.

When Aziz had driven the Range Rover slowly past the house, he must have seen the gardener in the yard cutting back hedges that ran the length of the house out back.

The yard was immaculately kept. Rupert supposed a man who enjoyed teaching others how to grow crops would be a good gardener himself. The place was quite an oasis in the middle of a desert town: palm trees, thick grass, fruit-bearing trees, and flowers of myriad varieties and colors. When his mind went to gardens, of course he thought of Solange, who grew orchids on her back porch. The delicate plants were not easy to care for, as anyone who'd ever grown them could attest. Rupert believed that Solange was such a good orchid grower because she was patient and kind, and genuinely loved them. It was as if they knew she loved them, and thrived to please her.

"Okay, Giles, you've been on stakeout too long," he said as he started the four-by-four and followed Aziz's Range Rover out of the Taya's neighborhood. Apparently, after seeing the gardener, Aziz had decided he needed to rethink his approach.

As he followed Aziz, Rupert hung back as far as he could without losing sight of him. Rupert had almost lost faith in the agency's ability to predict the actions of its targets.

He thought that maybe Aziz had gone to Switzerland, or somewhere else he had hidden assets that neither the Senegalese government nor the British government had been able to unearth. That would have been the wise thing to do. But, no, Aziz had to see to his human emotions first. Only when he'd punished Ashante to his satisfaction would he spend the rest of his life in the lap of luxury.

"I'll be the fly in your ointment, old buddy," Rupert said.

Up ahead, Aziz braked repeatedly. He wasn't used to Naouakchott drivers who didn't observe the rules of the road, nor even stay on their side of the road, for that matter. Rupert smiled. Driving in a place like this must be hard on an ex-dictator who was accustomed to being driven wherever he wished to go.

Aziz pulled into the parking lot of a restaurant. Rupert

was glad because he hadn't eaten anything substantial in nearly forty-eight hours. He would enjoy a sit-down meal.

He waited a good five minutes after watching Aziz go into the restaurant before getting out of his car and entering. The architecture was typical of buildings in northwest Africa. The main room was large and airy and had around thirty tables. Ceiling fans circulated the moderately cool air throughout the building. It was midday, and they were doing brisk business. Almost all of the tables were occupied.

Rupert stood at the entrance, sure he would have to be seated by a host. He was left standing only a couple of minutes before a young man dressed in a white jacket, black slacks, and black shoes appeared at his side. "Party of one?" he asked in French. Rupert supposed that when you worked in a place frequented by foreigners you came to recognize them by their dress and mannerisms. With his skin color, he certainly could have passed for a native but the waiter had known better. And the waiter had greeted him in French because many visitors spoke the language.

"Yes, I'm dining alone," Rupert told him.

"This way, please."

The aromas in the air were mouthwatering. Rupert recognized some of them: onion, chile pepper, and curry. His nostrils flared. "Is that Chicken Yassa I smell?" he asked the waiter.

"Yes, sir, it's one of the house specials," the waiter said proudly. "A generous portion is served on a bed of rice."

"I'll have that," Rupert told him as he sat down at the table the waiter had indicated. "Along with groundnut soup and yam Fu Fu." Rupert, who had dined all over West Africa, knew that if a restaurant served Chicken Yassa more than likely they served groundnut soup and yam Fu Fu. They were common West African dishes.

"What can I bring you to drink, sir?"

"Bottled water," Rupert said.

"Very good, sir. I'll only be a few minutes," the waiter said, and left.

Rupert had already spotted Aziz. He was sitting two tables to the left of him, his back to him. Good. Rupert hadn't wanted Aziz to know he was there until he was ready to make contact. He wanted Aziz to get comfortable and be in a relaxed frame of mind before he made himself known. Their meeting had to appear purely coincidental.

Ten minutes later the waiter returned with a tray piled high with Rupert's food. Rupert inhaled the heady smells. He felt like moaning with pleasure but resisted.

Solange would have done so, and with feeling. He smiled at the thought of her here with him, enjoying this meal.

"Bon appetit, sir," said the waiter after placing the food in front of Rupert.

"Merci, merci," said Rupert gratefully.

After one bite, Rupert knew that his nose had been on the money. The food was delicious.

A few feet away, Moustapha had grudgingly conceded that there was one thing about Nouakchott that was better than prison: the food. He ate with abandon, smacking his lips and licking his fingers. The people at the table next to his were aghast at his lack of manners. They screwed up their faces in disgust. Moustapha smiled at them and turned up the volume on his eating sound effects. They gave up and turned their backs to him. Even in a nice place like this, you ran the chance of encountering uncouth characters.

Moustapha burped loudly after he'd polished off every morsel. Then he raised his hand and bellowed for his waiter, who was clear across the room serving other patrons.

"More coffee!"

"Why don't you get up and get it yourself, you lazy bum?" Rupert said from behind him.

Moustapha's black eyes automatically narrowed. He'd had his main course. He would have this fool's ass on a platter for dessert. He rose with every intention of smashing the face of the man who'd insulted him, only to find his old friend and conspirator, Sam Booker, grinning at him.

Sam pulled up a chair and sat down. The fight gone out of him, Moustapha sat too.

Leaning toward him, Sam said in low tones, "What the hell are you doing here, my man?" Sam was from Texas. He spoke with a noticeable twang, but nothing over the top. Sam was the consummate salesman, a man who knew how to get whatever you needed in the way of weapons, whether it was a .22 or a tank. Sam could charm the pants off of anyone breathing.

The wheels in Moustapha's mind began spinning as he looked into the good-looking, all-American face of Sam Booker.

"Sam, my old friend. What the hell am I doing here? The question is, what are you doing here?"

"Business as usual for me," Sam replied. "I go where the business is. You know that." His voice got even lower. "Seeing you here, on the other hand, has to be a minor miracle. Last time I heard, you were cooling your heels in prison with no chance of getting out. In fact, they were still trying to decide whether or not to put you in front of a firing squad."

"What can I say?" Moustapha smiled smugly. "I got tired of the food."

Sam laughed. "Don't tell me you came to Nouakchott

for the food. You could have gone to any number of other places known for their cuisine. Believe me, I wouldn't be here if I didn't have to make a delivery tonight."

Moustapha's heartbeat accelerated. Tonight. That meant he had to move fast.

"I mean," Sam continued, making sure only Moustapha could hear him, "it would seem to me that you would try to get as far away from Senegal as possible. Crossing the border into Mauritania doesn't seem far enough away, considering that the Mauritanians and the Senegalese are now trying to get along. There's even a special Mauritania-Malian-Senegalese police coordination program to ensure greater border security. You were lucky to have made it into the country."

"Luck didn't have anything to do with it," Moustapha informed him nonchalantly. "I have powerful friends."

"Good for you," Sam said, rising. He extended his hand. "Well, it was good to see you again, my friend. I'm sure you won't mind if I don't tell anyone about running into you today. I'd like to stay healthy as long as I possibly can."

Moustapha hastily stood and pumped Sam's hand. "What's the hurry? I was just getting ready to go find a watering hole somewhere. Why don't you join me?"

"A bar in a country that's one hundred percent Muslim? You might have to sneak back across the border to find one of those." Sam thought a moment. "I'll tell you what, I brought a couple of bottles of fine whiskey with me. Don't ask me how I got them past customs."

So that's how they wound up back at Sam's hotel room.

Moustapha walked around the palatial suite—at least it looked like a palatial suite compared to the dinky room he was booked in—admiring the modern conveniences.

"You have a phone." He noticed right away.

Sam had gone to get a bottle of the whiskey he'd promised and two glasses. Moustapha had made himself comfortable on the sofa next to the picture window.

Sam handed him a glass and filled it half way with the golden elixir. He poured himself a glass, set the bottle on the coffee table in front of the sofa, and sat down. Looking at Moustapha, he said, "A toast to your freedom, my friend."

Moustapha raised his glass. "To my continued freedom." He smiled at the thought of him and Ashante enjoying a life of leisure in a country that had no extradition laws, someplace where they could raise a family and not have to worry about their children's father being dragged out of his bed in the middle of the night. He suspected Ashante still had nightmares about the night the authorities had come for him.

"And you, Sam, what shall we drink to for you?" Moustapha asked, full of good cheer and Irish whiskey.

"To my last sale," Sam said wistfully. "I'm getting out of the business. I'm getting too old for this crap. I'm going to get married and have a house full of children. I'm going to forget I was ever Sam Booker, the weapons broker."

"Is that what they're calling gunrunners these days?" Moustapha asked. "Weapons brokers? Sounds like even that is getting the politically correct terminology. I hate the way the world is going. Everything is becoming global. It used to be nobody cared what was going on in some remote part of the planet. But now, everybody's connected. The United States and Britain have made themselves the watchdogs of the world. Any little skirmish, they have to stick their noses in it." He swallowed the rest of his drink in one big gulp and grimaced as the whiskey burned his throat on the way down.

"Yeah, well, either way I come out smelling like a

rose," Sam said, and drained his glass, too. He refilled their glasses. Peering at Moustapha, he asked, "So, how is your beautiful wife? Will she be waiting for you at your final destination?"

Moustapha had never been able to hold his liquor. He rarely drank before he had been imprisoned because it made him emotional. Men like him did not like displaying emotions in public. Also men, in general, trusted another man more if he could hold his liquor, and Moustapha had imbibed in the company of males who needed to know he was in control. He had a reputation to uphold, after all. But he always knew his limit, two drinks.

Sam had caught him off guard when he'd asked about Ashante. Moustapha tried to avoid the subject by saying, "That's a long story."

"I've got nothing but time." Sam glanced at his watch. "I don't have to be anywhere for six hours. I'm all ears."

Moustapha bit his bottom lip, and took another sip of his drink for fortitude. "She didn't stick by me," he said harshly. He stared at the golden liquid in his glass. His eyes became watery. He sniffed. Perhaps five years in prison had rendered him even more susceptible to the effects of alcohol. This was the second drink he'd had in half a decade. He liked the taste of it on his tongue, how warm it made him feel inside.

The only thing that had made him feel warm inside had been his love for Ashante, and the assurance that she loved him in return. Now he could get it from a bottle.

He took another swig.

Sam had not uttered a word since he'd told him about Ashante's betrayal. Now, Sam shook his head and said, "Man, I don't know what to say. I would probably flip out if my woman left me to rot in prison."

Moustapha felt the tears on his cheeks and automatically brushed them away with his free hand. His other one possessively cupped the glass of whiskey. "She divorced me and married some maggot who makes farm equipment. Farm equipment! I bet he is short and has a potbelly."

"Probably," Sam said. "And he treats her like a piece of property. She's not going to like that after being treated like a queen by you."

"That's right," Moustapha agreed. "She's probably miserable."

In his inestimable opinion, that meant when he showed up on her doorstep she would be glad to see him, monumentally relieved that he'd come to rescue her from a life of drudgery and boredom. She would have to admit, being the wife of a dictator was anything but boring! Why, during uprisings she was obliged to ride in limousines with bulletproof glass. She had a foodtaster who tested each serving of food from her plate before she was allowed to eat it. They'd lost two good people that way, the taster and the cook who had to be executed after the food taster had died of arsenic poisoning.

From that point on, for some reason, Ashante refused to consume any food she hadn't personally prepared. Moustapha sighed. He had really spoiled that woman.

"You ought to send her a postcard from wherever you end up," Sam suggested. "Rub her nose in the fact that you're a free man and living well."

Moustapha finished off his second drink and set the glass on the coffee table. Licking his lips, he said, "Why would I send her a postcard when she's going to be right by my side?"

Sam threw his head back in laughter and slapped Moustapha on the knee. "You really had me going there, thinking that Ashante had left you, when she really is waiting for you somewhere!"

Moustapha looked Sam in the eyes. There wasn't a trace of humor in his dark gaze.

"It is as I told you. But she's still coming with me."

Grimacing, Sam said, "You're going to kidnap her? My friend, you're not thinking clearly. You should be on a plane making your way to a sympathetic country, not cooking up a plan to drag your ex-wife kicking and screaming with you."

Moustapha abruptly got to his feet, none too steadily, and glared down at Sam.

"They took everything from me when they arrested and jailed me for atrocities against my own people. I loved my people. Under my rule, unemployment dropped. School was mandatory, and starvation was becoming a thing of the past. How could my people have turned on me?"

Sam slowly rose and faced Moustapha. "I often wondered how you seemed to sleep so well at night. Now I know. You lived in a constant state of denial."

Moustapha wore a puzzled expression.

"You had nearly twenty thousand people killed for disloyalty, Moustapha. Unemployment dropped because you conscripted every able-bodied male and female into your 'volunteer' army. You made school mandatory because it was another way of exacting control. Anyone under the age of sixteen had to be in school. And any healthy persons between the ages of sixteen and thirty-two had to be a soldier in your army. Those who went hungry went down because some of them were in your army and were given two meals a day in exchange for killing their own people. Stop looking at life through rose-colored glasses, Moustapha. Look at me, I'm a gunrunner.

"I don't claim to be anything else. I am paid blood money for my wares. I know that. I know I'm going to hell when I die. So I'm going to have one hell of a good time while I'm here. You seem to be of the opinion that there is a heaven waiting for you somewhere."

"My slate was wiped clean by the past five years," Moustapha stated emphatically. "They got their pound of flesh. Now it's time for me to start a new life."

"Which you believe should include Ashante," Sam said, incredulous. "Man, you think that Senegalese prison was bad. Wait until you see the inside of a Mauritanian prison. And you will, if you try to kidnap Ashante. Take my advice, please. Leave here and get on with your life. There are lots of beautiful women in the world. I should know, I used to have one in every city I visited on a regular basis."

They went on like that for quite a while, Moustapha saying he was not going to leave Nouakchott without Ashante, and Sam, imploring him to forget about her. She would be his downfall. When it got close to seven P.M., Sam told Moustapha that he had an appointment and would be gone for two hours, but he was welcome to stay there and watch videos which the hotel provided because they didn't get very good television reception.

Moustapha accepted his hospitality (he couldn't stand up anyway) and was stretched out, snoring on the sofa before Sam left. It was the third glass of whiskey that was his undoing.

Sam did not really have an appointment. When he left the hotel room, he went straight to his four-by-four and got a bag he'd prepared earlier just for this occasion. In less than five minutes, he was back in the room. Moustapha's snoring had shifted into second gear. Rupert

stood looking down at the slumbering ex-dictator, the bag
in his right hand.

He unzipped the bag and removed a pair of leg shackles. The chains clicked against one another but not
loudly enough to wake the guest of honor. Rupert cau-
tiously approached him. He knew this could be tricky
because Moustapha outweighed him by at least thirty
pounds, and he was three inches taller, as well.

Moustapha turned over in his sleep and jerked his
right leg when Rupert slipped the cuff around his ankle
and snapped it shut. He rose up on his elbows when he
felt Rupert's hand on his left ankle. Eyes still closed, he
shouted, "How dare you come into my house like this?
Do you know who I am? I could have you shot for this!"

Rupert realized Moustapha must have been dreaming
about the night the authorities had broken down his
door and awakened him and Ashante out of a sound
sleep. A big, tough man like him, still having nightmares
about his imprisonment, but who didn't seem to have
any remorse about the many cruelties he'd inflicted on
innocent people during his reign of terror.

Rupert slapped the other ankle cuff on him before he
could fully surface from his dream, then grabbed
Moustapha by the ankles and dragged him off the sofa.

Moustapha hit the floor with a thud and woke up,
though the alcohol still had him in its intoxicating grip.
"What is this? What are you doing?" He tried to focus,
and rolled onto his side. Sluggishly getting onto his
knees, he grabbed the arm of the sofa to steady himself
and pulled himself to a stooping position. It wasn't until
he tried to walk toward Rupert that he discovered his
movements had been hampered.

Outrage flashed in his dark eyes. "What is the meaning of this?" he ground out.

"I would think it's pretty obvious that you're an escaped felon, and I'm taking you back to prison," Rupert calmly told him. "The reason I've put shackles on you is so that I can choose the second option of my imperative: to bring you in dead or alive."

Moustapha growled like some savage jungle beast. "Who are you with? CIA?"

Rupert stood several feet away with his arms akimbo. "It doesn't matter who I'm with, Moustapha. The only thing that matters is if you want to live, or if you want to die. I'm flexible. I left your hands unbound because it gives you a certain amount of movement. However, with your legs shackled, you're not going anywhere fast. It's your choice. You can go through me and, perhaps, beat me and be on the run again. Or you can peacefully come with me. Personally, I hope you'll choose door number one because I'd like the chance to get some exercise. I've been stuck in a car for two days waiting for you to show up, so I could use a good workout. Also, I'd like the opportunity to beat you within an inch of your life on behalf of all the people whose lives you've taken or, in Ashante's case, just screwed up."

"Five years ago, it was you who betrayed me, told them how to get to me," Moustapha said, the truth dawning on him at last. "You came to me as a friend, and you stabbed me in the back." His lips were curled in a nasty snarl.

"Don't take it personally," Rupert said with a cold smile. "I've helped bring down men who were much more powerful than you. Although none as blind to his actions as you are. Nor as stupid as you are. Come now, Moustapha, why would you make a beeline for the one person on earth we knew you couldn't resist?"

"She belongs to me, you bastard, and nobody's going to keep me away from her!"

Moustapha leapt onto Rupert, driving him back hard

against the wall. The plasterboard cracked under the on-
slaught of the men's combined four-hundred-plus
pounds. Rupert drove a knee into Moustapha's gut, and
after Moustapha doubled over, he aimed karate chops to
both ears. Howling in pain, Moustapha fell to his knees.
Rupert took a step backward for optimum leverage and
executed a kick to the side of Moustapha's head. The
former dictator fell, unconscious, to the floor, his rump
in the air.

"I never said it would be a fair fight," Rupert said as he
walked around him.

He promptly handcuffed his prisoner.

After Moustapha was properly restrained, Rupert sat
down on the bed, flipped open his cell phone and
pressed a button. A British man answered.

Rupert said, "The package is ready for pickup."

"Splendid," said the voice. "Someone will be there to
pick it up in under ten minutes. Thank you for using
Federal Express."

"My pleasure," said Rupert, and disconnected. He sat
there on the bed and looked around the room, at the
ravaged wall, and at the chair Moustapha had turned
over when he'd jumped on him, realizing that he hadn't
felt this alive in quite some time.

It occurred to him, then, that he'd accepted the assignment not simply because it would get the agency
off his back from now on, but because he missed the action as Thorne had accused him of three days ago. What
was wrong with him? Solange hadn't said yes to a spy
when she'd agreed to marry him. She'd said yes to a
man who had vowed never to go back to that dangerous
world again. Now look at him, sitting in a hotel room
thousands of miles away from her, relishing the fight
he'd just been engaged in.

He had some serious soul-searching to do.

* * *

Solange glided smoothly along the surface of the water in the pool. It was Sunday morning and, so far, she was the only swimmer doing laps in the Olympic-size pool.

She had on her favorite navy blue tank suit, and a sky blue swim cap that she wore more to keep water out of her ears than to prevent her hair from getting wet.

She swam to the far side and quickly turned by going under and coming up in the opposite direction. The slap of the water against the sides of her swim cap made hearing difficult, so she hadn't noticed someone had come all the way to the edge of the pool and was observing her. But when she got to the end of the pool and turned, shaking her head and blowing air out of her nose to dispel water, she saw him.

Treading water, she worriedly looked around her, wondering if anyone was within earshot.

Nicholas. She thought she'd never see him again after his heartfelt apology last week. Or had it all been a ploy? His presence here was unsettling. She held onto the side of the pool with her right hand, her legs working to keep her afloat in the deep end.

Looking up at him, she forced a smile. "Nick, I didn't hear you come in."

He grinned and moved a bit closer to her. "I figured you would be here. You always liked coming to the pool early on Sunday mornings. You usually have it to yourself."

"Yeah, for a little while at least. It could be filling up anytime soon."

"I'm on my way out of town," he said. "And I wanted to ask you one last question before I go: If I hadn't acted like a fool, would you have married me?"

"Maybe I should get out of the water," Solange said.

She grabbed the side with both hands, allowed her body to sink a bit lower in the water to give herself more buoyancy, and then hoisted herself up onto the side. She quickly lifted her legs from the water and got to her feet. She didn't like the way Nicholas was looking at her with his mouth hanging slightly open, and his eyes shining with . . . hope! She had left her engagement ring in her purse in the women's locker room. She never wore it when she swam for fear it would slip off her finger and be lost down the pool's drain. If she had it on, she could discreetly flash it under his nose to emphasize the fact that she was taken.

Her towel was clear on the other side of the pool. She had to walk over there with her body exposed to his increasingly possessive stare. He followed her, staying a few feet away from her, obviously sensing her nervousness.

Once the large towel was wrapped around her lower half, she smiled at him again and said, "Of course I would have married you, Nick. We were in love, or I thought we were. If I hadn't believed you loved me, I never would have told you that I couldn't have children. That's not something you share with someone you haven't invested your emotions in." She removed her swim cap and finger combed her locks.

"I know that now," Nicholas said quietly. "You were trusting me with your heart, and the only thing I could think about was how your revelation would affect me." He shook his head, thinking. "It's funny how certain things bother you after so much time has passed, but I just had to know, Solange." He turned to leave. "Thank you. Thank you for telling me you would have married me. I think that if I'm lucky enough to have love in my life again, I'll cherish it, and keep it safe."

Solange didn't know what to make of Nicholas Campion. She watched his back as he retreated, the sound of his footsteps echoing in the emptiness of the large area around the pool.

With each step she felt more relieved. She didn't care how much he said he'd changed.

He still unnerved her, and probably always would.

He was almost at the exit when he turned suddenly. "The man you're going to marry?" he asked. "What's he like?"

Okay, Solange thought, *now this is getting creepy.*

She was about to tell him where to get off when she heard the door opening and glanced up at someone entering the pool area.

She was excited and relieved at once, if that's possible. *Rupert.*

"He's like that guy over there," she told Nicholas, pointing to Rupert.

She began running toward Rupert, who was coming to meet her with his arms open wide and a huge grin on his face.

Nicholas spun around, his brows creased in a frown. "Who?" He stopped short when he caught sight of the liplock Solange was in with the tall, dark-skinned stranger.

A scene like that did more to crush any illusions he might have had about a second chance with Solange than hours of her telling him there was no hope for them.

He sighed deeply and left in a hurry.

Solange and Rupert didn't even come up for air after the door closed behind him.

Rupert's big hands were in her hair as he held her. He inhaled the soft, feminine smell of her. Even fresh from the pool, her unique scent was unmistakable to his discriminating nose. She smelled like wild jasmine to him. She tasted like strawberries.

Up on her toes, Solange felt as though she might combust at any moment. His strong hands were on her back, going lower to cup her buttocks, pulling her ever closer.

His lips were on her mouth, her throat, the side of her neck. How many nights had she imagined his hands and his mouth all over her? Too many. Now he was here, and she was breathing him in. Breathing in life again. He brought her fully to life.

Hello, his tongue spoke for him as it coaxed her lips apart and slipped inside her mouth. *I've missed you desperately,* it said. And hers said, *Dammit, cut the chitchat and take my clothes off, already!*

They might have stripped and made love right there if not for Professor Edith Pullman, who came into the room and loudly cleared her throat. She was an English instructor at the university. Eighty, if she was a day, she enjoyed Sunday morning swims too, but rarely walked in on foreplay.

Tall, and stately, with skin the color of toasted almonds, and a short, white Afro, she looked quite fit in her black, skirted swimsuit.

She smiled at them, her dark eyes full of humor. "Not that I object to sex, you understand," she told them. "It's just that I prefer it in the bedroom, and not by the pool. Run along, children. There must be a bed with your names on it somewhere close by."

Solange and Rupert both smiled at her, and executed playful bows as they left the room. "So sorry, Professor Pullman," Solange called, her cheeks hot with embarrassment.

"Just invite me to the wedding, Dr. DuPree," Edith Pullman said as she removed her sandals in preparation for diving into the pool.

Five

Rupert tried to go into the women's locker room with Solange, but she laughed and placed a hand on his broad chest, preventing him. "Oh, no, you don't. Wait for me here. I'll change, and we can go. I'll shower at home. Give me five minutes."

Rupert held her as though the thought of five minutes without her would be too painful to endure. He kissed her forehead. "Good God, woman, what do you think I'm made of, steel? I can't let you out of my sight for that long." He bent his head and nuzzled her neck. "Nobody's in there, we can lock the door and—"

Solange covered his mouth with her right hand. Shaking her head, she said, "Don't even think about it. I'm not going to get caught with my pants down in the women's locker room." She removed her hand and kissed his mouth. "Be a good boy and let me go."

She turned out of his arms and quickly went into the locker room.

In record time she was back with her shoulder bag on her arm, dressed in sweats and a pair of Nikes, her gym bag in her right hand. Rupert grinned at her and pulled her close to his side as they left the building. "It's good you're a creature of habit. When you weren't at home, I knew this was where you'd be. By the way, who was that man I saw you with?"

"Nicholas Campion," Solange answered. She pushed the door open, and they stepped outside into the bright sunshine.

Both of them automatically put on their sunglasses. They walked down the steps of the building and turned in the direction of faculty parking.

"*The* Nicholas Campion?" Rupert asked, frowning. She'd told him all about Nicholas. Finding the man who'd made her feel useless as a woman standing at the edge of the pool while she stood there in a wet bathing suit was the last thing he had expected when he'd gone into the pool area in search of her.

"No one was more surprised to see him again than I was," Solange said. The sun felt good on her skin. It was only around nine o'clock, and the heat was at a manageable level, around eighty degrees. A breeze blew her silken hair about her face. "He came to my classroom a few days ago after class had ended and told me he was a recovering alcoholic and as part of his twelve-step program he'd come to apologize for treating me badly. I actually found myself sympathizing with the guy, and told him I forgave him. When he showed up a few minutes ago, frankly, it scared me. I thought he'd started stalking me again. But he claims he wanted to ask me one last question: would I have married him if he hadn't freaked out after I told him I couldn't conceive?"

"What did you tell him?"

"I told him, yes, I would have."

Rupert sighed softly. "I see."

They had arrived at Solange's Mustang. Solange quickly unlocked the doors. Looking up at Rupert, she saw the somber expression on his face. "What?" she asked, curious as to why his light mood had darkened.

"Do you still have feelings for him?" Rupert asked, looking deeply into her eyes. Solange's full lips curved in a smile. "None whatsoever." The intensity of her gaze made Rupert's heartbeat quicken. He wondered how he could have doubted her for a moment. "I'm a jealous fool," he said, and bent to touch his forehead to hers.

Straightening up, he said, "Go on, get in. I'll follow you in the rental."

Solange got behind the wheel of the Mustang and looked up at him. "My heart belongs to you, Rupert," she said.

Rupert leaned in and kissed her. Their hunger for one another was nowhere near being sated, as evidenced by the deepness of the kiss and their reluctance to part.

But they couldn't make love in the parking lot, so they separated and Solange peeled out of the lot in the Mustang with Rupert behind her in the rented Ford Explorer.

With less traffic than on a weekday, the drive to Solange's bungalow from the campus of the University of Miami, which was in Coral Gables, took around fifteen minutes.

Solange pulled into the driveway and climbed out of the car. By the time she'd grabbed her purse and gym bag, Rupert was by her side. His long, powerful legs seemed to cover twice as much ground as her legs did. Besides, he was impatient.

He swept her up into his arms as she went to take the first step that led to the front stoop. Giggling, Solange wrapped one arm around his neck while she stretched downward and unlocked the door with her free hand. "Don't drop me."

As Rupert stepped into the foyer with her in his arms, he pretended to trip and Solange gasped, but he had her securely in his grasp. Laughing, Rupert set her down.

Solange put her purse and the gym bag on the hall table. Rupert was circling her like a lion trying to figure out which part of his prey's anatomy he wanted to devour first. Except he looked hungrier than any lion.

With eyes locked, in silent agreement, they began undressing.

Rupert unbuttoned his short-sleeve, off-white linen shirt with slow deliberation.

Solange sighed contentedly when she caught a glimpse of the dark chocolate skin of his smooth, muscular chest. Her gaze lowered to his six-pack, and when his hands went to his belt buckle, she licked her lips because her mouth had suddenly gone dry.

She might not have been as eager had she not known exactly what she was in store for. But she did. Since they had been together they had found myriad ways of pleasuring one another, all of them memorable. And it was impossible not to imagine all of those ways right now as she watched Rupert disrobe.

So mesmerized was she that she'd momentarily forgotten that she was undressing too. Rupert gave her a pointed look, and she smiled and took off her sweatpants.

Now she was dressed only in matching red satin bra and bikini panties, and her Nikes.

Five-foot-four and a hundred and thirty-five pounds, she was fit but voluptuous. Her breasts were full and womanly, the nipples dark brown and already hardening. Her hips were flared, giving her an hourglass figure since her waist was small in comparison.

She bent and loosened the laces on her sneakers. Rupert watched, enjoying the sight of her firm, round behind in the air. He was half tumescent, but seeing her bent over like that gave him a full hard-on. Solange sat on the floor to remove her Nikes. Her legs were wide open and he could see the outline of her sex against the crotch of her panties.

She finished taking off the sneakers and stood up.

Rupert was standing across from her with his pants still zipped, but from the bulge in them she knew he was near the point of ripping her clothes off. He'd kicked off his Italian loafers while she'd been busy with the Nikes.

His breathing was shallow as he approached her. Solange backed away. She smiled at him. His hands went to the zipper. He carefully lowered it and pulled his slacks down. The weight of the belt made them drop around his ankles. He stepped out of them. Powerful thigh muscles flexed as he moved closer. The white boxer-briefs he had on did little to conceal the size of his manhood, nor his state of arousal, huge and throbbing.

Solange felt a twinge of fear, which sent a thrill of desire through her. She always wondered, just before he entered her, if she would survive the powerful need in him.

Rupert was still an enigma to her. She knew he had once been a dangerous man and, deep down, he was probably still a dangerous man. But to love someone meant you gave all of yourself to him, and you accepted every part of him. She loved the dangerous Rupert as much as she loved the tender part of him that would lay down his life for her.

Solange had backed up against the foyer wall. She spread her legs, her buttocks pressed to the wall, her arms open and flat against it. Spread-eagled against the wall, she shot Rupert a smoldering look that was a blatant invitation for him to take her.

Rupert didn't have to be asked twice.

He went to her and made short work of taking off her bra and panties. She helped him out of his boxer-briefs. His body was dark brown while hers was a golden brown.

He bent and pressed his mouth to hers. Solange's arms went around his neck. She tasted and teased him, sucked his tongue with abandon, and writhed against his hard body. She was wet. Ready for him. Ached for him to fill her up. His mouth was sweet. His tongue was firm and insistent. Yet, she felt tenderness envelop her. Felt his love for her merging with her love for him. As though their spirits were becoming one. That was the strange thing about their coupling. Though it was often rough, it was always spiritual in nature. She could not fathom what they had. She was simply grateful for it. Any children they had would be conceived in love.

Her eyes stretched as it occurred to her that she had not told him her news. She turned her head, breaking off the kiss. "Rupert, I need to tell you something."

They'd stopped using condoms months ago. She was infertile. And since they were both healthy and faithful, why not enjoy sex to its fullest without the added barrier of a latex condom, they reasoned. But now things were different. Darrell had said she appeared to be fertile. Rupert needed to be apprised of the situation. They needed to discuss whether or not having sex without protection was the wisest choice.

Rupert's breath was hot against her neck. "Oh, baby, later. Please. I need you. You feel so good. The scent of you is driving me crazy."

"I'm sorry. I should have told you way before we got to this point, but I was hot for you. Still hot for you." Her nipples were so hard, the touch of Rupert's chest against them was painful, and a steady pulse was beating between her legs. Plus, having Rupert's fully erect penis jutting against her stomach didn't exactly have a calming effect.

Rupert wasn't listening. He lowered his head and took one of her nipples between his talented lips. His tongue wreaked havoc on her ability to reason. She moaned deep in her throat. Rupert's engorged penis jerked when he heard her make that sound. The tip was wet.

While his left hand cupped her breast, holding it gently as he suckled, he slipped his right hand between her thighs. She was so wet he had no fear of hurting her as he put his forefinger inside her and began massaging her clitoris.

With his tongue suckling her nipple, and his finger massaging her clitoris, Solange was swiftly approaching meltdown.

"Oh, baby, oh, baby," she cried. She moved up and down, up and down against the wall. Sensing she was close to the precipice, Rupert slowed down. This only increased the intensity of Solange's arousal, causing her to pant with the desire for release. Still, she tried to hold back. She needed to talk to him because she knew the moment she crossed the line, and succumbed to the impending orgasm, Rupert would penetrate her right there against the wall. Then, it would be too late for a condom. Millions of his little soldiers would be inside her, trying to penetrate her eggs and, if they were anything like the man whose body they'd come from, they would find their mark.

"Do you want to make a baby today?" she blurted out.

Rupert raised his head and looked into her eyes. His were drunk with passion. He was visibly trying to slow his breathing. "What did you say?"

"I had a test done at my gynecologist's. Darrell says it looks like my body has healed itself. He believes I can get pregnant now."

"That was the news you didn't want to tell me over the phone?" Rupert's voice was barely a whisper.

"Yes," Solange said, tearing up. She breathed through her mouth. Her lips were slightly swollen from kissing him so intensely. Her eyes glimmered. "There's a possibility that we'll be able to have a child together."

Rupert pulled her into his arms and held her tightly. "It's a miracle."

"That's what Darrell said." Solange's voice was muffled because her head was being held firmly against his chest.

Rupert eased his grip. Looking down into her upturned face, he laughed.

"You don't suppose it was that damned fertility goddess, do you?"

Solange laughed too, as though the thought had never occurred to her.

"Of course not. Darrell says it's a case of science not knowing enough about the human body. Apparently others have been miraculously cured. I guess I'm not a freak of nature."

Rupert squeezed her hard against him again. "This is what we've prayed for, isn't it?"

"Were you praying?" Solange asked. It was news to her. "You actually prayed for us to have a child together?"

"Didn't you?" asked Rupert.

"Of course, but I had no idea you were praying, too."

"Praying, hoping against hope. Whatever you want to call it," Rupert said. "We have been given a gift. Let's celebrate it."

"Now, don't get carried away," Solange warned. "What if Darrell is mistaken? He could be, you know."

"There's only one way to find out," Rupert said. The look of barely bridled desire had returned to his whiskey-colored eyes.

"You mean, do it without a condom?"

"We've been doing it without a condom for months now," Rupert reminded her.

"Yeah, but that was because we knew I couldn't get pregnant. If Darrell is right, you could knock me up before the wedding. I don't want to waddle down the aisle."

Rupert took her face between his hands and peered

into her eyes. "Solange, I'm going to marry you whether you're knocked up or not. If there's a remote possibility that we can have a child with your eyes and your joie de vivre, then I want to go for it! What are we waiting for? I know I love you, and I know I want you to be the mother of my children. Time waits for no one."

Solange's head was spinning. Logically, she was aware she could not have asked for a more positive response from Rupert. He wanted a child with her. And he didn't want to wait. But there were so many things happening in their lives. Having a child was a huge responsibility. In a few months, Desta would be coming to live with them. She would undoubtedly need some time to adjust to a new way of life. She might require their undivided attention. Shouldn't they wait until she was settled before bringing another child into the household?

Rupert did have a point about time running out, though. She was thirty-five. She didn't have that many more good childbearing years left. She closed her eyes, breathed in deeply, and exhaled. Opening her eyes, she met Rupert's gaze.

"God, I love you."

He smiled, knowing he'd convinced her.

"You won't be sorry. Come here."

Rupert picked her up, cradling her in his arms. "Let's do this right, shall we?"

He began walking in the direction of the master bedroom.

"How long are you here for this time?" Solange asked as she wrapped her arms around his neck. She looked him in the eyes. "Tell me now. What will it be? Two, three days of bliss, and then you'll be off to another exotic corner of the planet?"

Rupert smiled enigmatically. "I'll quit."

Solange's lips curled in a smirk. "Sure."

"No, seriously. I'll quit and come live here with you. We'll buy a house in Coral Gables. It's closer to the university, anyway. You won't have such a long commute."

Solange peered into his eyes long and hard, trying to discern whether he was pulling her leg or not. The thing about Rupert was, he had the best poker face she'd ever seen. "You're not going back to London?"

"Maybe for a visit," he said. "After all, my parents live there."

The door to Solange's bedroom was ajar. Rupert shouldered it open and strode into the room where he placed Solange on the queen-size bed that sat more than two feet off of the floor. He climbed in after her, using the bedside step in order to do so gracefully.

A naked man had to be careful not to bruise the merchandise. He straddled her on the bed, with Solange raised up on her elbows still looking at him intently. "Just like that, you're quitting your job? What are you going to live on? What about your pension?"

Laughing, Rupert said, "I told you, I've made good investments over the years. I could have retired a while ago, but I never had a reason to." He bent and kissed the tip of her nose, then lowered his body onto hers. He lay poised between Solange's legs. "I'm holding my reason," he whispered in her ear.

"You never cease to amaze me," Solange said, her voice low and awe filled. She pressed her pelvis into his. "My sweet Rupert."

Rupert's penis lay hard and heavy against her crotch. He raised his hips enough to position the tip at the mouth of her sex. She was slick with wetness from his earlier efforts. "Ah," he sighed as he penetrated her. "Don't make me out to be the hero. I'm doing it for purely selfish reasons, I'll get to be between your legs more often."

Solange's vaginal muscles squeezed his long, thick,

hard shaft, welcoming him. The tips of her breasts were erect. Holding himself up, Rupert's biceps flexed with each movement, as did the muscles in his backside and powerful thighs. "Wrap your legs around me tightly, sweetness. Give it up, because I've been dreaming about this ever since I left you the last time."

Solange put her arms around his neck, drawing him down to her. "You're not the only one who has missed this." With that, she coaxed him onto his side, and then she got on top.

Rupert grinned. "You know what I like."

"Yeah," Solange said. She slowly rode him. He loved watching as the lips of her vagina seemed to take his manhood and swallow it repeatedly. The insides were pink, and reminded him of the inside of her luscious mouth. He reached up and caressed her breasts, pinching the nipples, enjoying the look of ecstasy that came over her lovely face. Solange let her head go back as she moaned her pleasure. "And to think, all I was looking forward to after my swim this morning was brunch at Maman's. What a lovely . . ." She gasped. Rupert was hitting just the right spot.

"Surprise," Rupert finished for her. "And don't talk about your mother while I'm making love to you." The wonderful smell of their sex filled his nostrils. He was a man who thrived on being in touch with all of his senses. It made making love to Solange that much more enjoyable. She was a feast for his senses—golden-brown skin, covered with a thin layer of perspiration now. Her soft curves against his hard body. The sound of her voice in the throes of passion.

She wasn't aware of it, but she had a habit of licking her lips and forming an 'O' with them when she was close to release. She was doing that now.

Rupert smiled and grabbed her behind with both

hands, holding her firmly as he thrust upward. Solange let out a loud moan and collapsed onto his chest. Their eyes met.

"I want you on your back," Rupert said gently.

They rolled over in the bed and Solange clung to him as he threatened to rend her in two with his need. At release, he groaned loud enough to be heard next door. He bent his head and kissed her mouth. "I never expected to love someone as much as I love you," he said.

Solange, spent and happy, smiled up at him. "Neither did I."

They kissed again. This time slowly, softly, languidly tonguing one another.

The doorbell rang.

"Are you expecting anyone?" Rupert asked.

"No," Solange said as she scooted over to the edge of the bed and placed her foot on the antique cherry wood step beside the bed. "It's probably a neighbor."

Rupert got up, too. "Well, I'll be in the shower. You can join me once you get rid of whomever's at the door."

Solange quickly went into the adjacent bathroom, grabbed her bathrobe from behind the door, and then hurried through the house to the front door. "Just a second!"

She looked through the peephole. She had no idea FedEx delivered on Sunday!

Opening the door, she smiled at the Federal Express man. "A package for me on Sunday?"

"We deliver on time, ma'am, no matter what day it is. Funny name for a woman: Rupert Giles." He was of medium build and height, with white-blond hair and blue eyes.

He showed her the name on his clipboard. He held the package, a flat FedEx envelope, in his right hand.

"He's indisposed right now," Solange told him. "I'll sign for him."

He raised his brows, considering her suggestion. "Oh, okay. It's not anything valuable. Otherwise they would've insured it."

He held the clipboard firmly while Solange signed. When she was finished, he handed her the envelope. "Have a good one!" And he was gone.

Solange closed and locked the door. She peered down at the envelope. Rupert had been back less than two hours, and he was already getting packages? Obviously, he had told his company where he would be, and they'd sent him the paperwork for his next assignment. She smiled. They were probably going to be put out when he turned in his resignation.

"It was for you," she called as she walked through the bathroom door. "An envelope delivered by Federal Express."

In the shower, Rupert stopped soaping his body to listen. "It's probably something from the company. Leave it on the bed, please, and I'll open it when I come out. Are you coming in?"

"I'm taking off my robe as we speak," Solange told him.

"You're late," Marie said as she opened the door. "My, you look lovely in that sundress, though. And are those Jimmy Choos?" She was referring to Solange's white slingbacks.

"From his spring collection," Solange confirmed. "They're the one thing I've splurged on in the past few months." She glanced behind her. "Hold on, Maman. I'm not alone."

Rupert stepped up. "Hello, Mrs. DuPree."

Marie rarely was caught off guard, but this time she was nonplussed. She gazed up at Rupert with her mouth agape. Rupert removed his sunglasses so she could get a good look at his face. A mother-in-law-to-be had the right to peruse the man her daughter was thinking of bringing into the family.

"Well!" cried Marie. "It's about damn time!"

"Maman!" Solange exclaimed, laughing.

"Did I say something that wasn't true?" Marie asked, talking to Rupert. "You've been seeing my daughter for more than a year, and this is the first time I've laid eyes on you. I have the right to express relief. I was beginning to think you were a figment of my daughter's very vivid imagination." She smiled warmly at him. "I'm pleased to see that Solange and I both have a penchant for choosing handsome men. You are quite breathtaking, darling."

She led him into the foyer of her Coral Gables home, leaving Solange behind to close the door. The house was built in the 1920s. By Miami standards, it qualified for historical landmark status. It was rumored that it had been owned by a Cuban gangster who had run casinos on the island. Built in a hacienda style, it had an orange-tiled roof and was sprawling in design. Marie had refurbished it in the manner in which it had originally been built, restoring everything from the ceilings to the floors.

Today, Marie was attired in a peach-colored sleeveless pantsuit made of linen. On her feet were beige high-heeled sandals. She'd curled her hair and put on makeup, which she felt naked without. She knew good taste when she saw it. She was pleased that Rupert's clothes fit him so well. He wore a pair of cream-colored cotton slacks with cuffs, and a short-sleeve moss green shirt, also made of cotton. On his feet were Italian loafers in caramel-colored leather that looked as soft as a baby's bottom. He smells nice, too, Marie decided, breathing in deeply.

"Okay," she said, turning to look up at him as they stood in the foyer. "You're beyond handsome, you dress well, and you're obviously familiar with the importance of good hygiene. You can't be that perfect. Cough it up. What are you hiding, Rupert?"

Solange went and grabbed her mother by the upper arm. "Don't you think you could wait to grill him until after brunch? I'm ravenous."

Marie allowed herself to be led away by her daughter, who looked back at Rupert with an exasperated expression on her face that said, *I told you so!*

Rupert simply smiled and followed them through the house to the back patio, where Marie had set the table.

As soon as they entered the patio area, Marie became the consummate hostess.

"Rupert," she said. "You sit here so you'll be between the two of us. I'm not going to let Solange have you all to herself."

Rupert pulled out Solange's chair for her, then sat down next to her. Marie served them savory scrambled eggs cooked with chopped scallions; homemade croissants; crisp, thickly sliced bacon; and fresh strawberries, cantaloupe, and watermelon. When she was finished serving, she went to sit down. Rupert got up and helped her with her chair.

"Thank you," Marie said, smiling up at him.

They dug in, enjoying the meal and talking about mundane things. Rupert told them about his trip to Mauritania: "The people are friendly. But it's not at all tourist oriented. Accommodations are still hard to find, and most people agree that the weather is difficult to get used to. The sirocco winds off the Sahara can make the temperature even hotter than it normally is, which is hot enough!"

"Solange told me the story of how you were reunited with your biological father," said Marie. "The way you met is fascinating."

Rupert smiled, remembering. "If I hadn't met Solange, I probably never would have found my father and my sister, because it was Solange who my father was looking for."

"To help him find the Ark of the Covenant!" Marie exclaimed, her dark eyes sparkling with excitement. She met Solange's gaze. "Remember? You and Gaea must have gone to see *Raiders of the Lost Ark* a dozen times when it came to theaters back in the early 80s. You really loved that movie."

"I still do," Solange said.

"God works in mysterious ways," Marie said. "You two met, and then Rupert gets a whole new family."

"What was Solange like as a child?" Rupert asked Marie.

Marie's pretty brown face crinkled in a grin. "I'll do better than that, I'll show you what she was like." With that, she pushed her chair back and rose.

"Oh, Maman, not the photo albums!" Solange protested. She got up, too, but Rupert caught hold of her arm, preventing her from following her mother from the patio. She sat down. "Now you're in for it."

"I can't wait," Rupert said with a mischievous grin. "Eat, darling. You're going to need your strength later."

Solange resumed eating, her eyes on his face. "You're really enjoying this, aren't you?"

"Very much so. Your mother is delightful. She prepared a delicious meal for us, and if I have to look at every photo she's ever had taken of you to get in her good graces, I'll do it."

They were finished eating before Marie returned

carrying what looked like fifteen photo albums that she had to balance with her chin as she walked over to them.

Rupert got up, took the burden from her, and set the pile of albums on the tabletop. Then he helped Marie with her chair.

After they were all seated, Marie got the top album from the stack and placed it between her and Rupert. "This is her baby album. Georges and I must have supported Polaroid that first year. We had to have pictures of her every waking moment. The poor child nearly went blind from all the flash bulbs going off in her eyes."

The first photograph was of Marie with a pink bundle in her arms. She had apparently just come home from the hospital. She was standing in the doorway, wearing a pink shift that must have been one of her maternity dresses, and a pair of pink slippers.

"Look at my hair," she said. "Sticking up all over the place. I was exhausted, but it was a happy kind of exhaustion." She turned the page. The next photo was of Solange at five months lying on a thick pink blanket, her head raised with a grin on her face.

She didn't have a stitch on. "Her first cheesecake photograph," Marie commented. "Of course, it was nothing compared to the time she lost the top to her swimsuit in the waters of the Atlantic. She was sixteen then, and more filled out."

"So that's why you don't like swimming in the ocean," Rupert said. "I thought you'd had a near-drowning incident."

"I did nearly drown in the ocean. That came after the lost bikini top incident."

She and her mother shared a look. Neither of them liked talking about that day.

Solange didn't because the images of gasping for air when only water filled her lungs came back in living color.

Marie didn't like talking about it because that was the day she'd nearly lost her only child. She could still recall how she and Georges had pulled Solange's limp body from the waves. Marie had panicked when Solange didn't respond to the first round of mouth-to-mouth resuscitation and began slapping her daughter's face as hard as she could, crying, "Don't you die on me, dammit. You're not supposed to die before me." She'd alternated breathing air into Solange's lungs, slapping her, and shaking her. No one had been able to pull her off of Solange, not even Georges, who had been convinced Solange was gone.

After ten or more minutes, Solange began coughing violently, and they took her to the hospital.

Tears came into Marie's eyes now, thinking about it.

Solange reached over, grasped her mother's hand, and squeezed it reassuringly.

"I'll tell you about it sometime," she promised Rupert.

Rupert continued looking through the photo album, smiling and asking questions that Marie happily answered. The albums documented the DuPrees' lives up until the present. The last photograph was of Marie and Solange standing in front of Solange's house. It had been in the fall, following the redecorating project. Rupert breathed a contented sigh after he closed the last photo album. "Thank you," he said to Marie. "I enjoyed that very much."

"I'm glad," Marie said. She placed her fork on her plate. She'd completed her meal while they had looked through the photo albums. She smiled wistfully. "May I say something personal to you, Rupert? I don't want to embarrass you any more than I already have."

"Please, feel free to say anything you like to me," Rupert encouraged her. "I won't get embarrassed or offended. I promise. My skin is a lot thicker than it looks."

"Oh, no," said Marie. "It's nothing uncomplimentary."

She paused, appearing to need time to form her words correctly. "What I wanted to say was I'm so glad that you and Solange found each other. Solange is my heart. I haven't always shown her that she's my heart, but she is. I spent so much time hiding my emotions. I hope you and Solange won't waste time doing that. I hope your love spills out all over the place. I hope you'll always look at her the way you do now. Like you could scoop her up with a spoon."

"Maman!" Solange cried.

But Rupert only rose and pulled Marie into his arms and hugged her tightly. "Don't worry. I will always want to scoop her up with a spoon, a very small one to make the sensation last as long as possible."

"That's a good boy!" Marie said.

Solange sat watching them and shaking her head in amazement. Her life would never be boring with the two of them in it.

Six

"I don't know why I'm going to work. I won't be able to concentrate knowing you're here," Solange said to Rupert between kisses as he saw her off at the door. She looked up at him with such earnest longing that Rupert had to smile.

"Let's hope you still feel that way after I've been here awhile. I'm going to start looking for a place right away, so you'll always be glad to see me."

"Well, don't be too quick about it. I like sharing my bed with you," Solange said with a saucy smile. She playfully grabbed a handful of his butt. "Bye, sweetie."

Rupert watched her walk down the steps, admiring her shapely legs under the sporty pale yellow skirt suit she had on. Those legs were made even sexier by the three-inch heels she insisted on wearing. He'd told her she should not ruin her feet in those things, but she liked the extra height the heels gave her.

She waved to him as she backed the Mustang out of the driveway. Smiling, Rupert blew her a kiss. Once she was out of sight, he went to the bedroom and sat on the bed. Picking up the receiver of the phone on the nightstand, he dialed a number from memory.

Three rings later, Jason Thorne answered.

"You really shouldn't make calls from Dr. DuPree's residence. Have you forgotten everything I taught you?"

"Quit joking, Thorne. I'm going jogging. So are you. There's a park south of here. Be there in fifteen minutes."

"What if I don't want to go jogging, Giles? I think your adopted countrymen are way too obsessed with exercise. I see them all over the place, running as if they're trying to catch a bus, or something" Thorne joked.

"Don't screw around with me, Thorne," Rupert warned. "You wouldn't have sent me that message if the crap wasn't about to hit the fan. I'm leaving now."

He hung up and rose, peeling off the bathrobe he had on and opening the bottom bureau drawer to get some athletic clothes to change into. "Damned spies," he muttered as he dressed. "What possessed me to get involved with them again?"

Five minutes later, he was walking through the front door and running down the steps.

The neighborhood that Solange lived in was a multi-cultural enclave composed of single-family homes. Its streets were clean and, for the most part, quiet. It had wide boulevards and nicely manicured lawns. Rupert had jogged here many times before and enjoyed the scenery as he went: houses that, like Solange's, were southern-facing bungalows with weathered siding. Some with front porches, and some without. Other homes were more modern creations made of stone or brick, with touches of Spanish, Mediterranean, Chinese, French, and Dutch architecture.

"I see you're back," called Peter Wychowski, Solange's elderly next-door neighbor. He was taking his seven-year-old Jack Russell terrier, Jimbo, for his morning walk.

Seventy-six, tall, and gaunt, with a thick head of white hair, Peter made it his business to watch out for Solange and had introduced himself the first time he'd seen Rupert leaving Solange's house alone. Now, they were friends who, time permitting, enjoyed a rousing game of chess together on Peter's front porch.

"Yes, I got in yesterday. Surprised her at the pool," Rupert said.

"I bet she got a kick out of that," Peter returned with a warm smile. He was a widower of twenty years and still missed his wife Trudy with all his heart. Since he was fond of Solange, he enjoyed hearing that she was in a good relationship with someone like Rupert Giles who, in his opinion, was a man with lots of secrets but who was innately good.

Peter was okay with people having secrets. He'd survived Hitler's death camps. Most of his family had not. When he'd made it to the United States in 1944, he'd vowed that never again would he sit by while people were being annihilated. When he turned nineteen, he went to Israel and joined the army. He swiftly came up through the ranks and was chosen to join the Israeli Secret Service. It had been his pleasure to help bring in over thirty Nazi war criminals. Rupert Giles had the look of an ex-soldier even though he said he was an insurance investigator. Peter recognized the haunted aspect in Rupert's eyes. The look was always fleeting because Rupert knew how to mask his emotions, but Peter knew that look. He'd seen it too often in his own eyes.

"I think we both enjoyed it," Rupert said with a smile between men of the world.

"Yes, indeed," Peter said. He remembered how good it was to be young and in love. "I see you're getting in a little exercise now, but if you're up for a game of chess later, just knock on my door. I'll be home all afternoon."

"That sounds good," Rupert said. And it did. "Check you out later. Bye, Jimbo."

The little dog barked as if he knew Rupert was talking

to him; then he and his master continued down the sidewalk.

Rupert commenced running in the opposite direction. Several blocks later he spotted Thorne sitting at a picnic table by the volleyball court in the park. Thorne was reading the *Miami Herald* and pretending he hadn't heard Rupert approaching. His blond hair was sticking up on his head like spikes, and he hadn't shaved in days. Though it was a warm day, he was wearing a black leather jacket.

"What are you going for?" said Rupert. "The grunge look? If so, it's outdated."

"Very funny, Giles," Thorne said, abruptly putting the paper down and turning narrowed eyes on Rupert. "I wouldn't be in this sauna if you had just saved us all a lot of hassle and paperwork and put a bullet in Aziz's head."

Rupert sat down across from Thorne. The blood in his veins had chilled. Thorne couldn't possibly mean what he thought he meant! "The pick-up people let him escape?" he asked, his voice a lot steadier than his gut was feeling at that moment.

"I'm afraid so," Thorne said. He smiled as though the development was no skin off his nose. "But not until he'd tortured the female operative and gotten your name out of her. For some reason he was adamant about that, knowing your identity. What did you do to the poor man, Giles?"

"Sarcasm could get you killed right about now, Thorne. So, shut your face!" Rupert ground out, his jaws clenched with pent-up rage. "Don't give me that bull about his escaping. You people let him get away. You planned it this way from the start. Used me as bait! And I fell for it!"

"Don't be paranoid," Thorne said, showing his new caps. "Why would we do that? We wanted this case closed as soon as possible. You're the one who chose to take the second option and let him live. You could have killed him, and that would have been that!"

"You all knew I don't operate like that. If at all possible, I always bring them in alive." Yeah, he thought, and that's what they were counting on. They read me like a damned book!

Ultimately, he couldn't fault them for his predicament, though, because the fault lay with him. He'd allowed his ego to convince him that he was such a great agent that he was their salvation. All that baloney about his being close to Aziz, and never having been identified as an agent was just background. Window dressing that helped their scheme appear above board. Hadn't he learned his lesson with them? They were never truthful if being duplicitous helped them reach their objective quicker. The offer to wipe his slate clean had been the cherry on top. Throwing that in was designed to make him believe his accepting the case would somehow protect Solange and Desta from his past.

"You're betting that Aziz will make contact with Obed Bedele once he arrives in the States, aren't you? You want to get them on American soil. What is this, an American-British operation?"

"Really, Giles, you should become a writer. You're so good at dreaming up scenarios," Thorne drolly commented. He picked up the paper again. "All I was told was to warn you that Aziz is on the loose and he knows where you live. What you do with that information is entirely up to you, old buddy."

Rupert arose, lowered the paper, and popped Thorne in the mouth so fast that Thorne didn't have time to react. In pain, his mouth bleeding, and his new dental work loose, he gingerly touched his mouth with his right hand. "I'm going to let that one slide because I realize you're overwrought, Giles. But the next time you hit me, you're a dead man. I haven't been out of the game for five years."

He looked at Rupert with murderous intent in his cool blue eyes.

Rupert felt like hitting him again, but controlled the impulse. Glaring down at Thorne, he issued his own warning: "If the agency lets Aziz kill Ahmed and Ashante Taya, chalking them up as collateral damage, I will personally hunt you down and strangle you, Thorne. And if any harm comes to anyone I love, I will personally hunt you down and eviscerate you. That's a promise. You know I always keep my promises."

With that, he turned and walked away.

"Ahmed and Ashante Taya are at a safe house until this blows over," Thorne called after him. "Screw you, Giles."

Not even turning around, Rupert gave him the finger. "You already have."

"Checkmate!" Peter exclaimed.

Jimbo got up and chased his tail in excitement, celebrating the victory along with his master. Peter reached down and patted Jimbo on the head. "Settle down, pooch, settle down. It wasn't much of a victory since my opponent's mind has been elsewhere all afternoon." He gave Rupert a meaningful look.

Anyone looking on might not think the two men had much in common, except height; they were both over six feet tall. One was dark skinned. The other was melanin challenged. Rupert was thirty-six years younger than Peter, and in his prime.

Peter, though he had a touch of arthritis, enjoyed pretty good health, but he would never run the mile in under five minutes again the way he used to in his youth.

Both of them had loved only one woman deeply in his lifetime. Both of them had killed in the service of their countries. Those two facts made them brothers under the skin.

"Trouble in paradise?" Peter asked.

They were sitting on his porch, a card table separating them. Ice-cold beers had been their libation of choice that afternoon. Rupert was on his second bottle. Peter was still nursing his first. Peter sipped his, but it was barely cold. "Just tell me to butt out if it's none of my business. After all, we've only known one another about a year. It isn't as if we're lifelong friends."

"Shut up, Peter," Rupert said.

Peter shut up. He sat there and drained his beer bottle, looking out at the yard that needed weeding. He'd hire a neighborhood boy to do it this Saturday. He used to kill himself sweating in the yard, but no more. He was pretty well off. What was he saving his money for? He and Trudy had never had any children. He supposed that's why he'd allowed himself to care so much for Solange, and now Rupert. He didn't have anyone else to use up his emotions on. Plus, with his background of never sitting on the sidelines he had not become inured to other people's suffering. And Rupert was suffering.

"I apologize," Rupert said quietly.

"For telling me to shut up?" Peter asked. "It was probably good advice."

"Very good advice," Rupert said, and met Peter's gaze.

"I see," said Peter, still not shutting up. "Suppose I don't want to shut up, but would rather ask you countless questions until you break down and tell me what's on your mind? What if telling me what's bugging you is the only thing that will shut me up? Have you ever considered that?"

"No," said Rupert, not cracking a smile.

"You should," said Peter. "I'm a nosy, oldass man with nothing going on in my life. I might like a little danger to spice it up. Oh, and one more thing, I sleep with a nine-millimeter Glock next to my bed, and I know how to use it."

Rupert's facade cracked just a tad.

"I see you know the weapon," Peter deduced. "Good. Then you know it's very accurate and quite easy to reload in a pinch. I can protect myself, Rupert."

"Are there many other senior citizens around here packing heat?" Rupert asked with the smallest of smiles.

"Mrs. Brennermann packs an Uzi," Peter told him, straightfaced. "She's not very good with it, though. She scared the postman half to death one morning when she mistook him for a burglar and made Swiss cheese out of her front door."

This time Rupert laughed heartily. "I'm still not telling you anything, Peter."

Peter rose with some difficulty. His knees were aching. Must be going to rain this afternoon. "Excuse me, won't you?"

"Don't go get your gun, Peter. I'm afraid of guns," Rupert told him.

"I'm not going to get my gun, 'fraidy cat," Peter said.

Jimbo trotted after him, nudging the screen door open with his long nose.

Rupert waited patiently, wondering what Peter Wychowski had to show him that would convince him to spill his guts about the Aziz fiasco. He couldn't imagine anything that would induce him to change his mind. That's all he needed, someone else to worry about.

Peter returned ten minutes later, a manila envelope in his hand.

He sat back down across from Rupert and carefully unwound the string clasp that held the envelope together.

This done, he reached in and withdrew some yellowed papers.

He placed them before Rupert.

Rupert picked them up and began reading. They were honorable discharge papers from the Israeli Secret Service. Peter had been given an honorarium for twenty years of faithful service. Rupert was surprised by how small the amount had been. They certainly didn't pay spies very well back then.

When he'd finished reading the papers, he looked up at Peter. "I don't suppose Solange has any idea that her favorite neighbor is a former spy?"

"Does she know you're one?" Peter asked.

"Yes," Rupert said, realizing he'd crossed the line and there was no turning back.

"Then, what's your problem?" asked Peter.

Rupert sighed deeply. "All right, Wychowski. But don't blame me if you wind up dead."

"If that happens," said Peter. "I'll be quite beyond blaming anyone for anything."

Rupert smiled. "I still have my doubts about telling you. Someone could be listening right now."

"Well, then," Peter spoke a bit louder than he'd been speaking, and scanned the rather quiet neighborhood. There was a dark van parked in front of Mrs. Brennermann's house. Perhaps a surveillance team was using it. "If anyone is listening out there they should know that what you tell me won't go any farther. I'm seventy-six. There wouldn't be any point in killing me since my number's nearly up, anyway. I know how to keep my mouth shut." He looked up at Rupert and raised his eyebrows.

"I feel like an idiot."

"Shall we play another game?" Rupert asked as he began arranging the chess pieces on the board.

"Why not?" Peter asked. "This will be the first time I'll win two straight games."

"Don't be too hasty to claim another victory," Rupert told him with a smile. "I'm certain what I'm about to tell you will rattle you so much, you'll not be able to concentrate on the game."

"Do your worst," Peter said, taking up the gauntlet.

"I used to be with British intelligence. I left five years ago because I didn't agree with their methods. I knew when I left that I would always be on their crap list. You know, someone they no longer trusted and had to watch in order to make certain I didn't do anything stupid like write a bestseller about my days with the agency."

Rupert had made the opening move, and Peter appeared to be having a difficult time deciding what his next move should be. Finally, he placed his hand on the table without having made a move on the chessboard. "It's true, you don't walk away easily."

"I met Solange and we fell in love. I told her about my past without the specifics, of course. She told me she understood. That what I'd done was no different from what millions of soldiers all over the world have done for their countries. Though she said she was glad that I'd left that life, and didn't have any desire to return to it."

"But a few days ago," Rupert continued, "I was contacted by an operative and told that the agency wanted me to do them a favor, and in return for my cooperation I would be well compensated, and the eyes that had been on me for years would no longer be on me. The thought of a life free of fear that, out of the blue, they'd suddenly decide that I was a security risk and blow me away was too good to pass up."

"So, you took the assignment," Peter guessed.

"Yeah, I spent three days in Mauritania tracking down and capturing Moustapha Aziz, who'd escaped with the aid of his buddy, Obed Bedele. I let them convince me that I was the only man for the job because even after infiltrating Aziz's inner circle and leading them to him at his most vulnerable point, Aziz never knew I was an agent. He thought I was a gunrunner, and that I was a trusted friend."

"Subterfuge," Peter said. "One of the most important skills a spy can have."

Rupert nodded in agreement. "Yesterday, someone delivered a message to the house saying I should call a certain number. This morning I met an agent in the park—"

"While on your jog," Peter interrupted, following the story with keen interest.

"He told me that the transport crew had been overpowered by Aziz and, what's more, Aziz now knew where to find me because he'd beaten the information out of a female agent."

"Aziz," Peter said. "The Senegalese dictator? I thought they'd executed him."

"Isn't it funny how someone who is in the news one minute is forgotten the next?" Rupert commented dryly. "No, he was not executed. They're still trying to decide what to do with him. Believe it or not, some have even suggested he be sent into exile like Baby Doc, who is somewhere in France enjoying the good life as we speak."

Peter sighed and shook his head. Jimbo, hyperactive by nature, was running back and forth on the porch, letting off steam. Peter slapped his thigh. "Jimbo. Here, boy."

Jimbo came and leaped onto Peter's lap.

"It seems to me that they would have used more care when they were taking him back to prison," Peter said, as he rubbed Jimbo's head.

"My point, exactly," Rupert agreed wholeheartedly. "I

believe they used me to get Aziz riled enough so that he would consider me his mortal enemy. His betrayer. Which is what he called me, by the way. In his warped mind, I am to blame for his being sent to prison. I pretended to be his friend, and then I turned him in."

"In that case," Peter pointed out. "You were the only man for the job. They knew Aziz considered you a friend. They also knew you'd betray yourself as a spy when you captured him this time. They really got you good, Rupert."

"Yeah," Rupert said. His voice was cold, thinking of what a mess he was in, and because he was in it, so was Solange. That was the unforgivable part. "I came back here thinking I was free to get on with my life with Solange and Desta. Thinking that there was nothing standing in the way of our happiness. I've resigned from the insurance agency. I've got money to spare. Then, too, Solange told me that the doctor told her there is a possibility that she can conceive a child now."

"Wonderful news!" Peter cried happily. Of course, the excitement in his voice incited Jimbo to greater hyperactivity. He leaped from Peter's lap and ran down the steps, barking loudly at a group of children who were walking home from school.

"Oh, he does that every afternoon. They love it," Peter said of his behavior.

The children stopped to laugh at Jimbo, making barking noises themselves. "Hello, Mr. Wychowski!"

"Hello, Jaime," Peter called. "Tell your mother her hydrangeas are beautiful this year."

The children moved on, and Peter turned his attention back to Rupert. "You know, Solange has been here nearly ten years now. I remember when she moved in. She'd just started at the university. Had her doctorate degree at twenty-five. Looked all of eighteen. She still looks younger than her age. Anyway, it was about four years later that I got really sick and was unable to get out of bed, and she took care of me. She actually took a few days off from work, said they were coming to her since she never called in sick, and made me chicken soup as good as my mother used to make. It was during that time that we really got to know each other. I told her about Trudy. How the cancer had devastated such a vital, beautiful spirit. How I regretted that Trudy and I had never had children. That was when she told me about her condition. I prayed for a miracle in her behalf from that point on."

Rupert smiled. "It seems we were all praying."

Peter rested his chin in his hand, looking at Rupert. "You've got to tell her."

"She'll leave me," Rupert said, certain of it. "I know her. She won't ever be able to trust me again. She has issues with trust. And she's like a mother hen where Desta's concerned. She's preparing a home for Desta. A safe home. How can she insure that Desta will be safe if her adoptive father has royally screwed up by inviting a killer into their safe haven? She'd toss me to the curb so fast my head would spin!"

"You don't strike me as a man who can't take the heat, Rupert," Peter said sagely. "You made a mistake. You've got to own up to it and take your lumps. If you don't tell her and she finds out later, she'll be doubly upset. Believe me, especially if Aziz is gunning for you, as you suspect! What are you going to do, be on alert twenty-four hours a day? She has a right to know that her life could be in danger. In addition to telling her what's really going on, you also need to buy her a gun and take her to the shooting range and instruct her on the proper use of it."

"Logically, I know what you're saying is the right thing to do," Rupert said. "But what if she reacts the way I believe she will? If she gets angry and stubborn, she'll refuse to see me, then how will I protect her?"

Peter's brows drew together in a frown. "Then you'd have to refuse to budge until Aziz is caught. She would have to get the police to dispel you. I don't believe she'd go that far. She loves you, Rupert. She may get angry with you. She may even revile you, and treat you like something she stepped in. But ultimately love will win."

Solange's day was going pretty smoothly until she wrapped up her final class and began the trek across campus to the building that housed the archaeology department, where she had her office. As she always did, she'd slipped on a pair of athletic shoes for the long walk. She was making good time when a student on a bike misjudged the distance between Solange and the brick boundary of a decorative fountain, and hit her leg with the front wheel of his bike.

Solange lost her balance and flailed backward toward the huge fountain. She thought to drop her briefcase and shoulder bag onto the pavement before they, too, got soaked.

Luckily, she didn't hit her head as she went, butt first, into the fountain. The student on the bike righted the wobbly bike, looked back at her, and kept going. Two witnesses, both young women, went to her aid. They got on either side of her and hoisted her up and out of the fountain.

"Man," said the first girl who had a glorious cap of wavy black hair, a coppertone complexion, and brown eyes. "That creep just kept going. Are you all right?"

Solange's fall had immersed her from head to toe. Water dripped off of her hair, her suit clung to her wet skin, and her shoes squished when she walked. But otherwise she was fine. "I'm okay," she said, mustering up a smile for her Good Samaritans. "Thank you both."

The other girl, a petite African-American with dark brown dreadlocks and light brown eyes, smiled up at her as she bent and picked up Solange's briefcase, whose clasp had held, thank God, and her shoulder bag. "I hope you don't have a class to get to," she said. "You could use a change of clothes."

Solange gratefully accepted her belongings. "I have a pair of sweats in my locker at the women's gym. That'll have to do."

She turned to leave, feeling quite miserable with the wet clothes clinging to her skin.

"Thanks again, ladies."

The girls smiled at her and continued on their way.

Solange's shoes squeaked all the way to the gym, which, luckily, was closer than the building she was initially headed for.

In the women's locker room, she carefully peeled off her wet clothes. She had no clean underwear in her locker, and would have to go without. The athletic suit was dark blue, so no one would be able to tell she wasn't wearing any.

There was an old pair of athletic shoes on the bottom of the locker. They'd seen better days, but she was glad to see them. After putting on the clothing, she sat down on a nearby bench and put on the Adidas. Her cell phone rang as she was tying them.

Grabbing her shoulder bag, she slipped her hand inside and got the phone. Flipping it open and bringing it to her ear, she said, "Hello, Solange here."

"Solange, this is Gary Hardwick."

Solange's heartbeat accelerated. Her attorney never phoned unless there were new developments in Desta's adoption. He was not the type of man to phone just to chitchat or to reassure her while she waited for the process to be over with. He did his job, and left the handholding to her friends and relatives.

"Hello, Gary, how are you?"

"Well, thank you." His voice sounded peculiar to Solange. He was usually all business. Not wasting a minute of time. Today, his tone was relaxed, almost happy.

"It's done, Solange. You can go pick up Desta any time."

Solange was astounded. She sat on the bench in the empty women's locker room with her jaw slack with surprise. "Two months early?" She had to have further evidence of her good fortune.

"James Tan of the American Embassy had a hand in it," Gary told her. "Remember him? He felt very strongly about your case and wanted to see it end with positive results. He lit a fire under all concerned. This was the smoothest foreign adoption case I've ever handled, thanks to him. He told me he has a gift for Desta, as well. I gave him your mailing address. I hope you don't mind."

"Of course not!" Solange said, so happy her eyes were tearing up. "A gift on top of everything he's already done. I'm going to have to go by his office and give him a big hug when I go to Addis Abbaba to pick up Desta."

"That's another thing," Gary said. "Desta doesn't want to wait for you to come get her, although that's what I suggested. She says she'd like to come alone. She looks at it as a big adventure. I told her she'd have to discuss it with you. Just a warning, she's very sold on the idea. She's quite the independent young lady."

Solange's first impulse was a resounding no. There was no way she was going to allow Desta to travel thousands of miles by herself. But then, she remembered what Desta had already been through in her short thirteen years: witnessing the deaths of her parents and her older brother, Tesfaye. Living on the streets and surviving by picking pockets. She was tough. She was resilient. She's my daughter, Solange thought with a sudden rush of pride.

"Gary, I can't thank you enough," she said into the phone's receiver. "You came through for us, and I'll never forget you for it."

"I was just doing my job," Gary told her modestly. "It was a pleasure, Solange. Well, I guess you'd better get on with those travel plans."

"Yeah, I'd better," Solange said, excited. "Bye, Gary."

She closed the cell phone and screamed with delight. She danced around the locker room for a few minutes, then remembered she needed to get in gear. She grabbed her wet clothes and shoes, shoved them in a plastic bag she'd found at the bottom of her locker, grabbed her briefcase and shoulder bag, and ran from the locker room.

She made record time getting home.

Rupert met her at the door with a smile. "Hey, baby, welcome home."

The air was redolent with the aromas of Solange's favorite dish, arroz con pollo, Cuban style. She dropped her things onto the hall table and went into Rupert's arms. He smelled like he'd just gotten out of the shower. The arroz con pollo. Freshly showered. Something was up. She tiptoed and placed a chaste kiss on his mouth. Rupert reached up and smoothed her hair when they parted. "What happened? Your hair's damp."

She told him about the mishap with the rude student on the bike.

"While I was getting changed I got a call from Gary Hardwick. Desta's adoption came through. I can go get her. We can go get her if you have time between assignments."

"I told you I was quitting," Rupert said. "It's final. I'm all yours."

Solange gave him another quick buss on the lips. "Thank you, sweetie." Her eyes danced with excitement as she turned away, heading to the bedroom. "I don't know what to do first. Call her, I suppose. I can't wait to hear her voice." She turned suddenly and looked back at him. "Is that chicken and rice I smell?"

Rupert nodded in the affirmative. He couldn't think of a reason why he should tell her what was going on with him. Not right away, anyway. He'd wait until after dinner. She looked so happy. He didn't want to burst her bubble, bring her down off her high.

Solange went to him and hugged him tightly. "I don't know what I'd do without you. You take such good care of me."

"Save the praise until after you taste it," Rupert joked, lightening the mood. "I got the recipe from your mother."

"I bet she was glad to hear from you," Solange said with a mischievous smile. "She probably took the opportunity to ask you more personal questions."

"She wanted to know if we'd set a date for the wedding yet. I told her no. She suggested a June wedding."

"That's only a month and a half away!" Solange protested.

"She said she and Dani could pull it off if we were willing. I told her it's up to you. I'm ready any time."

He felt like a heel, telling her all of this, when in about two hours she would know the whole truth. Then she wouldn't be able to look at him without hurt and disappointment mirrored in her lovely brown eyes.

Solange kissed his clean-shaven chin, and said, as she backed toward the hallway, her eyes never leaving his dear, sweet face, "Okay, sweetie, I'm off. I want to phone Desta and get our plans together. Gary Hardwick told me she wants to fly here all by herself. Can you imagine that? Her first time on a plane, and she's going to be alone? I don't think so! After I speak with her, I'll take a shower and join you for dinner." She eyed him with obvious appreciation for how handsome he looked in his relaxed-fit jeans and polo shirt, both in shades of blue. Blue was her favorite color on him. "Unless you have something else in mind before dinner?"

Seven

Rupert indeed had something else in mind he dearly wanted to be able to do before they sat down to dinner. He wished he could take a trip back in time to correct his mistake so that it wouldn't be necessary to make the confession he was about to make. Of course, a safe way to travel back in time had not yet been discovered by the quantum physicists currently working on it. Therefore, he had to bite the bullet and deal with his real-time mistake. He was understandably in no rush to start spilling his guts.

While Solange was in her bedroom gabbing on the phone with Desta, he checked on the arroz con pollo in the oven. He made certain the tossed greens were crisp in the fridge. He opened a bottle of cabernet sauvignon to let it breathe.

In the bedroom, Solange was arguing with Desta. She'd showered first and was pacing the floor wearing her favorite white terry bathrobe and a towel wrapped around her freshly washed hair.

"I can be there in two days," Solange told Desta, who had just laid out her plan to fly to Miami by herself. "There is no need for you to travel by yourself."

"But I want to," Desta whined.

"You're a thirteen-year-old girl. It isn't safe."

"I'm a thirteen-year-old young woman," Desta begged to differ. "I've been doing research."

"Research?" Solange said.

"Yes, online. The flight attendants will make sure I don't miss my connections. And they will keep an eye on me while I'm on the plane, keeping me safe from perverts," Desta informed her confidently. "That's what you're afraid of, right? That some pedophile is going to try to kidnap me."

Solange was getting a glimpse of what it was going to be like to be the mother of a teenager. "That, and the fact that if anything ever happened to you, I'd never be able to forgive myself," Solange said. "Have pity on me, and let me come for you."

"I read about this somewhere," Desta said. Her English was even better than it had been a year ago. Must be all those books she's read, Solange thought. "You're laying on the guilt," Desta accused her.

Solange couldn't believe Desta had said that! She stopped pacing, and sat down on the bed. The little devil *had* been doing her homework. "So what if I am?" she said, now that she was busted. "I still think my way is the safest way to bring you home."

"We would waste two days your way," Desta pointed out. "Online reservations could get me out of Addis Ababa tomorrow morning. I would arrive in New York City late that night. I would immediately get on a plane for Miami. I'd sleep on the plane. You and Rupert could pick me up at Miami International Airport at around noon the next morning." She paused. "Please, Solange. I can't wait to see you, and Rupert, and my new grandma. She said I could call her that. I've never had a grandma before."

"She would have an apoplexy if she knew you were traveling alone."

"Then don't tell her. Let me surprise her," was Desta's reply.

Frustrated, Solange said, "I'll call you back. I've got to give this some serious thought. Give me a few hours."

"Okay," Desta said, eager to be cooperative. She figured the longer Solange thought about it, the better her chances were of getting her way. "I love you, Solange."

"I love you, too, Des," Solange said. "Bye."

"Bye."

Rupert stood in the doorway with a glass of red wine in his hand. He walked into the room and handed it to her. "Looks like you could use this."

Solange accepted it and took a sip. "That's delicious." She gave the glass back.

With a sigh, she turned and went into the closet to find something to put on. "She is really sold on coming here by herself. That girl could be captain of a debate team. She has so many logical reasons why she should win this argument."

Rupert simply watched her, his insides tense, his mind a jumble, thinking of what could happen in the next few minutes. Solange removed the robe and hung it on a hook in the closet. Naked, she went to the see-through shelf of drawers, selected a pair of silken pink panties, and slipped them on. "I don't want to discourage her strong streak of independence. But the world is a dangerous place, and I don't want anything to happen to her, either!"

She looked up at him. Usually, if she walked around topless, like she was doing now, he couldn't keep his hands off her. Now, he stood there and observed her with the kind of intensity that made her nervous. Earlier she'd thought something was up when she'd smelled the chicken and rice cooking. Could she have been right?

Rupert wanted to close the space between them and

pull her into his arms. He wanted to breathe in her essence and revel in the touch of her skin against his. Lose himself in her one last time. One last time. Damn, I'm getting maudlin, he thought. He smiled at her as he leaned against the door jamb. "You're worrying about a kid who survived on the streets by herself for years. Don't you think she can manage to fly here without getting lost?"

Solange removed the towel that had been wrapped around her head and fingered her damp locks. A quick blow-dry would whip her hair into shape. The cut allowed her the freedom of not having to use a curling iron every time she did her hair.

"Want me to blow-dry your hair for you?" Rupert asked.

He'd done it many times, so the question didn't surprise Solange. He enjoyed pampering her, and she enjoyed being pampered. She smiled at him. "Thanks, but, no, you've made dinner," she said as she walked past him, heading to the bathroom. Rupert could barely resist reaching out and touching her as she came within a hair's breath of him. But he didn't.

For her part, Solange wondered at his new ability to ignore her nakedness. Normally, he would've forgotten about dinner and had her on the bed with her legs spread by now.

She tried not to read anything into it as she went into the bathroom, bent and retrieved the blow-dryer from under the sink, and started drying her hair.

Rupert placed the glass of wine on the bureau's top and stood a few feet away from Solange, watching her dry her hair. Solange let him stand there while she finished the job and smoothed a small amount of moisturizer throughout it. Then, she turned to see if he was still there. He was, looking at her with that same strange intensity he'd been observing her with earlier. It was as if he missed her! When he was only a few feet away from her!

Solange decided to forgo wearing a bra tonight. She went to the closet and chose a short cotton sundress in royal blue. It had a low-cut neckline and spaghetti straps. Her breasts filled out the bodice rather nicely, if she had to say so herself. Based on Rupert's sudden ability to resist her, she obviously was the only one to appreciate the view. He was about to get on her nerves!

He stood, like a bump on a log, watching her.

Solange went and shook him. "What's wrong with you, Rupert?"

Rupert pulled her into his arms and held her so tightly she could hardly breathe.

"Baby, I've messed up," he said softly.

Solange went weak in the knees. For some reason, she could think of only one way he could have 'messed up' as he'd referred to it. He was having an affair. A long-distance relationship left a lot of room for someone else to slip in and fill up the spaces your partner wasn't filling. Maybe he'd gotten lonely one night and weakened when an attractive woman had pushed up on him. She wasn't naive. She knew he encountered lots of beautiful women in his travels.

In the few seconds that had elapsed since he'd told her he'd messed up, her mind had gone from panic, to a reasonable mode. Now, she tossed out the reasonable mode in favor of anger. She pushed out of his embrace.

"Just call it what it is, Giles. You cheated on me! You took some floozy to bed. Saying you 'messed up' makes it sound like a little mistake. If you think I'm going to be a woman of the world and be civil about this, then you're deluding yourself, buddy! I am pissed!" She paced the carpet, talking with her hands as well as with words, she was so upset. Cutting eyes remained trained on him. He didn't seem in the least perturbed by her tirade. In fact, he was smiling. That enraged her further. She ran to him and pounded his chest with both fists. "What the hell are you smiling about? This isn't a laughing matter!"

Rupert calmly grabbed her by the wrists and held onto her. "I love you, Solange. To me that means that you and I are exclusive. I'm faithful to you, and I always will be."

Solange felt deflated. The anger went out of her in an instant. She was left breathless, though. And it was a few seconds before she could say, "You haven't cheated on me?"

"You're all the woman I need."

"Then what did you mean by you've 'messed up'?" she asked, confused.

Rupert took her by the hand and led her from the bedroom. "Come on, you need something in your stomach. It's apparent to me that this is going to be an emotional night. We could both use the sustenance. Eat first; then I'll tell you the whole sorry story."

"You can't drop a bomb like that and then clam up!" Solange shouted, stomping her feet. "I want to know now."

"You know me well enough to know that kind of behavior will get you nowhere with me," Rupert told her. She refused to go any farther than the entrance to the bedroom. She dug in her heels, which was difficult because she wasn't wearing shoes.

Rupert picked her up and carried her to the dining room.

She shot daggers at him all the way. "One of these days, you big bully, I'm going to gain so much weight you're not going to be able to pick me up so easily."

"I'd still love you," Rupert said.

His comment made her all warm inside. That's what

love does for you, makes you a sucker for a compliment. "I can't believe you're torturing me like this, making me wait for you to lower the boom. If my life is going to be ruined by your revelation, I demand to be told this instant!"

He set her down on one of the chairs at the dining table. He'd set the table earlier, and now he sat next to her and began serving them. "You're going to need your strength in case you want to tell me to get the hell out of your life once I reveal what I have to tell you. So, eat."

Solange looked down at the food on her plate. She had no appetite. Not when their future might hang in the balance. She returned her gaze to his eyes. Tears sat in hers.

"Is this something that's going to break us up?"

"It could," Rupert said. "You might decide that you'd be better off without me."

"I could never be better off without you."

Rupert picked up his cloth napkin and dabbed at the tears on her cheeks. "For God's sake, don't cry. I can't stand it when you cry," he said tenderly.

Solange took the napkin from his hand. In doing so, their fingers touched and the tension of the moment coupled with their natural desire for one another ignited a fire between them. They leaned in and kissed. "Make love to me," Solange said against his mouth.

Rupert summoned the strength to pull away. He took her by the shoulders and forced her sit back down. "I can see that I was wrong to postpone telling you what I need to tell you. I was procrastinating because I'm afraid of losing you. But, for what I've done, I deserve whatever's coming to me."

Solange closed her eyes and sighed deeply, trying to steel herself.

Opening her eyes again, she sought his golden brown gaze. "Go on."

Rupert began talking, choosing his words with care.

He made certain that she knew he took full responsibility for his actions. He'd been foolish, and now he was ready to face up to that foolishness.

Solange remained perfectly quiet until he'd finished telling her everything. From his past, when he'd posed as a gunrunner to infiltrate Aziz's camp, to the present, when he'd been duped into recapturing him. "The truth of it is, I believe I took the assignment because on some level I missed the life. Maybe I thought I could have one last fling. When I was subduing Aziz, I admit it—I got a shot of adrenaline like I haven't felt in years. But then, when I learned what had really gone down, that it had all been a ruse, I realized what I stood to lose—you. I was a fool, Solange. In a way, I have cheated on you. I promised I was done with that life, and I went back to it."

When he'd finished, he heaved a sigh of relief.

Solange slowly rose, and looked down at him. "I guess there's something to be said for genetics. Because if I weren't my mother's daughter, I would be freaking out right about now! Moustapha Aziz may be on his way to Miami right now with a vendetta against you and, possibly, me and Desta. Also, Desta is eager to come here, where she'll be with people who love her. I bet you were disappointed when I told you her adoption had come through. You were probably hoping her arrival wouldn't come this soon. Maybe by the time she got here, the Aziz thing would have been taken care of."

"You're right," Rupert said. "I had hoped to take care of Aziz before Desta got here."

Solange was back to pacing, this time with her hands on her hips. She turned to face him. "Take care of Aziz. You mean to kill him?"

"I mean to protect the people I love, Solange. If it means I have to kill to do that, then so be it," Rupert said. He was standing across from her looking very much like the dangerous man she knew he could be, but that she had hoped would never have to come to the surface again.

"What if he really did take off for some country that has no extradition, like you advised him to do?" Solange asked, grasping at straws.

"He won't do that," Rupert said with conviction. "People like Aziz thrive on revenge. He can't get to Ashante. He will turn his attention to me and the people I care about. In his estimation, I took away his life. He will try to take away mine."

"And your former agency provided him with the information he needed to come after you," Solange said. "To use you as bait. Therefore they will have you under surveillance twenty-four-seven, right? Maybe they'll catch him before he strikes."

"Maybe," Rupert conceded. "But we've got to be ready in case they decide that they can kill two birds with one stone, and decide to let Aziz assassinate me for them. I don't want you and Desta to get caught in the crossfire."

"So, we arm ourselves," Solange said. "Isn't that what Mr. Wychowski suggested?"

"He'd like for you to call him Peter," Rupert said.

"Can't," Solange explained. "Mr. Wychowski's old enough to be my grandfather. It's my southern upbringing. Respect and all that." She looked at him, her brows deeply furrowed. She turned to leave the room. "I need time to process all of this. I'm going to bed. You can sleep on the couch tonight."

Rupert glanced down at his watch. It was only a little after six-thirty. It was going to be a long night.

He watched her retreating back. Then he turned and went into the living room, sat down on the couch, and picked up the remote. Bart Simpson was making another crank call to Moe's bar. Maybe Bart would cheer him up. Miracles can happen.

Solange awoke at around midnight. The room was pitch black. She felt on Rupert's side of the bed before she remembered that she'd asked him to sleep on the couch tonight. Everything he'd told her came rushing back. Fear snaked through her.

When she'd laid down, she'd been too mentally exhausted to collect a nightgown from the bureau drawer, so she was wearing only panties. It was funny how bad news caused lethargy to set in, sapping your mental, emotional, and physical strength. But now that she'd had the chance to think, she knew she couldn't remain passive. Rupert was right: if Aziz came for them, they would have to be prepared for him.

She rose and went to the bathroom. While she was sitting on the toilet, she realized she hadn't phoned Desta like she'd promised to. She tried to calculate what time it would be in Addis now. There was an eight-hour difference. Midnight here made it eight o'clock in the morning there. Desta had gone to bed without having heard from her. Solange knew the staff of the orphanage rose early, so she wouldn't be waking anyone if she phoned now.

She grabbed a T-shirt from the bureau drawer and put it on before sitting on the bed and picking up the receiver of the phone on the nightstand.

The phone in the office of the director of the orphanage rang three times before Mr. Manawi answered with a cheery greeting in Amharic.

"Good morning, Mr. Manawi," Solange replied. "This is Solange DuPree."

"Ah, Dr. DuPree. It's a pleasure," said Mr. Manawi. "What can I do for you?"

Solange thought the best thing to do was to be honest. "Mr. Manawi, we've got a problem on this end. My fiance used to be in law enforcement and he helped put a really horrible man behind bars several years ago. We've learned that he has escaped from prison, and the authorities believe he could be bent on revenge. We don't think it would be safe for Desta to come here right now. We were hoping she could stay there a while longer."

"She's going to be very disappointed. You should see how happy she is at the prospect of coming to live with you and Mr. Giles. But Desta is certainly welcome to stay as long as she needs to. We all love her here."

Solange was relieved. "Thank you, Mr. Manawi. I feel better already knowing she's going to be in your care."

"Do not worry, Dr. DuPree. We will not let her out of our sight until either she gets on a plane to you, or you come for her. Now, shall I go get her for you?"

"Yes, please. And thanks again, Mr. Manawi."

Desta's voice was a bit breathless when she got on the line. "What's wrong? Mr. Manawi is giving me sympathetic looks," she said right away.

I can't get anything past this girl, Solange thought, rolling her eyes. "Sweetheart, I have some disappointing news for you. We're going to have to postpone plans for you to come here. Just for a little while."

"Why?" The hurt and confusion was evident in her tone.

"Desta, I'm not going to make excuses that will leave you feeling even more insecure than you're already feeling. The truth is, Rupert had another job before he was an insurance investigator. He was in international law enforcement. He helped put this guy in prison and now the guy has escaped and the authorities think he might be thinking of coming after Rupert. It's not safe for you to be here. I'm sorry, but that's how it is.

"Until this guy is captured, and I know no harm will come to you, you're going to stay where you are. Now, don't start giving me all the reasons why you should come anyway, because I've made up my mind."

Desta surprised her by saying, "All right, Solange. I understand." Then she started talking a mile a minute. "This is so exciting! Rupert used to be an agent, didn't he? Like James Bond. I love James Bond movies. One night last week, when Mr. Manawi was asleep, we sneaked into his office and watched *Die Another Day*. He'd die if he knew we'd gotten into his private movie collection."

"You're too young to watch movies like that!" Solange cried, upset by Desta's confession but relieved that she'd taken her news with such ease. They chatted about Mr. Manawi's movie collection which, Solange was glad to find out, didn't include any really racy films. Desta's immersion in the Internet, movies, and books was making her a bit too worldly wise for Solange's comfort. But she knew Desta had a good head on her shoulders. She didn't worry too much about her.

"I've got to go now, Des. Do your best to behave for the remainder of your stay there, all right?"

"I'm not making any promises," Desta joked. "I guess you and Rupert had better hurry up and capture the escaped maniac and get me out of here."

"Deal," Solange said. "Bye."

"Bye."

Solange hung up the phone and went in search of Rupert.

Rupert was asleep on the sofa in the living room. Before he'd crashed on the sofa he'd put the dinner that he'd cooked away without eating a bite of it, cleaned the kitchen, took the bottle of wine with him to the living room, and sat in front of the TV. He'd ignored the wine, too. He drank only a glass of it before falling into a troubled sleep. He dreamed that Aziz had somehow gotten on campus and kidnapped Solange. Before he could track him down, Aziz had taken out his rage on Solange, beating her so severely she was barely breathing when Rupert found them at an abandoned house in the Everglades. Aziz had put Solange's limp body in a boat and was preparing to escape with her into the marshland, when Rupert came upon them, drew his weapon and shouted, "Get out of the boat, Aziz. Slowly."

But Aziz picked up Solange instead and held her aloft over the murky water. He grinned at Rupert. "Put the gun down, or she'll be food for the alligators."

Suddenly, the water was full of alligators, huge leviathans with their mouths open, revealing razor-sharp teeth.

"Don't do it!" Rupert pleaded. He held his arms out. "I'm putting the gun down." He slowly placed the gun on the dock.

Aziz laughed villainously, and dropped Solange into the mouth of a twelve-foot alligator.

Rupert yelled and launched his body into the water, going after her while Aziz stood in the boat and roared with laughter.

"Rupert!"

Rupert opened his eyes to see Solange leaning over him. He was so grateful to see her alive and well that he pulled her over the back of the sofa and on top of him. He didn't say a word as he held her, and buried his nose in her hair. Then he started raining kisses on her face and throat.

Solange didn't try to wiggle out of his embrace. She closed her eyes and sighed. She gave herself over to the sensation he incited within her, and knew that she would forgive him because that's what you did when you loved somebody. She felt the incidents with Nicholas had been a precursor to this moment. If she could forgive Nick, then she certainly could forgive Rupert, who loved her with all his heart. She could not bring herself to judge him. He was human, and human beings made mistakes.

For a moment, after Solange had awakened him out of his dream, Rupert thought he was still dreaming. She had come so willingly to him, as though she felt no animosity whatsoever toward him. As if being in his arms was the only place she wanted to be. He felt like crying, he was so happy to have her this close again.

His body came alive. His heartbeat sped up. His senses reeled with the heady notion that she might have forgiven him. Then she kissed him. He held back at first, still confused by the miracle of her being here in his arms. Then he put his hand behind her head and hungrily devoured her mouth, accepting what she was offering.

It suddenly became imperative that there be nothing to prevent their skin from touching. Solange pulled her T-shirt over her head, tossing it somewhere in a darkened corner of the room. Rupert was wearing a pair of boxer briefs. He loathed having to relinquish his position on the sofa, and the feel of her on top of him, but there was no getting around it.

He pulled her down for another kiss and, while their lips were locked, he gently eased her onto her back on the opposite end of the sofa. Then, he got up and quickly doffed the briefs. There seemed to be a silent consensus between them that no words would be spoken. He kept it as he knelt over her and pulled her to him. Solange opened her legs to him. He entered her. She breathed in sharply, exhaled forcefully. Grabbed his behind with both hands and took all of him inside of her. Their loving was fierce and rough. Passionate in a way that neither of them had ever experienced before.

It was as if they were sealing a pact, making it known that nothing, and no one, could sever what they had, because this was their truth. Their love was unbreakable.

They were ravenous. At one o'clock in the morning, they warmed plates of arroz con pollo in the microwave and sat at the kitchen nook to eat it. Solange had put her robe on, and Rupert had put on his jeans.

"What are we going to do?" Solange asked around a mouthful of chicken and rice. It was delicious. The various spices, some savory, some with fire, merged to make a taste that encouraged gluttony. And it was even better now because the spices had had time to soak in.

"We're going to carry on as usual," Rupert said.

"You mean I should go to work? And we should go forward with our wedding plans?"

"No to work," Rupert said, remembering the dream. He'd probably had it because guilt was eating him up but, still, it had been too vivid to ignore. He might not be able to protect Solange on campus. There were too many people around, for one thing. Aziz might be able to blend in. "Take a few sick days. I need to take you to a firing range and teach you how to shoot, and there are other things we should be doing. But, yes, let's go ahead and set a date for the wedding. We need to appear normal to friends and family. We can't tell them anything, of course. But if we start acting too strangely, they'll know something is up."

"All right," Solange agreed. "That'll make Maman and Dani happy." She met his eyes across the counter. "About Dani: she's kind of eccentric, in a nice way. I hope you like her."

"Darling," Rupert said, smiling at her. "If you like her, I'm sure I will, too."

* * *

Solange held the automatic with her right hand, supporting her right arm with her left hand around her wrist, just as Rupert had said she should. "This is for you to be able to maintain as much control as possible," he explained as he stood behind her on the firing range. Both of them wore earplugs to muffle the sound of weapons going off around them.

"I hate to ask where you got this gun from," Solange said.

"If you have the money, you can buy a gun on nearly every street corner of the city," Rupert told her.

"Tell me you're exaggerating."

"I'm exaggerating. On every other street corner."

Solange squeezed off a shot and hit the target in the area where his genitals would have been if he were a real man. "Oops, my bad."

"Aim a bit higher, sweetness," Rupert encouraged her.

She breathed in deeply, and exhaled. As she exhaled, she pulled the trigger and this time she hit the target in the center of its chest. She grinned back at Rupert.

"That's better. Try it again," he said.

Solange shifted her body weight, rolled her shoulders, and closed her right eye.

She hit the target right between the eyes. "I think I've found my method," she said. "I've just got to imagine I'm Angela Bassett in *Strange Days,* close my right eye, and go for it."

Someone laughed behind them. Rupert knew that voice. Solange lowered her weapon and turned slowly to find the same man who'd delivered the Federal Express package to her house a few days ago. "You must be the Thorne in Rupert's side," she said.

Thorne, who was still sporting his grunge look, smiled roguishly. "It's a pleasure to meet you, Dr. DuPree."

Solange's eyes flashed fire as she came to stand within inches of him. "You people are loathsome. Using innocent people as bait."

Thorne held up both arms as if he were surrendering. "I come in peace! And I have good news."

Eyeing him suspiciously, Solange took a step backward. "What?"

Thorne lowered his arms and looked at Rupert. "Well, good news and bad news. Aziz led us to Obed in New York City. Obed has been arrested, but Aziz was able to somehow slip away during the raid."

"You sound like a broken record!" Solange said derisively. "Why do you even bother showing up?"

Thorne seemed at a loss for words. He started to say something, but Solange cut him off with, "Oh, I know, you're just following orders. Tell me one thing, Thorne. Do you people have our backs? Or are you satisfied with catching Obed, who was your prime objective anyway? Are you going to leave us high and dry?"

Frowning, Thorne looked at Rupert. "She's like a pit bull, only prettier." He smiled at Solange. "Yes, ma'am, we have your back. We're not going anywhere until Aziz is back in custody."

Solange looked deeply into his eyes. "You'd better not be lying to me."

"And risk your wrath?" Thorne said. "Never!"

He smiled at Rupert as he slowly backed away from Solange. "You're a lucky dog," he said sincerely. With that, he turned and left them.

In his absence, Rupert said, "I once saw that man single-handedly dispatch four men."

"He doesn't scare me," said Solange.

"Then why are you trembling?"

"Because he scared the crap out of me!" Solange said, laughing. She returned to her stance in their booth at the range and tried to hold the gun as Rupert had taught her, but failed miserably. Her hands were shaking too much. Rupert took the gun from her hand.

Solange looked up at him. "I guess this spy business is not for me, huh?"

Rupert pulled her into his arms. "Just keep being my little pit bull."

"Welcome," Solange said to Theophilus Gault and his daughter, Samantha.

Theophilus bent his big, square head and kissed Solange on the cheek before going into the house. He was casually dressed in a pair of slacks and a short-sleeve shirt. Both were black. He wore black, highly polished English wing tips. He frequented the same shoe shop as his son. Their tastes in attire were similar. That wasn't where the similarities ended. Both men were tall and solidly built. Both had dark chocolate skin, and eyes the color of a Key West sunset.

Theophilus spied the petite, very attractive woman standing behind Solange, and smiled warmly. "You can be none other than the lovely Marie DuPree," he said.

Solange was busy hugging Samantha. Samantha was several inches taller than her soon-to-be sister-in-law, and had to stoop down to greet her. The smiles on their faces came from their hearts. Solange adored Samantha. The feeling was mutual.

Samantha smacked her on the cheek. "Hey, girl, you look fabulous. Like my brother is taking care of business." Luckily, she said this close to Solange's ear.

Solange laughed. "Thank you, sis. You look divine, as always."

Indeed, Samantha was invariably turned out in the latest fashion. Tonight she wore a beautiful sleeveless fitted sheath in red, whose hem fell just above her knees. Strappy sandals in red leather completed the outfit. The color red beautifully complemented her mocha-colored skin.

She tossed her long, dark brown wavy hair behind her with a little neck action.

Looking down at Solange with the same color eyes as her father and brother, she asked, "What are those delicious aromas? I know I'm not gonna even think about my diet tonight!"

Meanwhile, Marie was trying to quell the flutter of butterfly wings in her stomach. Theophilus Gault was overwhelming her rusty femme fatale skills. For too long, she'd allowed her feminine wiles to remain dormant. She was finding it hard to breathe in his presence, let alone carry on a coherent conversation.

Rupert came to her rescue with a tray of margaritas. "Dad," he said. He referred to both his fathers as 'dad' nowadays. "Have a drink. There is plenty of time for you to get acquainted with Maman."

Marie smiled up at him. She liked it when he called her that.

Theophilus reached for a long-stemmed glass, and Marie took the opportunity to grab her daughter by the arm with the intention of dragging her back to the kitchen.

But first, Solange had to introduce her to Samantha.

Solange clasped the hand her mother had clamped onto her upper arm. "Maman, I'd like you to meet Rupert's sister, Samantha. Samantha, my mother, Marie."

Samantha smiled graciously. "It's a pleasure, Mrs. DuPree."

Marie immediately warmed to Samantha, who radiated

the same charm as her father, but was not in the least bit threatening. Marie stepped forward and took Samantha by the arm, leading her away. "My dear, is that fragrance you're wearing called Miracle?"

Surprised that she knew her fragrance, Samantha grinned. "How did you know?"

"It's one of my favorites," Marie told her.

Solange joined Rupert and Theophilus, snagging a margarita from the tray Rupert still held. She came in on the tail end of their conversation. "Head of security?" Rupert was saying. "How do you know I'd be any good at the job?"

Theophilus laughed shortly. "With your military background and the sort of work you did for your former employer, you would be perfect for the job. At least go down to the office and speak with Tomas Garcia. Let him explain what your duties would be. Then you can decide whether or not it's for you." He smiled at Solange, appealing to her. "Believe me, son, a new wife rests easier when her husband is gainfully employed."

"I don't know," Solange said. "I'm enjoying having him all to myself."

Theophilus looked so crestfallen that Rupert threw him a bone with, "Give me a little more time with Solange, and I'll go down and speak with Mr. Garcia."

Theophilus instantly cheered. He struck Rupert on the back. "That's good enough for me." He then looked around them. "Where did your lovely mother get to?" he asked Solange.

"She and Samantha went into the living room, I think," Solange said. "It's right through there."

Theophilus beat a path for the living room.

"He's going after your mother like she's an attractive acquisition," Rupert commented dryly in his absence, referring to his father's knack for taking over businesses.

Solange looked worried all of a sudden. "Is that a good thing or a bad thing?"

Eight

"He's just a man," Solange said as she pulled the pork roast far enough out of the oven to baste it. Her mother's heels could be heard clicking on the tile floor behind her. "Admittedly, he's a bit larger than life. And he can be like a missile aiming for a target when he wants something. But Samantha has told me how tender he was with her mother. How much he adored her. I think that's a good quality in a widower, that he truly loved his wife." She shoved the roast back into the oven, and peeked at the sweet-potato souffle while she had the oven door open. She straightened up and looked at her mother. "If he makes you nervous, talk about your work. You're always comfortable talking about your work."

Marie paced, talking to herself. "This is ridiculous. I'm a woman who knows her own mind. I'm a successful businesswoman. I eat men for lunch! The last man who came on to me, I sent limping off like a whipped dog." She met Solange's eyes, confidence shining in hers. "He's toast!"

Solange went and hugged her. "That's my Maman. Now, get out there and show him he can't intimidate a DuPree woman!"

Marie smoothed the pant legs of her bronze sleeveless pantsuit and raised her chin. "He'll be putty in my hands."

"That's right. He should fear you!"

Solange watched her go. *Oh, Lord, help her,* she thought.

Theophilus was in the middle of a conversation with his son and daughter when Marie reentered the living room, but his attention was diverted to her as soon as she put in an appearance. She went and sat beside Samantha on the sofa.

Samantha turned her head and smiled at her. "I'm glad you're back. Now it's two women against two men. My father and brother were telling me that I should finish law school before getting serious about anyone. But, I've met this great guy. We're like night and day, but I'm completely in love with him."

Marie smiled wistfully. "Tell me about him."

Theophilus observed how she crossed those elegant legs of hers. She had perfect posture, and her sloe eyes were the prettiest dark brown he'd ever seen. He had been surprised when he'd met her. She and Solange didn't resemble each other. He had expected the two women to practically be mirror images. Possibly because his children looked so much like him, especially Rupert. Perhaps Solange took after her father. Except for those lips. She had her mother's full, heart-shaped lips.

He had not heard what Samantha was saying. He was studying Marie too intensely.

He caught Marie in mid-sentence. "Montana? How did you ever meet a black cowboy from Montana in Washington, D.C.?"

"His little sister, Clancy, was my roommate. One weekend, Chad showed up looking for her. Clarisse Nancy, that's Clancy's real name, had gone home for the weekend with her boyfriend. Chad wanted to surprise her, and wound up surprising me. I never knew a man could look that good in a pair of Wranglers!"

"Then it's physical attraction," Theophilus put in,

finally breaking free of the spell Marie's lips had him under.

"No, Daddy," Samantha insisted. "I'm old enough to know the difference between lust and love. We have great chemistry. It's true. However, and let me clarify this—"

"She's sounding more like a lawyer all the time," Rupert said with a grin.

"Let me clarify this," Samantha repeated, smiling at her brother. "He listens to me when I talk, he cares about my opinions. And I know this sounds strange, but he seems to be able to anticipate my needs. I know from conversations with women who've been married for years that that doesn't always happen to a couple, even in a happy marriage."

She sighed contentedly. "I'm in love with a cowboy."

"Now, when you say cowboy," Marie began. "Are you referring to his being raised on a ranch? Or does he work as a professional cowboy? Don't tell anyone, but I get a kick out of watching the rodeo on television." Her eyes stretched. "Oh, my, oh, my. You're not talking about Chad Roberts, are you?"

"Yes!" Samantha exclaimed, delighted that Marie knew her sweetie.

Marie dramatically placed her hand over her heart. "Be still my heart. He's one of the best bronco riders in the country today. And talk about gorgeous!"

She looked at Samantha with newfound respect. "I'm so happy for you."

Samantha spontaneously hugged Marie. "Thank you, Mrs. DuPree."

"Oh, honey, call me Marie."

Theophilus couldn't believe his ears. This petite, lovely woman enjoyed watching dirty, sweaty men ride farm animals on TV. He smiled. There was hope for him.

"What else do you like to do?" Theophilus asked Marie.

Marie's brows arched in surprise. "What do you mean, Mr. Gault?"

"If you and Samantha are on a first-name basis, surely you and I should be. We're closer in age."

"And how would you know my age?" Marie parried. "I could have had Solange when I was a child bride."

"My dear, you're beautiful, whatever your age is," Theophilus lunged, going for the jugular. "I repeat my question: What else do you like to do besides watch young men in tight jeans risk their lives on bucking broncos?"

Samantha and Rupert were enjoying the repartee between their father and a woman who was able to match him remark for remark. Samantha had brief flashbacks of her mother and father. Her mother, Francesca, had been able to hold her own with him, too.

"I like entertaining," Marie told him, her eyes boring into his. "I like to travel and take photographs on my trips. On cool mornings, I like to putter around in my garden. Solange inherited her green thumb from me. We can grow just about anything. I enjoy doing simple things like taking a walk. I'm partial to Cuban music. Celia Cruz was one of my favorites because I love to dance, and she did the best dance music ever!"

Finished, she tossed him a challenge with her eyes. "And you?"

"I like seeing you blush, Marie," he said.

Marie grabbed a decorative pillow from the sofa and threw it at him. Theophilus caught it. "I love a woman with spirit."

Solange came into the room at the moment her mother tried to brain Theophilus with the pillow. She laughed. "Can't you two behave? I'm going to have to seat you far apart at the dinner table."

"Don't you dare," said Theophilus. "Seat us right next to each other."

A panicked look flashed in Marie's eyes for a split second, and Solange knew her mother had lost her battle with Theophilus Gault. She liked him. She liked him a lot.

Hands on her hips, Solange surveyed everyone in the room. "Well, all right then. Dinner is served!"

Rupert, Theophilus, and Samantha led the way to the dining room. Marie hung back to whisper to her daughter, "I'm going to be a nervous wreck before this night is over with."

"Turn the tables on that outrageous flirt," Solange advised.

"You heard what he said?"

"I was standing just outside the room, listening," Solange told her. "He's unbelievably cocky. Reminds me of someone else I know."

They joined the others in the dining room.

Theophilus held Marie's chair out for her. "Thank you," Marie said politely.

He sat down beside her, leaving Samantha, who had expected him to pull her chair out, too, standing. "Thanks, Daddy," Samantha said, pulling out her own chair and sitting down.

Rupert helped Solange with her chair and sat down beside her. He couldn't resist a quick kiss to the side of her neck as he sat down. Samantha caught him in the act and said, "You two can't keep your hands off each other, can you? You've kept us in suspense for a while now. When's the wedding? And I hope I'm going to be a bridesmaid or something. I'll settle for being an usher. I won't be happy about it, but I'll take it."

Solange and Rupert looked at each other.

"Go ahead," Rupert said, giving Solange the floor.

"We're getting married the last Saturday in June. The twenty-sixth."

"That's only a little over a month away," Samantha said. "How will you pull everything together by then?"

"We have two very competent women working on it," Solange said, looking at her mother.

Marie smiled. "Actually, we started making plans a couple of weeks ago. The invitations have been printed. They go out on Monday. The wedding planner, Dani Chevalier, pulled a few strings and got the garden at the Biltmore, and the reception will be there as well, which will save the guests from having to fight Miami traffic twice in one day."

"Sounds wonderful," Samantha said. "Will Desta be here for the ceremony?"

"Yes, we're positive she will be," Solange said. "Things are going very well on that front."

"I'm glad. She's such a sweet little girl."

"She's a devil," Theophilus disagreed. "She cheated me out of a hundred bucks."

"Let it go, Daddy," Samantha said with a laugh. "She beat you fair and square. You're just sore that a thirteen-year-old was a better poker player than you were."

"She's a card shark," Theophilus said with a mischievous glint in his eye.

"That's my granddaughter you're talking about," Marie put in.

"Well, she's my granddaughter, too," Theophilus countered. "And she's still a card shark!"

Everyone laughed.

"If you all let my food get cold," Solange warned. "I'm going to be highly upset. Dig in."

They dined on southern fare: pork roast with corn-bread stuffing, sweet-potato souffle, and collard greens. Theophilus gave Solange a sloppy kiss on the cheek after the repast. "My son's gonna gain thirty pounds the first year with this kind of cooking."

An Important Message From The ARABESQUE Publisher

Dear Arabesque Reader,

Arabesque is celebrating 10 years of award-winning African-American romance. This year look for our specially marked 10th Anniversary titles.

Plus, we are offering *Special Collection Editions* and a *Summer Reading Series*—all part of our 10th Anniversary celebration.

Why not be a part of the celebration and let us send you four more specially selected books FREE! These exceptional romances will be sent right to your front door!

Please enjoy them with our compliments, and thank you for continuing to enjoy Arabesque.... the soul of romance bringing you ten years of love, passion and extraordinary romance.

Linda Gill
PUBLISHER, ARABESQUE ROMANCE NOVELS

P.S. Don't forget to check out our "Great Romance Contest" with a grand prize valued at $10,000! Contest opens January 26 to April 30, 2004. For more details visit us at www.BET.com

A SPECIAL "THANK YOU"
FROM ARABESQUE JUST FOR YOU!

Send this card back and you'll receive 4 FREE Arabesque Novels—a $25.96 value—absolutely FREE!

The introductory 4 Arabesque Romance books are yours FREE (plus $1.99 shipping & handling). If you wish to continue to receive 4 books every month, do nothing. Each month, we will send you 4 New Arabesque Romance Novels for your free examination. If you wish to keep them, pay just $18* (plus, $1.99 shipping & handling). If you decide not to continue, you owe nothing!

- Send no money now.
- Never an obligation.
- Books delivered to your door!

We hope that after receiving your FREE books you'll want to remain an Arabesque subscriber, but the choice is yours! So why not take advantage of this Arabesque offer, with no risk of any kind. You'll be glad you did!

In fact, we're so sure you will love your Arabesque novels, that we will send you an Arabesque Tote Bag FREE with your first paid shipment.

* Prices subject to change

THE "THANK YOU" GIFT INCLUDES:

- 4 books absolutely FREE (plus $1.99 for shipping and handling).
- A FREE newsletter, *Arabesque Romance News*, filled with author interviews, book previews, special offers, and more!
- No risks or obligations. You're free to cancel whenever you wish with no questions asked.

INTRODUCTORY OFFER CERTIFICATE

Yes! Please send me 4 FREE Arabesque novels (plus $1.99 for shipping & handling). I understand I am under no obligation to purchase any books, as explained on the back of this card. Send my free tote bag after my first regular paid shipment.

NAME _____

ADDRESS _____ APT. _____

CITY _____ STATE _____ ZIP _____

TELEPHONE ( ) _____

E-MAIL _____

SIGNATURE _____

Offer limited to one per household and not valid to current subscribers. All orders subject to approval. Terms, offer, & price subject to change. Tote bags available while supplies last.

Thank You!

AN044A

ARABESQUE

Accepting the four introductory books for FREE (plus $1.99 to offset the cost of shipping & handling) places you under no obligation to buy anything. You may keep the books and return the shipping statement marked "cancelled". If you do not cancel, about a month later we will send 4 additional Arabesque novels, and you will be billed the preferred subscriber's price of just $4.50 per title. That's $18.00* for all 4 books for a savings of almost 40% off the cover price (Plus $1.99 for shipping and handling). You may cancel at any time, but if you choose to continue, every month we'll send you 4 more books, which you may either purchase at the preferred discount price. . . or return to us and cancel your subscription.

* PRICES SUBJECT TO CHANGE

THE ARABESQUE ROMANCE BOOK CLUB
P.O. BOX 5214
CLIFTON NJ 07015-5214

PLACE
STAMP
HERE

THE ARABESQUE ROMANCE CLUB: HERE'S HOW IT WORKS

* * *

Across town, at the Colombian restaurant Patacon, Dani was enjoying her appetizer, crisp cornmeal turnovers called empanaditas. They were stuffed with potato and ground meat and were generally dipped in green chile sauce. Dani enjoyed spicy foods.

She was dining alone, which was usually the case. Forming any attachments at this stage of her transformation would be foolhardy. It would take a very special man to understand why she was putting herself through such a process.

A simple little black dress adorned her trim figure tonight. Her auburn hair fell down her back. A black headband kept it in place. She'd opted for comfort tonight instead of glamour and wore a pair of black sandals with two-inch heels. Though she liked the looks she received from men when she wore her four-inch heels, tonight she was simply chilling out. It was her thirtyninth birthday. Twelve months from now, she would be the big four-oh. The thought depressed her. Forty years old, and she'd never been in love, or been loved by someone special, someone who could accept her for who she really was.

She took a large swig of her white wine.

The man at the table across from hers smiled and raised his glass to her. His skin was so black, it was blueblack. She had a weakness for very dark men. It had led to heartbreak more times than she cared to remember. She raised her glass to him and smiled anyway.

He was broad shouldered and wore his black natural hair cut close to his big head. She judged he must be well over six feet tall to look as tall as he did seated. *Dressed nicely, too,* she thought admiringly. Her gaze lowered to his hands. Big hands. She tried to discreetly get a gander at his feet. No luck, not from this distance, anyway. The tablecloth was too long.

They flirted with their eyes throughout their meals.

He finished eating first, and wiped his mouth with his cloth napkin in such a suggestive fashion that it actually aroused Dani, something that hadn't happened in a very long time. She bit her bottom lip as she watched him rise, place his napkin on the table, go into his wallet for some money, and leave a tip on the table.

He smiled at her one last time before turning to leave.

Dani was, frankly, disappointed that he hadn't come over to her table and introduced himself.

Though, in this day and age, it was probably best that he hadn't. She certainly wasn't the type of girl who would welcome the attentions of a perfect stranger, even if she had spent the better part of an hour smiling at him.

She put him out of her mind, as she broke the surface of her plum pudding with a dessert spoon. It was much safer to eat your way to happiness than to find it in some stranger's arms. It was hell on her thighs, though. She would have to do half an hour on the Stairmaster when she got home.

Two weeks after Thorne had reported the capture of Obed Bedele there had been no signs of Moustapha Aziz.

One night as they were preparing for bed, Solange posed a possibility. "Maybe, after he'd had two close calls, he decided to take your advice and cut his losses after all," she said.

She was crossing the bedroom to the bathroom where Rupert was standing in front of the sink, flossing. She joined him, picked up the package of floss, unwound a length of it, cut it, and began flossing. "All of this waiting is making me antsy," she said.

Floss. Floss. "How long are we supposed to wait before we can get on with our lives?"

Rupert finished flossing and threw the waxed string into the wastebasket. "He's trying to lull us into a sense of complacency. Make us let down our guard. I know in my gut he's not giving up this easily. I humiliated him. I made a fool out of him. A man like Aziz doesn't forget that. What does he have left except his pride? Who does he have left to prove anything to? Himself. He'll try to kill me in order to regain his self-respect."

Solange finished flossing and picked up her toothbrush. "I can't believe the entire British Intelligence Agency can't find one big, bald African with murderous intentions. How many of those are running around?"

Rupert spread toothpaste on his brush, then hers. "A lot more than you think. Try to be patient for a little while longer."

Solange sighed and began brushing.

She wanted to go back to work. She wanted to get on with her life. She felt like a vacationer who had gone to a beautiful island and it had rained every single day, forcing her to hole up in her hotel room.

Rupert finished brushing and put his toothbrush away. "Let's go out."

Solange had to rinse before she could speak. "It's nearly midnight."

"On a Saturday night," Rupert said. "We're not old yet. Let's go dancing at Cristal's."

Solange cocked her head, considering. "Okay."

Cristal's, located between Lenox and Michigan Avenues, boasted live Latin, R & B, hip-hop, and reggae music. Tonight, there was a decided Latin beat in the air. In fact, the salseros, or salsa dancers, were out in force.

Solange and Rupert were in their element, as they frequented the club whenever Rupert was in town, and the dance floor was where they wanted to be practically the entire time they were there.

Salsa, Miami style, is called rueda or casino-style salsa. It had its origins in Cuba's social clubs in the 1950s. Depending on the proficiency of the dancers, the rueda can be swift or slower. Usually, the moves are done quickly, and there isn't much eye contact between partners. You definitely won't be partners for very long, either, because partners are exchanged as in a square dance. It's not uncommon to have a hundred people or more in a circle, with inner circles forming, on the dance floor.

Solange had worn a dress made for salsa dancing. Hot pink, it swirled about her legs with her movements, and was cinched at the waist and low cut. Rupert looked very cool in black slacks that clung to him in all the right places, and a billowing long-sleeve white cotton shirt open down his chest.

They got lost in the crowd of other dancers on the floor. Solange got spun, held, picked up, and dipped by men she'd never met before. Rupert had strange women brushing against him, their perfume mingling with perspiration.

The beat of Latin music drummed in their ears, loud and sensuous. The band was live and, if not superb, they were certainly enthusiastic. The crowd appreciated enthusiasm. There were broad smiles on their faces. Sweat trickling down between women's breasts. Men's brows beaded with it. The air was musky.

Solange was right in there with the best of them, doing fancy footwork she'd learned years ago when she'd first come to Miami. There was always somebody who would teach you how they danced salsa. And everybody's way was different. Over the years she'd developed her own style which was fast, sexy, and done with abandon.

Tomorrow morning her muscles would be telling her

she was too old for this. But as for tonight, she just didn't care.

She'd lost sight of Rupert a few minutes ago, but that didn't disturb her. Sometimes the rueda went on so long, your initial partner might go sit out the last of it, or have to take a bathroom break. The hearty souls lasted until the end. Rupert was usually among them.

Suddenly a tall, muscular man clasped her hand. Solange expected him to let go of her immediately, as was the usual manner in which this part of the dance was done.

Instead, he held onto her. In fact, his grip was hurting her hand. Crushing it. She looked up at him, but the overhead flashing lights obscured her vision. He leaned down close to her, so close she could smell his alcohol-laced breath. "So, you're his little pet. Be careful who you sleep with. He might get you killed."

With that, he let go of her and disappeared into the crowd. Solange turned and tried to make her way through the crowd of dancers. She didn't know where she was going, but she had to get as far away from him as she could. Her hand was throbbing painfully.

She rubbed it with her other hand. Where was Rupert?

Her heart was pounding. Why wouldn't these people let her off the dance floor?

A few men reached for her, thinking she was still one of the participants. She pushed their hands away. "Sorry, I'm sitting this one out." "Please, I'm leaving the floor."

A strong hand clasped her upper arm.

She jerked free of it. "I said I'm not dancing this one!"

"Whoa!" said Rupert. "What's the matter?"

Solange's face was a mask of frowns. "He was here. He grabbed me. He nearly crushed my hand."

Rupert pulled her into his arms, and together they made their way off the dance floor. They walked outside into the muggy night air. Other couples were standing around, smoking, or wrapped in one another's arms. One couple was arguing.

"Calm down," Rupert said gently. "Now, tell me what happened."

Solange continued to rub her hand. The pain was lessening; however, it was the fact that Moustapha Aziz had touched her that bothered her more. The hands of a merciless killer had held hers. She'd smelled his breath, known the bone-crushing strength he possessed. If she wasn't scared before, she was now!

"I was dancing, going from partner to partner when he grabbed me by the hand, but he wouldn't let go. He said, 'You must be his little pet. Be careful who you sleep with. He can get you killed.' Then he let go of me and left. I panicked and tried to get off the dance floor and that's when you showed up. Where were you?"

"I'm sorry, baby. Bathroom break," Rupert said with sincere regret.

Still tense and angry, Solange said, "Sorry doesn't cut it. You're supposed to be there when I need you, dammit! He's right, you could get me killed!"

Rupert willingly took her abuse. He felt guilty enough for bringing her into this mess. Now for this to happen! He felt useless. But emotions had to be subdued. He took her hand, "Let's get out of here. You can cuss me out in the car."

Solange sniffed. "His touch made my skin crawl."

Rupert pulled her along with him. "I know, I know," he commiserated.

"His voice was so slimy. That's what it would sound like if a snake could speak."

Rupert picked up his pace. They were vulnerable out in the open like this. Aziz could be anywhere. He didn't like the feeling of being the prey. He was usually the one who went hunting, not the other way around.

They arrived at the Mustang, and Rupert quickly unlocked the car and handed Solange in. She was still mumbling about Moustapha Aziz as he got behind the wheel.

"I couldn't see his face clearly because of the lights. But I got a sense of his size. He's big, Rupert. Bigger than you are."

Rupert started the car and backed out of the parking space. "Three inches taller and probably thirty pounds heavier. The last time, I got him drunk so I'd have the advantage. This time, I'm going to have to shoot him to stop him."

"Stop the car," Solange suddenly cried.

Rupert didn't ask why, he simply pulled the car over and put it in park.

Solange opened her car door, leaned out and vomited. It had been the excitement of dancing the salsa, the two glasses of beer, and, most of all, being threatened by a cold-blooded killer that had given her the nervous stomach.

She felt better after her stomach was empty. "I should have thrown up on him. That would have shown him," she joked as she closed the car door.

Later that night, after Solange was sleeping soundly, Rupert got out of bed and went to sit in the living room with all the lights off and the TV on. Earlier, when he'd told Solange that he felt in his gut that Aziz would not give up easily, he had been hoping he was wrong. Now that he knew he was right, and Aziz seemed to be bent on playing a game of cat and mouse with them, he was even more worried about Solange.

He might be able to take this in stride, almost making it a game, if it were not for Solange's involvement.

Even when he'd been in the thick of it, he'd survived by having a certain mindset: the one who was the best player always emerged triumphant.

He was the best player. Of course, he had never had to factor in the woman he loved. He reached over and picked up his cell phone from the coffee table. Quickly dialing a number, he waited impatiently. After the sixth ring, Thorne answered. "What the freaking hell do you want at this hour, Giles?"

"Aziz is in the city. He frightened Solange tonight while we were at a dance club. He grabbed her. Left bruises on her. Do you feel me, Thorne? Where were you?"

"There is a team watching your house twenty-four hours a day. They didn't report anything unusual except that you and Solange left after midnight. They didn't see anyone following you. Another couple of agents followed you to the club and waited outside until they saw you and Solange leave at around two A.M. There's a team outside your house right now, and everything's quiet."

"Well either Aziz has become an expert at camouflage, or your people are incompetent, because he was definitely inside the club tonight. Those bruises on Solange are very real!"

"What am I supposed to do about it, Giles? You're by her side all the time and you let him get close enough to her to slit her throat. You should be happy bruises are all she came away with. You know, I respect Aziz more and more the longer he evades us. I mistook him for a two-bit ex-dictator. But obviously he has skills we're yet to discover. This case is getting more interesting by the minute."

"Before this is over with, you and I are going to settle things between us once and for all, Thorne."

"Oh, I'm shaking," Thorne said with a laugh. "Why don't you admit it. You're rusty, old buddy. Five years ago, you would have put a bullet in Aziz's brain and been done with it. Love has made you soft. Though, I must tell you, she looks like she's well worth it. Is she a wildcat in bed, as well as on the firing range?"

Rupert told him to go have intercourse with himself, and hung up.

"I like this one best," Marie said as she stood with Solange in front of a full-length mirror in one of Miami's most exclusive bridal shops. The gown Solange had on was by Vera Wang. The sleeveless Chinese-inspired dress in champagne-colored satin had a square bodice with a vee neckline at the center, which made the front look like the petals of a white tulip. Ankle length, there was a slit in the back. The waist was tapered, and the skirt fit snugly. There was a see-through train attached to the waist that fell a couple of inches below the hem of the dress.

Solange smiled. She loved it. "It's my favorite, too."

Marie kissed her cheek. "Then it's settled. This is your dress."

Solange hated to ask the next question of the salesperson who was standing a couple of feet away watching them as they made up their minds. "How much is this one?"

"I thought we decided that I was going to worry about the price," Marie said. She stepped away from Solange and crooked a finger at the salesperson. The two of them went off by themselves and all Solange could hear was whispering. Her mother loved to haggle. But Solange didn't think her mother was going to be able to convince the salesperson to lower the price by very much—not when the salesperson's commission came out of the exorbitant price.

Solange admired herself in the dress. The color went perfectly with her medium brown, red undertoned complexion. It also accentuated her figure. She'd always had a small waist and full hips. The cut of the dress seemed to be made for her particular figure. She sighed. *I can't let Maman spend a small fortune on a dress I'm only going to wear once.*

She looked over at her mother and the salesperson, a tall, full-figured African-American woman in her late forties. She and her mother were apparently arguing about the price.

Her mother was driving her point home by pounding her fist into her palm. Solange smiled. She hoped there wasn't going to be a fistfight in here this afternoon.

"Maman," she said.

Marie looked up. "Yes, sweetie?"

"The dress is lovely. But there are lots of lovely dresses out there."

"Okay, it's a deal," the salesperson told Marie. She stuck out her hand. She and Marie shook on it.

A few minutes later, Solange and Marie were walking down the sidewalk heading to a favorite bistro for lunch. "What did you say to her?" Solange wanted to know.

"Well," said Marie, "she owns the shop, so I told her that if she would eat her profits and let me have the dress at wholesale, I would eat my fee for redecorating her house. Believe me, she got the better deal. You ought to see that woman's house!"

"Then you're acquaintances," Solange guessed.

"We met at a mixer for area black business owners last year. She knows someone who has used my services, and she's been after me ever since to do her house. I even went as far as to go to her house to look at it. Talk about overdoing the Miami theme. I thought pink flamingoes went out in the fifties. But, no, she has about ten wrought-iron pink flamingoes stuck in the grass of her front yard. Plus a black lawn jockey holding up a lantern that actually works! That child needs help!"

"Shows how much I know about decorating," Solange said. "I always thought those flamingoes were kind of cool. Especially the ones that are shown wearing sunglasses."

Marie laughed. "You don't have any in your front yard."

"It never occurred to me to buy any. But now that you've brought them up, I might go by Kmart and pick up a few."

"Over my dead body!" Marie said, laughing even harder. "And I don't think your favorite discount store sells them. They have more taste than that."

"Then I'll order them from an online novelty store," Solange said. "People who love pink flamingoes, unite!" They both laughed until they had tears in their eyes.

Once Marie got her breath, she said, "Seriously, though, Romana's good people. She gave me a really great deal on the dress and I'm going to do her proud on her redecorating project."

They arrived at the bistro and were greeted by a very handsome Cubano in his early twenties. He was around five-eleven, and wore the bistro's signature colors, black and gold. His black slacks and long-sleeve gold shirt looked good against his brown skin. "Ah, the lovely DuPree girls," he said. "Now, which one is the mother, and which is the daughter?" He eyed them appreciatively.

Marie laughed and playfully punched him on the arm. Indeed, she appeared younger than her years in her trendy white vest and matching skirt. She wore a chocolate-colored T-shirt under the vest that was practically the same color as her eyes. White sandals with three-inch heels allowed her to be the same height as Solange, who was wearing flats. "If you can't tell I'm the mother, you need your contact lenses cleaned, dear boy." She looked around at the busy bistro. Practically all the tables were taken by a vivacious lunch crowd. "Is your mother here today?" The bistro was called Lily's.

Lily Calderon was the owner. Adriano was her eldest son.

"She's in the kitchen insulting the cook," Adriano joked. "You know Mama, picky, picky, picky."

"She's a perfectionist," Marie said with a smile. "That's why she's been such a success. She cares about every little detail."

Adriano showed them to a table in the center of the restaurant. He helped both ladies with their chairs, then smiled down at them. "Yes, but it's so hard to live with a perfectionist. Do you know, when I was a small boy, she would iron my school clothes the night before and, then, the next morning she would iron them again. She said the moisture in the air had made them less crisp. Crisp! Why do clothes have to be crisp?"

"Are you telling that story again, Adriano?" a female voice chastised him. Lily Calderon came up behind her son and goosed him. She grinned at Solange and Marie.

"The DuPree gals," she said with a warm smile. "How are you, ladies?"

"We're doing well, thank you, and you?" Marie answered for both of them. "We've been shopping for a wedding dress and we're worn out. I'm craving some of your lemon sole, with a glass of that divine Chablis I had the last time I was here."

"I'm great," Lily said. "And you're in luck, we got some fresh sole in this morning."

She smiled at Solange. "And the bride-to-be?"

"I'm not very hungry," Solange said. "I'll just have a bowl of ratatouille, if you have it, and French bread on the side. I'll take a glass of iced tea to go with it."

"You heard the ladies, Adriano, go give Cesar their

orders. I'm going to stay to find out more about Solange's upcoming wedding."

Adriano bowed to his mother. "Mein Capitan!"

"Smartass," Lily said as she made herself comfortable on the spare chair at Solange and Marie's table. In her mid-fifties, Lily wore her black hair in a severe bun. Her skin was a light golden brown, and her eyes black as coal. When she smiled, they seemed to take on a warmth that radiated outward to make the person she was looking at feel cherished, but if you crossed her, those black eyes could cut right through you.

Marie admired her. They were both women in their fifties who were single: Marie due to divorce, and Lily due to death. Her husband, Mario, died of a heart attack three years ago. She'd been running the restaurant ever since.

"Okay," she said, smiling at Solange. "I got my invitation in the mail, and I can't wait to come. What I want to know is, will there be single men my age at the reception?"

"I know of at least five unattached males who are a little older than you who will be there without dates," Solange said. "Bring Adriano. There are always single women at weddings hoping to be swept off their feet."

"That's his problem," Lily told them frankly. "He does all that sweeping, but he never brings anyone home to meet me. He must think I'm going to take one look at her and start issuing orders: Stand up straight! Suck in that gut, girlie, what do you think this is, a game? You're going to have to be shipshape to date my son!"

"You definitely have him spooked," Marie said.

"What my children don't understand," said Lily. "Is that I have certain standards because they help me be the best I can be. However, I don't require them to live up to my standards. I want them to be who they're going to be. I am proud of all of them, just as they are. Warts and all."

"Can I quote you on that?" Adriano said. He held a

tray with Marie's Chablis and Solange's iced tea on it. He served them with a flourish, then set a basket of fresh-baked bread sticks on the table.

"How would you like to escort your mother to Solange and Rupert's wedding?" Lily asked him, looking up at him with a humorous expression in her eyes. She expected him to come up with some kind of an excuse. Her son preferred the excitement of the dance clubs on South Beach, where the women were hot and the music loud.

"When is it?" he asked.

"The afternoon of June 26," Solange supplied.

"My schedule's clear on that date," Adriano said. "I'd love to go." He looked down at his mother. "But once we're there, I don't know you. No self-respecting woman would ever take a man who brings his mother to a wedding seriously!"

To which the three ladies at the table burst into laughter.

"You're wrong," Solange said once her laughter was under control. "Some women would consider themselves lucky to find a man like that."

Back on the sidewalk, heading to Marie's black Mercedes, Solange spotted the unmarked car that was supposed to stay several car lengths behind her whenever she was on the street. As they were leaving Lily's she'd also seen the female agent who had been following them around all day. She'd gone into Lily's and had lunch, too, while Solange and her mother had dined.

In fact, Solange had paused at the entrance as she and Marie were leaving to give the agent a chance to pay her bill and fall into step behind them.

"Rupert told me Theophilus phoned to ask you to

show him around Miami, and you refused him," Solange said as they walked.

Marie put on her sunglasses and sighed. "That's true."

"I thought you had your attraction to him under control."

"Dear, there's something primal about that man. I don't trust myself to be alone with him. He looks at me like I'm something delicious to nibble on."

Solange smiled at her. "Am I hearing correctly? You're afraid you'll end up in bed with Theophilus?"

"Honey, if we're ever alone together our clothes would fall off by themselves. It's like that. I've only felt this way about one other man, and I married him!"

Solange laughed delightedly. "I say go for it!"

"Are you crazy? He's going to be your father-in-law."

"One of my fathers-in-law. Benjamin and Helena Giles will be my parents-in-law, too. I, for one, won't feel the least bit uncomfortable if you and Theophilus got together. I doubt if Rupert would either. He says you two make a cute couple. He's still talking about that exchange you and Theophilus shared the first night you met. So is Samantha, who is very fond of you already. So, you see, Maman, the only one standing in the way of whatever's going to happen between you and Theophilus is you."

"Rupert thinks we make a cute couple, huh?" Marie mused. She pursed her lips, thinking. "Well, maybe I'll take pity on the poor man and give him a quick tour of the city. You never know where it will end up."

Things between Solange and Rupert had been strained ever since she'd been accosted by Moustapha Aziz at Cristal's. The incident had happened two weeks ago, and Solange could not bring herself to make love to

Rupert. They tried to pretend that they were fine as a couple. They had not stopped speaking to each other. Solange had gone back to work, feeling fairly safe due to her being aware of the agents who were watching them. Rupert kissed her goodbye at the door every morning. He greeted her each afternoon. He cooked her favorite meals. She cooked his. They did things any normal couple might do. They watched TV together, ate out, went to the movies. But when they got into bed at night, Solange stayed on her side of the bed. Rupert would put his arms around her and pull her close to him in bed, and she would freeze up.

Thinking she needed time to adjust to being under a microscope twenty-four hours a day, Rupert let it slide. Besides, he felt he was the reason why she was stressed out. The least he could do was be patient with her. She'd come around.

Though the sex had always exceeded his wildest expectations, sex was not the be-all and end-all of their relationship. They'd gone without it for weeks, although that was when he was working out of town. Whenever they were together, sex came as naturally to them as any other thing they did in order to sustain life: breathing, sleeping, eating, drinking water. Sex had been just as vital to them.

He worried that she'd never be able to truly forgive him for his mistake. She had said she'd forgiven him, but perhaps, deep down, she hadn't. She came home from work one day in early May with a briefcase full of papers, which, to Rupert, was another way she avoided intimacy. Lately, she'd been coming home and, following dinner, would say she had work to do, and disappear into the little den in the back of the house where she kept her desk. Sometimes he would go back there to tell her goodnight, but instead of finding her hard at work, she would have slipped out onto the deck to tend her orchids. He would not disturb her, but would stand there silently in the shadows to watch her face. She looked so sad, it broke his heart. It made him think that he'd killed the joy inside of her by bringing his past into their present. He thought, perhaps, she'd be better off without him and that leaving her once this business with Aziz was finished would be the selfless thing to do. She deserved someone who wouldn't inadvertently get her killed just for loving him.

Therefore, tonight, after the dinner dishes had been done and Solange made the excuse of having to work, Rupert looked at her and said, "Do you have to work, or are you trying to avoid any kind of intimacy between us?"

The air went still. The room was silent except for the ticking of the clock on the wall. Solange stood barefoot, wearing a pair of well-worn jeans riding low on her hips and a white off-the-shoulder midriff top. She did not lower her gaze. Her mouth was stubbornly set, as though she wished he would start a fight. She was itching for one.

Rupert was dressed for jogging. He'd taken to running at night now that she was usually holed up in the den pretending to work. The running took his mind off of making love to her since it provided mood-boosting endorphins. It was no substitute for sex, though, and he was developing shin splints, when what he'd rather be developing were rug burns on his knees.

"Come on, say what's on your mind," he taunted her. "I'm tired of listening to your silences. If you want me out of here, say so. If you want me to stay, say so. But say something! Lately, you've mastered the art of speaking without saying anything! I'd almost prefer it if you didn't say anything to me at all instead of being so damned civil without any sort of intimacy."

"How can you be so smart and be so dense?" Solange asked, her eyes riveted on his. She smiled pityingly.

Rupert's eyes narrowed. "Explain yourself."

Solange breathed in and exhaled. "I'm still angry with you!" She let that soak in for a few seconds, then continued. "Spies, lies, and alibis are all such integral parts of what makes you who you are, Rupert, that the impact of what you've done hasn't hit you yet. Or it doesn't seem to have hit you. You went off to Mauritania to do a job for people whose methods you find morally wrong. Yet, you were able to put aside your distrust in favor of taking the chance on being free and clear of them for our sakes: yours, mine, and Desta's. But what if you'd been killed? I would never have known what became of you. It irks me that you found it so easy to lie to me. You phoned and told me where you were going, yes. But you said it was just a routine insurance investigation. Oh, no. I'm sorry. You didn't exactly say that. So, perhaps you can get away with not having lied to me. You simply didn't give me all the facts."

Rupert started to say something, but Solange walked up to him and put her hand over his mouth. "I've got the floor. You wanted to hear this, so listen," she said.

"If the stuff hadn't hit the fan, I would never have known what you were really up to in Mauritania. But since your work followed you home, I'm faced with having a killer in my town, hoping to murder my fiance while we're in the middle of planning our wedding. Yesterday, my mother asked me how things were between us, and I lied and said everything was glorious! Everything is not glorious, Rupert. I'm scared half the time, and the other, I'm terrified." She let her hand fall and turned her back to him. "If you're wondering why I haven't wanted to make love to you, it's because I'm afraid to let down my guard with you. I don't know you anymore. I'm not sure you're not an adrenaline junkie, after all. I'm not positive that you'll never again put your life in jeopardy just for the thrill of it. I've had to admit to myself that I never really knew you. That's the terrifying part."

She walked through the doorway, heading to the den.

"Now wait just one damn minute!" Rupert yelled. "You said you forgave me."

Solange spun back around, her eyes fierce and unyielding. "I know I said I forgave you, but those platitudes obviously haven't reached my heart yet. I guess it took me a few days for the realization of what you'd done to sink in. Forgiving something like that isn't going to be easy. Sure, you made an error of judgment like any human being might, but given your background as a spy, perhaps you should have given it more thought. And if I'm being too hard on you, too bad! Because we're both going to have to live with the consequences of your actions the rest of our lives, whether they get Aziz before he gets to you or not! You might not have cheated on me with another woman, Rupert. But you have definitely broken the trust that existed between us!"

Stunned, Rupert could not form the words that he wanted to say. He turned and walked away. Solange let him go. She continued to the den, her sight obscured by tears. She had to stop midway to lean against the wall because she was suddenly weak with the fear that she'd said things that were irretrievable. She heard the front door close. She had thought that he would slam it, but he hadn't. She slid to the hall floor and cried until she was cried out. Then, she got up, washed her face, and went outside to water her orchids.

Rupert ran flat out for fifteen minutes, and then settled into a slower pace for the next thirty minutes. He'd covered five miles before it occurred to him that he shouldn't leave Solange alone for such a long period of time. He almost regretted goading her into letting her anger out. Almost. It was always best to have everything out in the open. He didn't want her hanging on to her resentment of him. She had every right not to trust him. He would have to earn her trust again after what he'd done. His confidence in himself had been shattered, too. It would be a long time before he would automatically trust his judgment. He hated feeling vulnerable. But he'd get through this. He'd always been a fighter, and he wouldn't stop now.

He was a few blocks from the house when Thorne leapt from behind a tall hedge and started jogging alongside him. "Hey, buddy. Sounds like you and Solange aren't on the best of terms. Does that mean the wedding's off?"

Rupert laughed. "I don't know what I'd do without your comic relief, Thorne. Are you here to tell me you've found Aziz?"

"No, 'fraid not. Fourteen days, and the only sighting of him was when he tried to crush Solange's hand. Maybe he died in his sleep or something. I should check the morgue to see if any bodies fitting his description have been brought in in the last two weeks."

"So, how long do you think the agency's going to allow you to stay on the case? They must be losing patience at headquarters by now."

"No word on that. But you're right. They might pull the plug, then you and Solange would be on your own."

"You all haven't exactly been Johnny-on-the-spot," Rupert reminded him.

"Nor have you. But we are trying. It's the general consensus of the agents on this case that we like Solange and don't want anything to happen to her. You, on the other hand, are not well liked. Except for Harris. She thinks you're dreamy. Her words, not mine."

Rupert laughed again. "Thank you for the update, Thorne."

"Just threw that in as an ego boost after that tongue-lashing you got from Solange."

"You're a sweetheart, Thorne."

"Yeah, I hate you, too." He veered off to the left. "Enjoy your night on the couch."

Rupert went straight to the bathroom to take a shower when he got in. Solange was on the deck, sitting on a lounge chair with her feet stretched out before her, looking at the stars. The night was not as muggy as it usually was. It felt like a front was trying to move in. The air smelled of the wild jasmine that was growing near the back fence.

She had her eyes closed. After tending to her orchids she'd gone inside to get her portable CD player, and Sam Cooke was serenading her with "*You Send Me*" right now.

His mellow voice was soothing her frayed nerves. Did Rupert think he was the only one who missed intimacy? Every night as they lay side by side, she was at war with her emotions. The distrustful part of her told her she couldn't possibly share her body with a man who could go out tomorrow and provoke someone to shoot him. The horny part of her said what's love got to do with it? You're tense. You need a good session in the sack. It'll relax you. Use him. Use him up, girl! The distrustful part had won so far. No telling when Miss Lustful Panties would KO the distrustful part of her and jump Rupert's bones, though.

After showering and brushing his teeth, Rupert went in search of Solange. He had heard the music when he came in, and followed the sound of it. Barefoot, wearing only his white cotton robe, he stepped onto the deck and saw Solange lying on the lounge chair with her eyes closed. He went to stand next to her and bent low to determine if she was sleeping or simply had her eyes closed.

Solange smelled him the moment he walked outside. Now, she felt his body heat as he leaned over her. She kept her eyes closed, hoping he'd go away, and soon. His proximity had kick-started her libido.

Rupert didn't go away, though. He leaned even closer and placed his mouth over hers. He licked her lips with sensual intensity, taking his time. Solange moaned softly and opened her mouth to him. Rupert's tongue entered her mouth and gently touched hers. He tasted clean and sweet. Her mouth was nectar to him. It was difficult for him not to groan with pleasure, but he sensed the spell might be broken if he were too enthusiastic. He pulled away for a moment, trying to assess the situation. He didn't think the lounge chair, which was made of lightweight aluminum, would hold both of them. He bent on one knee beside her. "I am the man you thought I was, Solange. I had a temporary lapse in my thinking, that's all. I don't crave the life of a spy. Sure, I'm somewhat of a thrill-seeker. But, then, so are you. You wouldn't make love the way you do if you were not adventurous, and bold, and slightly nuts, just like I am. I love all those things about you. If it takes me the rest of my life, you will believe in me again. I swear it. But don't stew in your anger. Let it out. Take it out on me. Come on, show me how you feel. I can take it."

He rose and held his hand out to her. Solange took it and allowed him to pull her to her feet.

"I didn't want to hurt you," Solange said, her voice rife with regret. "But you asked, and I'd been holding it in for so long that I needed to get it off my chest. I know you're in pain, too, and that you regret what you did. But if I made love to you tonight, it would be because I want you so badly, not because I've suddenly forgiven and forgotten."

"I understand," Rupert said, letting go of her hand. He smiled wistfully as he turned to go inside. "I'll sleep on the couch tonight."

Solange watched him go, then she went straight to the bathroom and took a nice, long shower. When she emerged she was clean, if not satisfied.

It was cake sampling day. Solange and Rupert were to meet Dani at Celestial Creations, a bakery that specialized in wedding cakes, on Friday evening. Dani was driving there now in her white late-model Toyota Camry. She had a smile on her face because she had a date tonight, her first date in nearly a year. Not counting that one-night stand with Marc, who did not understand the concept of 'get lost.' Dani had chalked that night up to loneliness. She came to her senses the next day and told him to stay gone for good.

But this guy, the new guy, was intriguing. They had kept seeing each other all over town. At Patacon's, at her favorite fruit stand. At the strip mall where her favorite stylist had her shop. Now *that* was out of the way. It was in Hialeah. Not her normal stomping grounds. That incident had made Dani think he must be following her. With no shortage of nerve, Dani had walked up to him and asked him if he was following her, and he'd said, "Yes, I am. Does that make you nervous?"

Dani had copped an attitude then. "Damn straight, it makes me nervous. So I'm gonna tell you now: you don't scare me! I will kick your butt and then call the police! You'd better find yourself another hobby, sweetheart!"

"Please forgive me," her secret admirer had said with a regretful smile. "I'll leave you alone."

That was two days ago. Yesterday, Dani had gone back to her shop after lunch and found two dozen calla lilies sitting on her desk. Roses were her flowers of choice, but she couldn't ignore the fact that calla lilies were imported from South Africa and those babies cost an arm and a leg. Whoever her secret admirer was, he was loaded. Dani was no gold digger, but if she was going to be wined and dined, she'd prefer to be wined and dined in style. It was that touch of diva in her. She'd read the card with bated breath: I'm really harmless. It's just that you're so beautiful I momentarily lost all ability to think rationally. I'm sorry I frightened you. Then, he'd written his phone number down.

She'd phoned him when she got home last night, and tonight they were going to meet at Patacon's. She would drive her car. He would drive his. Dani had no intentions of getting involved with him. But he'd piqued her curiosity. She wanted to know more about him. She had a can of mace in her purse in case he turned out to be a creep. She'd wear stilettos in case he turned out to be a real creep. They'd do some damage.

Dani parked the Camry on the street and got out of the car. She spotted Solange and that divine Rupert waiting for her in front of Celestial Creations. She'd only met Rupert once before, when they'd met with the chef at the Biltmore Hotel to sample the menu he was planning for the reception. Rupert had treated her with respect, even though she sensed he knew her secret. To Dani, that showed real class.

"Good afternoon, darlings," she greeted them. She and Solange touched cheeks.

She got between them, taking each by an arm and directing them toward the shop's entrance. "Shall we go inside? Andre is waiting for us."

Andre turned out to be a tall, rather dour-looking

black woman in her mid-forties. She didn't smile once when they were introduced. She wore a hairnet over her black curls. She had on khakis and a long-sleeve white shirt underneath her baker's apron.

The shop smelled wonderful. And it was spotless. Atop the glass display cases were all sorts of cakes of various sizes done in plaster of paris. The real cakes were inside the display cases. There were two other employees in the shop, and both of them were helping customers.

"Please come this way," Andre invited them as she walked through a beaded curtain toward the back of the shop. The room she led them to was brightly painted in pastel ice cream colors. There were several small, white wrought-iron tables with matching chairs with bright cushions on their seats. She directed everyone to the middle table, upon which sat three small, iced cakes. "Have a seat," Andre told them.

Her three customers sat down, and Andre began serving them. She placed a piece of each of the cakes on china plates and gave them shining utensils to eat with. While they sampled her creations, she talked. "The recipes are my mother's, God rest her soul. I'm afraid we lost her recently. She ran this shop for twenty-five years."

When Solange tasted the vanilla cake with vanilla cream frosting, it took all of her willpower to prevent her eyes from rolling back in her head in ecstasy. It was ambrosial. There was no other word for it.

She looked up at Andre. "I'm sorry for your loss."

Andre smiled and, when she did, her eyes glistened with tears. "Thank you."

Solange returned her smile. "This is the best cake I've ever eaten in my life."

"I agree," Rupert said, looking at Solange.

Andre's smile became broader. "You have to sample the others before you decide. Next, we have the Die

Happy chocolate cake. Momma called it that because a woman once told her that after eating it she could drop dead at that moment, and she would die happy, it was so good."

"Oh, let me at it," Dani said, fork poised. She gently broke off a piece of the cake with her fork and brought it to her mouth. She placed the fork in her mouth and slowly withdrew it. Then she licked the icing off the fork. "Good Lord, girl. This cake will make you hurt yourself! What did your mother put in it, some kind of aphrodisiac? Look at those two."

Indeed, Solange and Rupert were feeding each other the Die Happy chocolate cake and gazing into each other's eyes as though they were the only two people in the room.

"She put a lot of love in it," Andre said, pleased to see her mother's cakes were a hit so far.

"Let's move on to the third and final cake. Momma called this one A Piece of Heaven. It's lemon chiffon. It's as light as a cloud."

Solange placed a small piece of the lemon cake on her tongue, and closed her mouth, savoring it. Andre was right. It was so light, it practically melted on her tongue. The flavor was also light, with no bitter aftertaste. Another winner.

After she, Rupert, and Dani had sampled all three cakes, Andre looked at them expectantly. "Well, what do you think? Which flavor would you like?"

Solange and Rupert locked gazes. Then, they looked at Andre. "All three," they said in unison.

"The cake will have six tiers, right?" asked Solange.

Andre nodded in the affirmative. "Yes, that's right."

"Then we'd like you to alternate the flavors. A Piece of Heaven on top because it's so light, it's almost like an appetizer. Then the vanilla cream. What's the name of that one?"

"A Kiss on Your Lips," Andre replied.

"Very appropriate," Rupert said, his eyes on Solange's mouth.

Solange had trouble concentrating. "Okay, A Kiss on Your Lips second, and Die Happy on the bottom."

Andre smiled her pleasure. "It'll be the first time we've done a cake like that. I'm sure Momma would have enjoyed creating it. In her absence, I'm going to do it for you."

"Wonderful," said Dani, rising and putting her purse on her shoulder. She shook Andre's hand. "Thank you, Andre."

Solange and Rupert thanked her as well, then, hand in hand, they hurried from the shop. Once on the sidewalk with Dani ahead of them, they paused in their steps to briefly kiss. Dani peered back at them, her auburn hair whipping about her face in the Gulf Stream breezes. "Would you two please take it off the street? Go home, go home. It's hot enough out here without you steaming up my air. And I just got my hair done. This humidity is awful on a girl's 'do."

They waved to her as they ran across the street to Rupert's new SUV.

"That's right, children," she said in a low voice. "Go home and teach each other what love is all about. I might give a lesson or two myself tonight."

She turned and walked swiftly to her Camry.

Nine

Rupert insisted that Solange wear her seat belt as he drove them home; otherwise she might have been in his lap. She had to be satisfied with touching his cheek, gazing rapturously at him, and sighing with contentment because she'd finally come to realize that her love for him supplanted the distrust that his actions had caused to take root in her heart.

"Can you drive faster?"

"I'm already going ten miles per hour over the speed limit. I want to get you home without being pulled over by a patrolman."

"You should have let me drive."

"You drive like a maniac."

"No, I drive like a native. You drive like someone from England."

"I am from England."

"There you go!"

Rupert sighed and cut a brief glance at her sweet face. "I adore you."

"I adore you more."

"I saw it in your eyes the moment you decided to end the standoff. But I still want to know why," Rupert told her quietly. "For weeks we have been living in the same house, lying awake in bed burning for each other. Yes, I saw you tossing and turning. I heard you taking late-night showers. Still, you wouldn't budge. What was it that changed your mind?"

"It was because I could feel Andre's pain when she told us about her late mother. I thought to myself, I know I love Rupert and I never want to be without him. Why am I wasting precious time by denying our passion for each other? Life gives us no guarantees. I think I was angrier at you for risking your life than for deceiving me. How could you be so cavalier about the very thing I hold most dear, your life? I'm still angry about that! But I can't bear to be without you any longer, so I'm giving up the acrimony, and getting on with the matrimony."

Rupert reached across and grasped her hand in his. "I'm so relieved. I was going crazy sleeping on the couch while you were a few feet away in that big bed. All by yourself."

"Time," Solange said with a smile. "I needed time to figure things out."

He pulled into the driveway and parked. They unbuckled their belts, leaned toward each other, and kissed. The cab of the SUV was large enough so that Rupert could pull Solange onto his lap. He did. "Nineteen days," he said as his hands encircled her waist.

"What?" Solange asked. They were crotch to crotch now. Both had on jeans; hers were buttonfly, while his were zippered.

"Nineteen days since we made love."

"I can't believe you kept count!"

"It became a habit when I was away from you. I would count the days until you'd be back in my arms again."

Solange bent and kissed him deeply. His hands cupped her buttocks, squeezing them as she pressed closer to his already hard manhood, causing him to get even harder.

Solange turned her head, breaking off the kiss. "Why didn't you get tinted windows in this thing?"

Rupert smiled up at her. "Why, so that you could have your way with me in the car?"

He reached for the door's handle. "We're not going to give the neighbors something to talk about. Though Peter would probably love to rib me about it for the rest of his days."

He lifted her off of him and set her down on the pavement of the driveway. Solange turned and ran up the steps of the house. She heard Rupert slam the car door as she put the key in the lock and turned it. By the time she stepped into the foyer, Rupert was at her side. He closed and locked the door, then turned to her.

His eyes swept over her with a biological imperative to mate. Hunger, dark and passionate. Solange sometimes felt a twinge of fear when she saw that look in his eyes. Of course, the fear only heightened her subsequent satisfaction. It was born of anticipation and a primal need.

He reached for her hand. She placed it in his. He in turn put it on his chest, over his heart. "Feel that?" he asked. "How powerful an effect you have on me? It would stop beating if you ever left me. I would will it to."

That was enough for Solange. She began tugging at his shirt, pulling the hem of it out of his waistband. This done, Rupert finished yanking it over his head. She went for the top button of his jeans next. "Better let me," Rupert said, and unzipped his jeans.

"Now, it's your turn," he said as he stood before her shirtless and with his jeans unzipped. His hands were on her crisp, white blouse. He undid each button with slow deliberation, while Solange got more and more impatient.

"Patience is a virtue," he said.

"Funny, I'm not thinking about virtue right now," Solange told him.

Rupert finished unbuttoning the blouse, and allowed it to hang open while he worked on the buttons of her jeans. "You went a little button crazy when you got dressed this morning. Is there a Victorian lady locked somewhere in your psyche?"

"Maybe. I hear those Victorians were pretty lusty," Solange answered. "Faster, baby, faster."

Solange suddenly went still. "We need noise." She met his eyes. "You do the bedroom, and I'll do the living room. Meet me in the bathroom."

They went off to turn on stereos in the two rooms.

Outside, in a dark van parked across the street, Thorne cursed. "Sorry, Harris, looks like they've kissed and made up."

"Too bad," said Harris, an attractive brunette with brown eyes. "I was preparing to become his rebound woman."

She and Thorne were alone in the van. "You know, Harris, if you want a man who has stamina, you're looking at him."

"Sod off, Thorne. I know your reputation with women. You have never had a relationship that lasted more than one night."

"It goes with the job," Thorne said.

"Keep making that excuse, and you'll always be alone," Harris told him. She opened a magazine. "Nothing going on here. I might as well read."

Thorne simmered. Here he was alone with an attractive woman who wouldn't give him the time of day, and Giles was in there with a woman who was about to shag him within an inch of his life!

"What if I told you my reputation isn't what it's all cracked up to be," he said confidentially to Joanne Harris.

She raised her eyes from the magazine. "You would have to prove it."

"How?"

"The next time you speak with Giles, you have to tell him you're jealous of him, and that's why you behave the way that you do."

"What?" Thorne yelled.

"It's the truth, isn't it? I've studied you, Thorne. Okay, I admit it. I find you terribly attractive in a tired playboy kind of way. You intrigue me. I'd like to see what's underneath your rough exterior. If you're capable of human kindness. Because when it comes down to it, only kindness matters. Surely you know that."

"And if I do it?" Thorne wanted to know. Not that he was seriously considering kowtowing to Giles. No way. But he wondered what the advantage would be if he actually did what Joanne asked. Joanne. He might humiliate himself just to run his hands through her wavy hair. Man! He was one spy who needed to come in out of the cold! "Not that I would do it. Giles and I go back a long way. We've never gotten along. He hates my guts, and I hate his."

Joanne raised her shirt, and bared her tanned and toned belly. "How do you feel about my gut, Thorne?" She raised her shirt a little higher. "There's more where that came from." She eyed him speculatively as she lowered her shirt. "How far I'll go depends on whether or not you're willing to show your sensitive side."

"I certainly hope you're not toying with me, Harris," Thorne said, his tone serious.

"I don't play," Joanne Harris said, eyes narrowed. "I want you, Thorne. But I don't make love to callous men."

Otis Redding's voice filled the bedroom. Try a "Little Tenderness," his emotionally charged vocals advised. On the bed, tenderness was being explored in every manner physically possible.

At that moment, Solange was on top, with Rupert inside of her. Her skin was slightly flushed and had a thin layer of perspiration on it. It glistened too, because Rupert had rubbed her down with body oils earlier. She closed her eyes, relishing the feel of his hard, hot shaft moving against her clitoris. Erect, his penis pointed a bit upward, making it very versatile when it came to pleasuring her. Rupert was gently squeezing her nipples between his thumb and forefinger, causing her to drift between exquisite pain and intense arousal. He loved watching her when she was close to reaching a climax. Her face mirrored the state she was in—pain, pleasure, sheer joy, release, and ultimately letting go of all inhibitions.

She threw her head back and growled deep in her throat. Of course, it wasn't one of his growls, which were loud and guttural. It was more the sound of a lioness claiming her territory. She had to get her breath, regain her rhythm of breathing. Rupert watched her breasts rise and fall, enjoyed the sight of her flaring nostrils, became even more aroused when her tongue flicked out and licked her lips.

Though she had ridden him to her satisfaction, he had not found release. But it was so close he feared that she would bring it on with one thrust of her hips. So, he said, "Don't make any sudden moves, baby. I want you on your back with your feet in the air. Slowly get up off of me, and lie down on your back."

Solange rose with great care. She looked down at him as she got up. His penis was covered with her bodily fluids. It stood up, and waved at her. That's how she thought of the movement his penis made when it was fully erect.

Rupert smiled at her as he grabbed her about the

waist and threw her onto the bed, onto her back. He
straddled her. He took his heavy member in his hand
and tapped it on her flat belly. "Open wide, and wrap
your legs around me, sweetness."

He entered her then. The cool air in the room had
brought the temperature of his penis down, but that was
a nice change for her sensitive insides. Rupert reached
down and raised her buttocks up off the bed. He pumped
her while Solange kept her legs wrapped tightly around
him. He thrust harder and deeper until surcease could be
found only in the explosive sensations contained in his
impending climax. He came. His seed flowed into her. It
felt like he might go on ejaculating inside of her forever,
because it had been a long time since his last orgasm. He
had saved himself for her, hoping she would take him
back into her bed. And now he was here, and if they
hadn't made a baby tonight there was no hope for them
to ever make one in the future. He felt it in his heart.
They would have a child together in about nine months.

He bent and kissed her mouth. Lay on top of her for
a few seconds without putting his full weight on her. Let
out a contented sigh. Rolled off of her onto his side and
pulled her close so that their faces were only inches
apart. "Let's buy a house with a huge skylight in our bedroom so we can look up at the stars after making love."

Solange laughed shortly. "Sure. I also want a balcony
so that you can climb up and surprise me sometime."

"With a rose between my teeth," Rupert said. He
kissed her again. "Seriously, though, babe. I want to buy
you a house as a wedding gift. Let's start looking for it
tomorrow."

Solange sat up. "A house as a wedding gift? Real estate
prices have shot up since I bought this house ten years
ago. Do you know how much a house in Miami costs?"

"No more than ten percent of my net worth, I hope,"

Rupert said. He yawned. "I was figuring on $1.5 million. And I was thinking of Coral Gables."

Solange rapidly did the math in her head. "That means you're worth about $15 million."

"Give or take a million," Rupert said. His eyes were getting droopy.

He didn't see it, but Solange looked at him bug eyed. He'd closed his eyes. "You never told me you were that rich!"

"We never discussed finances," he reminded her, not bothering to open his eyes. "Can we talk about this later, sweetness? I'm down for the count."

Solange lay back down, mumbling, "You never tell me anything!"

Rupert chuckled. "I thought your engagement ring would give you some clue as to how much I was worth."

"You said you got a good deal on it," Solange said, still clueless.

She peered at the five-carat white diamond solitaire. It sparkled even in the dimmed light. "I don't go around pricing jewelry, you know! I trusted you to have given me a ring comparable to your salary."

"I did. It's worth a hundred grand."

"A hundred grand! Are you crazy? I've been walking around campus with a hundred thousand dollar ring on my finger? I've been leaving it in my locker while I swam. Somebody could have stolen it!"

"It's insured," Rupert said, yawning yet again.

Solange sat up and swung her legs down off the bed, remembering to use the footstool to get down. "You go to sleep. I'm too upset. I can't believe you let me walk around with a ring this expensive on my finger without telling me how much it was worth."

Rupert smiled, turned over in bed, and went to sleep.

* * *

Dani's date was already seated at their table when she arrived fifteen minutes late.

She had not meant to be late, but she couldn't get her hair right to save her life. She'd ended up putting it in a French roll and forgetting about it. The restaurant was nicely full tonight. Dani loved the buzz of human voices in the background. The sounds of people enjoying themselves. It relaxed her. She'd worn a black skirt suit with a double-breasted jacket. Under the jacket, she wore a white camisole. The jacket was buttoned. Dani did not show cleavage. She wore a lovely white scarf around her throat.

She smiled at Sidney as she approached the table. He got up to greet her. Dani's eyes kept going up, and up, and up. He was at least six-foot-four, if he was an inch! Broad shouldered, rakishly handsome with that blue-black skin, wide-set eyes, square chin, and a wide nose, a real man's nose. It was a nose that could probably smell a woman's perfume at a hundred paces. Nice lips, too. Not too thick, not too thin. Just right.

"Danielle," he said in his French-accented voice. When she'd phoned him to thank him for the calla lilies, he'd told her he was Haitian. Dani had never seen a Haitian this tall before, but she didn't say anything. "You look beautiful," he said next to her ear.

He held her chair for her. Dani sat down and placed her clutch purse on her lap.

Sidney sat down across from her, his appreciative gaze raking over her. "I was getting worried that you might have had a flat tire or something."

"No, I had trouble with my hair. I'm sorry I'm late," Dani sincerely apologized. "I'm rarely late for anything. It really upsets me when something happens to make me late for an appointment." She smiled, showing the space between her two front teeth. Sidney thought that space added to her beauty. He realized in America there was an exaggerated standard of beauty that most women would never live up to. He could not understand it. Didn't they know all women were beautiful in their own way?

Dani's beauty was in the way she carried herself. He'd never met a more feminine woman. She reveled in her femininity.

He was nervous in her presence. He had never felt nervous in a woman's presence before. He'd always known his power to charm them, bend them to his will. Now, he was uncertain and at a loss.

"I wrote a poem for you," he said suddenly, feeling like a schoolboy trying to impress a girl.

Dani smiled, delighted. "Then let me hear it!"

Sidney cleared his throat. "You're like a unicorn; one of a kind, unique. Something that legends are made of. A whisper of fables. The feminine mystique."

Dani reached across the table and grasped one of his big hands in both of hers. She held his gaze captive. "No one has ever written a poem for me before. That was lovely. The feminine mystique. I like it. I like it a lot."

Sidney gently squeezed her hand and swallowed hard. "I'm glad."

Their waiter arrived, a blond kid with brown eyes who had surfer's knuckles. Dani recognized the affliction because she'd dated a surfer back in the day. They developed knots on their knuckles, their knees, and anywhere else they repeatedly hit themselves with their surfboards. The knots were caused by calcium deposits. "Good evening folks," he said. "Have you had time to peruse the menu, or should I give you more time?"

"I'm ready to order now," Dani spoke up. "I'll have the

fried red snapper with green beans and a baked potato. Butter on the side, please. And I'll have a glass of the house white wine." Finished, she looked at Sidney. "You don't mind if I go to the ladies' room while you order, do you?"

Sidney immediately got up to pull her chair out for her. "Of course not, my dear."

He watched her cross the room, and then turned his attention to the waiter. "Bring us a big platter of the empanaditas while we wait for our meal, would you? I'll have the sancocho as my main dish tonight. Ice-cold beer is my drink of choice."

The waiter smiled his approval. "Yes, sir. It'll only be a few minutes." He turned to leave, and Sidney sat back down.

He observed the other diners while he waited for Dani's return. Their table had a clear view of the entrance. While he'd been there, the restaurant had enjoyed a rather swift turnover of patrons. He thought, perhaps, he might want to invest in one of the chain's restaurants. His portfolio could use a bit of diversity.

In the women's room, Dani vied for space at the mirror with three other women. They all seemed to know each other and were chattering about the men in their lives. One, a redhead with large lips and emerald green eyes that Dani bet were contacts, laughed loudly and said, "I can't stand it when he thinks all he has to do is buy me dinner and rent a video every Saturday night. I'd like to go dancing some time. We're in a rut. All he wants to do is eat, sleep, and watch TV on the weekends. If I had known he'd turn into such a slob I never would have married him."

Dani reapplied her lipstick. *How ungrateful can you get,* she thought. *At least you had the option of marrying the slob. If you want to go dancing, tell him!*

"Yeah," said the dishwater blonde with blue eyes. "Jeff mows the lawn on Saturday morning and crashes on the couch the rest of the day. The kids miss him. I miss him. I don't understand it. We're not even in our forties. Jeff's too tired to do anything!"

The brunette piped in with, "I hear you, girl. It has been more than a month since Harry and I did the horizontal mambo. I never asked him to work as hard as he does. But he's got to have the biggest house, the most expensive car, when all I want is for him to hold me like he used to."

Dani could stay silent no longer. She turned and went to stand in front of them, tapping her small stiletto-shod foot. "Ladies," she said. "I couldn't help overhearing your laments about your tired men, since I'm standing right here. I hope you don't mind if I make a tiny suggestion?"

She waited to see if they were curious enough to hear her out. They were.

"My suggestion is, stop bellyaching and seduce your husbands. Seduce them the same way you did before you got those rings on your fingers. Be whores in the bedroom, ladies, and your men will not fall asleep on you. And that's free advice from Miss Dani, roving sex therapist!"

With that, she walked out of the room, leaving them with their mouths agape.

Dani smiled all the way back to her table.

Sidney rose and held her chair for her. "I took the liberty of ordering a platter of empanaditas. I saw you enjoying them the night we met." He gestured to the appetizers. Dani smiled at him as she reached for one of the cornmeal turnovers and dipped it in the green chili sauce. "You're spoiling me, Sidney." She bit into the turnover and chewed with sensual intensity. Sidney picked up one of the turnovers and popped it into his mouth without the chili sauce. Watching her eat was a spicy enough experience.

"Tell me about yourself, Sidney. What do you do for a living?"

"I import African art," Sidney told her sheepishly.

Dani smiled brilliantly. "Don't tell me you're a man who doesn't like talking about himself. I didn't think such a creature existed."

Sidney laughed. "Guilty. I would much rather hear about you."

Dani wiggled a finger at him. "Oh, no. This should be an equal exchange of information. Since you've told me what you do for a living, I'll tell you: I'm an events planner. The bulk of my business is planning weddings, but I also do other kinds of events like birthday parties, retirement parties, and even bar mitzvahs. Okay, how long have you been in Miami?"

Sidney took a sip of his beer before replying. "Only a few weeks, actually."

Dani's brows raised in surprise. "Oh, you're just visiting?"

"Yes, I'm afraid so. I hope you don't think I've been leading you on by not disclosing that bit of information before now."

Dani was disappointed, but didn't let it show on her face. An interesting man, and he was just passing through. Ah well, that would keep her from allowing herself to get too carried away. "No, of course not." But her eyes glanced at his ring finger, just in case. She saw no faint outline where a ring might have been. It was her way to ask, though. "You're not married, are you, Sidney?"

"Not anymore," Sidney said. "And you?"

"Never been lucky enough to find that special man," Dani told him.

"What kind of man is that?" Sidney wanted to know.

"A man who will accept me for who I am underneath the image I project," Dani said. "A sensitive man who will love me with all of my flaws."

"From what I can see, you don't have any flaws," Sidney said with a gentle smile.

"Oh, we're all hiding something," Dani assured him. "It's just a matter of time before the layers are peeled back and the true person is revealed."

"You're right," Sidney said, a serious expression in his dark eyes. He brightened.

"But for our first date, let's leave the layers on. Shall we?"

He raised his glass and Dani clinked her wine glass against his beer glass. "That's all right with me."

When the doorbell rang, Marie's stomach muscles constricted painfully. She checked her reflection in the bedroom mirror one last time. She was wearing a deep burgundy pantsuit with a beige camisole underneath. The safari jacket had a tie belt. She had buttoned it because when it was open, the camisole revealed her cleavage too much for her taste. She didn't intend to remove the jacket anytime during their outing.

Why she'd let Solange talk her into calling Theophilus Gault in the first place she'd never know! It wasn't as if there was any hope of their hitting it off on any level except physical attraction, and she wasn't the type of woman who would be kept. Who knew how Theophilus Gault, multimillionaire, treated the women in his life? Perhaps he had a harem somewhere at his beck and call. Marie DuPree wouldn't be a part of anyone's harem. She pulled a face in the mirror. She was being silly. A harem. Yeah, right!

She sighed and hurried through the house to the front door. She'd let him wait long enough. Besides, the sooner this date began, the sooner it would be over with.

She opened the door, gazed upward, and was about to say hello when the words caught in her throat and she inhaled sharply instead. My, but this man was gorgeous.

She didn't know how her brain had let her forget that. Curly salt-and-pepper hair cut close to his big, handsome head. Beautiful eyes that seemed to look right into her soul and discern her deepest desires. A mouth made for kissing.

He smiled at her. "Hello, beautiful." Had she forgotten that voice? It was a sexy rumble. She felt it in the pit of her stomach. No, blast it. She felt it lower than that. She blew a frustrated breath through full lips. Theophilus's eyes zeroed in on her pouting mouth, and before she knew it, he'd leaned down and kissed her.

She felt as light and loose as a rag doll when he finally let her go. She tried to work up indignation, shock, even a modicum of embarrassment, but all of those things were beyond her acting ability. Instead, she reached up and pulled him down for another kiss. When she twisted her head to the right, thereby breaking off the kiss, he was the one who was dizzy. But they were both breathless.

"Lady, if that's how they say hello in Miami, I'm moving here," Theophilus said between breaths.

Marie smiled up at him. "I forgot my purse. Give me a minute."

She walked back to her bedroom to get her purse, all the while repeating the mantra: Don't invite him in when you get back home, in her head. She said a silent prayer for willpower as she returned to the foyer where she'd left him, and saw him still standing there, looking for all the world like a man who knew he had this date in the bag. She would show him!

His car, a black late-model Lincoln Town Car, had a driver. Theophilus opened the door for Marie and handed her in. Then he jogged around to the other side and got in. The driver apparently knew where they were going, but Marie was at a disadvantage. "When I phoned you, it was to take you up on your suggestion that I show you around Miami. Now, we're going someplace you've chosen, instead," she said. "Do you always get your way with women?"

Theophilus seemed to take up the whole backseat. Or maybe it was Marie's nervousness that made her think that. There was plenty of room in the car. "As a matter of fact, this is the first time in over a year that I've done this," he said.

"Done what?"

"You're gonna make me work, aren't you?"

"You always appreciate what you work for."

Theophilus laughed shortly. "A date," he said. "I was seeing someone, but she wanted to get married and have children. She was in her early forties and figured she didn't have much time left. I'm fifty-nine, Marie. I don't want any more children. Do you?"

Marie laughed. "That's the least of my worries, Theo. And I'm not going to tell you my age."

"Like I told you before, you're beautiful no matter what your age is," Theophilus told her. "And in answer to your question, we're going to the marina."

Marie sat further away from him on the seat. "You're a pirate and you're kidnapping me."

"Thanks for the suggestion, but no. We're having dinner on a friend's yacht."

"Will the friend be there?"

"No, just you and I. Oh, and the chef and the waiter."

"Of course," Marie said with an enigmatic smile.

Theophilus was pleased that she wasn't easily impressed. He liked a challenge.

"You're divorced from Solange's father. But you remain friends. I find that commendable. So many marriages end in acrimony."

"Oh, ours ended in acrimony, believe me. He cheated on me and I was mad as hell. I was angry for years. It's only been within the past two years that I could forgive him and wish him well in his marriage to his present wife. I'm definitely no saint."

"We sinners have very little use for saints, Marie. Except to corrupt them."

Marie laughed. "Let's see who corrupts whom."

They arrived at the dock, where the yacht, the *Ana Maria,* was anchored. It was a double-decker cruiser, at least fifty feet in length, painted white with royal blue trim.

Theophilus got out and went around the car to open Marie's door for her. He offered her his hand. Marie took it. Their eyes met, and Marie had to look away. His gaze was too intense for her. She looked down at her three-inch heels instead. "If I had known we were going on a boat I would have worn appropriate shoes."

"No problem," Theophilus said, and swept her up into his arms. He looked at the driver. "James, old man, be back here in three hours."

"Yes, Mr. Gault. Enjoy your evening," said the driver, who couldn't be more than thirty. He smiled as he got behind the wheel of the car. He could see old man Gault in the rearview mirror carrying that pretty lady in his arms as if she weighed next to nothing. That Viagra must be kicking in, he thought good naturedly. Marie copped a feel or two before Theophilus placed her down again next to the gangplank. Theophilus's biceps were as hard as rocks. Pretty good shape for a man of fifty-nine. "You can walk up the gangplank barefoot. And I had my secretary buy you a pair of deck shoes. They're on the boat. I guessed you were a size six."

"Do you have a foot fetish, or something?"

"Okay, Solange told me," Theophilus admitted.

"This is a conspiracy," Marie joked. "You and my daughter planned this."

Theophilus was busy removing her pumps. Marie was glad she'd recently had a pedicure and didn't have sweaty feet. If her feet smelled at this juncture, she might have died of embarrassment.

Theophilus gestured for her to precede him up the gangplank. The sun was just going down and there was a light breeze. The boat was well lit on the main deck, and as they reached it, she could see the chef at work in the galley. A table had been set for them on the aft deck. Theophilus took her arm and directed her toward the table. Atop the table was a shoe box. He placed her heels in a storage compartment on deck.

"Please sit," he said.

Marie sat and he bent and put the deck shoes on her feet, tied their strings, and rose again to his full height. "There you are, safe from slipping into the drink."

Marie smiled her thanks. "You think of everything."

Theophilus sat down across from her. He willed her to look at him. Marie raised her gaze to his. "I'm not one to play games, Marie. I don't have the time or the patience for it. I'm told that I can be too single-minded about a lot of things. I wouldn't be the man I am today if I were not single-minded, stubborn, and unwilling to take no for an answer. I grew up in Guyana. We were poor, but I don't remember feeling deprived. I felt loved. I felt cherished. But I found out we were poor when I finished the mandatory schooling and was told there was no money for me to go to college. At that time, I wanted to become a doctor. Well, that never came about.

"At eighteen, I was in love with Rupert's mother,

Maryam. She was the first woman I ever loved. But I knew that if I ever wanted to amount to anything, I couldn't stay where I was, so I stowed away on a ship headed to New York City. I wound up in Philadelphia. From Philly, I went to Washington, DC, where I went to electronics school, and found I had a talent for all things electrical. I never would have tried any of that if I were not so stubbornly single-minded."

He paused, wondering if he'd been too longwinded. "I said all of that to make a point. From the moment I saw you, I knew you and I would be simpatico. I get these feelings about people. You're a powerful woman, Marie. What I felt coming off of your body that night we met was like volts of electricity. It shot off of you and hit me right between the eyes."

Marie threw her head back in laughter. She met his eyes again. "Theophilus Gault, you're absolutely full of it!"

Theophilus laughed too. "Maybe I am, but tell me I'm not right about that spark we both felt. I know you felt it, too. You can try to deny it, but you did."

"I'm not going to deny anything," Marie said. "My body reacts to your closeness. The question is, what do we do about it?"

Theophilus leaned toward her. "I think we ought to do what comes naturally."

"And forget that my daughter is about to marry your son?"

"What's that got to do with anything?" Theophilus wanted to know. "We're going to be related by marriage. I still don't get you."

"When you grow tired of me and drop me like a hot potato, nine times out of ten, we're not going to be able to totally avoid each other. We will share a grandchild, for one thing. I don't know about you, but I'm going to attend every event in Desta's life. I may only have one grandchild in my lifetime, and I'm going to enjoy her."

Theophilus smiled. "You're already foretelling the downfall of our relationship? What makes you think that once I get you in my arms, I'll ever want to let you go?" He looked deeply into her eyes. "Oh, I see. Because your ex cheated on you, you have it in your mind that every man on the face of the planet will do the same thing. Get a grip, Marie. I'm not like any man you've ever known. So don't go lumping me with the rest of them."

Marie cocked her head to the side. "You're something special, huh?"

"Damn right, I'm something special. I'm the man who turns you on. I'm the man you grabbed and kissed not thirty minutes ago. I'm willing to bet you've never done that before, Miss Marie. I'm willing to bet everything I own. Would I win?"

Marie hesitated before saying, "You'd win."

The waiter, a young African-American, cleared his throat as he approached them on the deck. "Good evening, Ms. DuPree, Mr. Gault. Your wine has been chilling. May I pour?"

He wore a formal uniform, black slacks and shoes, a short white jacket with a white shirt underneath, and a black bow tie. Over his left forearm hung a pristine white cotton towel. He held two wine flutes in his right hand, and a serving trolley stood next to him with two bottles of wine atop it. "Does madame prefer her white wine from the Sauternes, or a blanc de blancs?"

Marie laughed shortly. "That's the first time I've ever been asked that question."

She was sure the waiter wasn't trying to be pretentious. He was simply trying his best to give her what she preferred. However, it was presumptuous of him to assume she knew the difference between the two wines.

Actually, she did know a little about wine, but what if he'd asked a poor wine-ignorant guy trying to impress his date?

"I prefer the light white wines," she told him pleasantly. "Wines from the Sauternes are too sweet for my palate."

After the waiter had served them and gone, Theophilus said, "I'm glad you knew what he was talking about, because I was lost."

"Then you don't have a wine cellar in your home?"

"I have one, but it's stocked and maintained by my butler, Danyael. He knows enough about wine for both of us."

"Oh, you have a butler. I had no idea there was such a thing as a butler until I came to the United States."

"Neither did I," Theophilus said. "Where were you born?"

"I was born in Port-au-Prince, Haiti."

Night had fallen around them. There was a light breeze with the smell of the sea on it. Marie thought she felt a raindrop on her face, but figured it was a fluke. She saw no lightning in the distance, which usually preceded a rain shower in springtime in Miami. Nor had she heard thunder.

They were leaning toward one another as if they were already lovers who craved the proximity of each other's bodies. Theophilus inhaled the heady scent of her, from the fruity smell of her shampoo, to the more sensual, spicy aroma of the cologne she wore. He was a man who appreciated a woman's need to smell pretty. Marie smelled good enough to eat.

"Aren't you warm in that jacket?" Theophilus asked.

"No, not really," said Marie. "The temperature's nice tonight."

"I'm not going to get you out of that jacket, huh?"

"Not tonight," said Marie confidently.

Ten

The night was still young.

Solange put on her robe, went to the kitchen and grabbed a carton of Ben & Jerry's ice cream. As she ate it from the carton with a tablespoon, she paced the floor.

She would pause every now and then to gaze at the engagement ring on her finger.

One hundred thousand dollars! That amount of money would have put her through college. How could Rupert be so blasé about it? She supposed rich people had a different perspective on money. She could not empathize with them, since she'd never been rich. She wished she could be sophisticated and think nothing of having a fiancé who was worth $15 million. But she couldn't wrap her mind around it. Maybe if he'd been forthcoming from the very beginning, she might be used to it by now. Then, again, if he'd told her he was a millionaire when they'd met, she might have been too intimidated by him to date him.

She spooned the Chunky Monkey into her mouth faster.

Boy! What other surprises did that man have up his sleeve?

* * *

"Neither Georges nor I have much of a formal education. He went to night school and got his certificate in auto mechanics. He owns a garage nowadays. He's been successful. After we divorced, I didn't know what I was going to do. All I had was a high-school education. Solange and I stayed in Key West for a while afterward. I worked in a dress shop as a salesperson. I was hired because I had a certain flair for fashion, and the owner thought customers would buy more merchandise from an attractive person, not for any talent I had as a salesperson. That rankled. Anyway, one day I just up and told Solange, 'We're moving to Miami.' She was upset because that meant leaving her best friend, Gaea, behind. Oh, she gave me a hard time for months after we got here. But soon she was making friends, and she got into a college preparatory program at the University of Miami called Upward Bound. That's when she started thinking seriously about becoming an archaeologist. She was inspired by the other black professionals she met."

"And by her mother's fiercely independent spirit," Theophilus put in.

"I worked hard," Marie admitted. "I went to technical school and earned a certificate in interior design." She laughed. "It wasn't much of a course, actually. But what it did was bring home to me the fact that I was good at making people's surroundings pleasant. I'd always done it. On a shoestring budget. I still have a hard time spending huge amounts of money even when my wealthy clients tell me to spare no expense. I'm naturally frugal."

They had dined and moved inside after it turned out the raindrop Marie had felt on her face earlier in the evening had been a warning. Shortly after finishing the delicious grilled salmon, the wind picked up and the rain came in at an angle, instantly soaking Marie's jacket. Theophilus had ushered her below deck, and that's where they were now, sitting in the stateroom on the comfortably cushioned couch. Marie had had to remove her jacket, and now she wore just the beige camisole with her burgundy pants.

She sat with one leg underneath, turned toward Theophilus, who was enjoying the view. For a petite woman, Marie's breasts were full, and the cut of the camisole displayed them at their best. Theophilus was listening to her tell him about how she got started in the decorating business, but his attention was split between her mellifluous voice and her enticing cleavage. Now he knew why she hadn't wanted to take off her jacket when he'd joked with her about it earlier.

Marie suddenly narrowed her eyes at him. "Are you listening to me? Or are my breasts distracting you?"

"Both," said Theophilus truthfully, not the least bit embarrassed. He met her eyes.

"A man would have to be dead not to be drawn to your body, Marie. When God put you together he patted Himself on the back for a job well done."

Marie laughed. "I'm fifty-four years old. Don't expect these babies to defy gravity. I'm in pretty good shape, but like any woman my age, I'm softer in certain areas than I used to be. And I'm not the type of woman to resort to plastic surgery. What you see is what you get."

"Well, I like what I see. When do I get it?" asked Theophilus, not missing a beat.

Marie's body reacted to his blatant sexual innuendo. Her nipples grew hard, and in the camisole, her state of arousal was more than evident.

Theophilus smiled when he saw how his words had affected her. She was very responsive to stimuli. He knew that when he did get an invitation to her bed, it would be well worth it. He was willing to be patient.

"Don't answer that," he apologized. "I was out of line."

Marie blew air between her lips. Then remembered that she'd made the same gesture just before Theophilus had kissed her. "We were both getting too familiar, too fast."

She rose suddenly. "Maybe you ought to take me home now."

The rain had let up, and she'd spotted the Town Car a few minutes ago when James had returned with it earlier than Theophilus had asked him to come for them. She'd been relieved to see him.

Theophilus got to his feet. Marie glanced down and realized he'd become aroused too. Her cheeks grew hot with embarrassment. Theophilus saw where her gaze had gone. He smiled at her. "I'm a healthy man with healthy desires. Like I said, I don't play games. I want you. I'm all yours whenever you decide that you want me, too."

Sidney walked Dani to her car and opened the door for her. After he helped her in, he closed the door firmly and leaned down to peer at her. "Thank you for a most pleasant evening, Danielle."

Dani felt treasured. She had, frankly, never felt this protected by a man. She couldn't remember the last time a man had walked her to her car and made sure she was safely behind the wheel. "I had a great time, too," she told him.

"May I call you?" Sidney asked.

"Darling, you can call me as soon as I get home," Dani said, hoping she didn't sound too enthusiastic. Even though she was! She'd fallen under Sidney's darkly handsome spell.

"Wonderful," said Sidney. "That way I'll know you made it home without mishap."

Mishap, Dani thought. I've never heard a man use that word before. She was even enamored of his word usage. Lord, help me, I'm falling for him. Let me get out of here.

She turned the key in the ignition.

Sidney stepped away from the car. "Good night," he said softly.

"Good night!" Dani called, and put her foot on the accelerator.

Rupert woke around two in the morning and went in search of Solange. He found her curled up on the couch in the living room, the empty ice-cream carton on the coffee table. He picked up the empty carton and the tablespoon, went into the kitchen, disposed of the carton, and tossed the spoon into the sink. Then he went back out to the living room and scooped Solange up in his arms.

She slowly opened her eyes and yawned in his face. Her breath, not unpleasant, smelled of milk. She hooked her right arm around his neck. "Hello," she said sleepily.

"So," Rupert said. "Am I going to have to apologize for not telling you I'm filthy rich?"

"'Course not."

"Good, because I woke up hungry for you. Remember, you haven't been feeding little Rupert on a regular basis."

"Sick, sick," Solange joked. "Men and their pet names for their penises."

"Be quiet, woman, or Little Rupert might sulk and not want to come out and play."

Solange laughed even harder. "I'm sorry. I'll try to be a good girl."

"Don't try too hard," Rupert told her, and buried his face between her breasts.

Solange giggled and said, "I'd like a shower first, please. I feel kind of funky."

"You smell fine to me," Rupert said.

"I'll make it worth your while," Solange bargained.

"With an offer like that, how can I refuse?" he replied, and took her straight to the bathroom instead of the bedroom. He set her down, and stepped back to watch her peel off her bathrobe.

He hadn't bothered to put a stitch on when he went looking for her. Solange had never known a man who was more at home in his body. Shy, insecure? Not her Rupert.

"I was a shy, retiring educator until I met you," she said as she removed the bathrobe.

"Don't lie to me, sweetness. You've never been shy and retiring. You might have been voluntarily celibate for a while, but you've always enjoyed sex. I knew it from the moment we made love for the first time that you were my match, and then some."

Solange raised a brow at him. "As I was saying." She hung the bathrobe behind the door, and faced him again. "I was a shy and retiring educator when I met you, but you are slowly awakening the goddess in me."

Rupert got it then. She was role-playing.

"I am terribly attracted to you, but I am reluctant to go any further than heavy petting because I'm afraid of what I'll become: a wanton woman."

She went and turned on the water in the shower, got a fresh bar of soap and stepped inside the shower stall. Looking at Rupert with eyes filled with longing, she continued.

"I've never met a man as virile as you. I'm used to staid professors who smoke pipes and wear cardigans. They smell like mothballs. I never knew a man could look, smell, or taste like you do. So, I've invited you here to watch me, but not to touch. No touching allowed. I don't know if I'm ready to take you yet."

She stepped under the spray of water. Allowed it to run over her head, down her golden brown body. Her nipples hardened right before Rupert's eyes. Rupert swallowed hard but didn't move.

Solange rubbed the soap between her hands, working up a lather. Then she put the soap in the shower caddy and ran her hands over her breasts, and between her thighs, all the while looking Rupert in the eyes with a lascivious gleam in her own. She moaned with pleasure.

Rupert's penis waved at her.

"If I let you touch me, will you promise to be gentle?" she asked, her eyes on his distended member.

Rupert already had one foot in the shower stall. "Hell, no. I promise I'll have you climbing the walls, though."

Solange was glad the floor of the shower stall was slip-free, because her man didn't know the meaning of caution. He grabbed her about the waist, pulled her roughly against him and kissed her while his big hands grabbed her bottom and pressed her closer to him.

She felt drunk with passion, as wanton as the little educator might feel right now if she, indeed, was about to make love for the first time. Rupert's hands went lower until they were on the inside of her thighs. He turned his head, breaking off the kiss long enough to say, "Open up for me, baby."

Solange spread her legs a bit more. Rupert used the pad of his forefinger to gently massage her clitoris, lubricating her. He pressed her back against the wall of the shower stall so that she could gain purchase, then he reached back and removed the detachable shower massage and rinsed off the soap that Solange had put down there with her hands. He replaced the shower massage and turned off the water. This done, he knelt on one knee, brought Solange closer to him, bent his head, and took his fill of the nectar between her thighs.

Solange held his head with both hands while he whipped her into a frenzy with his tongue. And oh, what a talented tongue it was. It dipped and teased. Glided over her clitoris and vulva, giving equal attention to both sensitive areas. Took its time, too. None of that fast and furious action. No, this was designed to ensure her optimum pleasure. It was done, dare she think it, lovingly, as though doing it gave him as much satisfaction as it gave her.

She was deliciously weak in the knees when he stopped for a moment to look up at her. "I told you I woke up hungry for you."

Then he continued, and did not let up until he felt her body quivering in an orgasm whose impending arrival he'd felt with his tongue. He rose and held her in his arms for a moment before saying, "Turn around, sweetness."

Solange turned around and placed both palms up on the shower stall's wall. Rupert took her from behind. He groaned when his penis entered her vagina. He loved taking her any kind of way, but her bottom was gorgeous and he enjoyed looking at it while he made love to her. That, and the way her vagina looked to him as his shaft went in and out of her. He supposed it was true, men were visual creatures. They enjoyed looking at their women when they were making love to them.

The thing about Solange was, even after she had come, she was a willing participant. Right now, she was giving him thrust for thrust. Guiding his hands over her body. Encouraging him to squeeze her nipples. Turning her head around so he could kiss her. Licking his lips the way that he liked it done. She'd never been a shrinking violet in the bedroom. Hence, each time they made love, and they'd made love plenty of times, she always rocked him down to his toes.

He came. He had been thinking about all the other times they'd made love so intently, that it practically came as a surprise when he exploded inside of her. He pulled her closer, issuing all of his seed into her. Then they embraced.

"Thank you, baby. Thank you for loving me the way that you do," Rupert said.

It was a Sunday, and today marked the first time Solange would have both her parents to dinner. There would be six of them; her mother had phoned to inform her that morning that she was bringing Theophilus. That meant there were be three couples having Sunday dinner together: She and Rupert, her father and her stepmother, Elena, and her mother and Theophilus.

Frankly, Solange was surprised her mother wanted to bring Theophilus. She had not mentioned him since she phoned the morning following her date with him on the *Ana Maria* to say, "He was a gentleman."

When Solange had pressed her for more information, her mother had said, "I don't think I'm going to see him again."

"Is it because of your scar?"

Marie had a scar on her left breast from a biopsy nearly two years ago.

"It isn't easy getting naked in front of a man like Theophilus."

"What's so intimidating about it, Maman? He hasn't got anything you haven't seen before."

"Don't waste your breath, baby girl. I've made up my mind."

And that was the end of the conversation.

Her father and stepmother were the first to arrive. Solange and Rupert had decided on a barbecue in the backyard. Rupert was out there now, making sure the chicken didn't burn on the grill. They had grilled shrimp for appetizers. Garden salad and corn on the cob that would go on the grill later. Solange was making watermelon martinis and, for dessert, strawberry shortcake.

Georges DuPree, fifty-seven, stood six feet tall, was trim, and had medium-brown skin and a fabulous mustache that Solange used to love to touch when she was a little girl.

It was still as thick and luxuriant as it used to be, although it was salt-and-pepper gray now. He hugged her warmly at the door and kissed her cheek. "Mon petite, you look wonderful."

"So do you," Solange told him. It was true, Georges looked healthy and happy. She'd asked everyone to dress casually, and he had on a pair of jeans and his favorite Miami Dolphins jersey. A cap with the team's emblem on it covered his short, graying natural hair. "Like the outfit?" he asked.

"Love it," Solange told him. "Go on back to the deck; Rupert's out there. I want to say hello to Elena."

Elena was ten years younger than her husband. She was also about an inch taller. On the plump side, she had cafe-au-lait skin, deep brown eyes, a pert nose, and full lips. She always wore makeup. Solange used to think that it was because she was vain, but later found out Elena had a skin condition that had left her skin discolored in spots. Makeup evened her skin tone.

Over the years, Solange had grown to love Elena, and was thankful to her for taking such good care of her father.

The two women hugged. "I'm glad you came," Solange told her.

"I started to fake a headache or something," Elena confessed. Solange knew Elena was never comfortable around her mother. In the past, Marie had not sought to make Elena comfortable around her. Elena was the woman Georges had left her for.

Elena put a lock of her long, dark-brown hair behind her ear. "If things look like they're going to fall apart, Georges and I will leave before making a scene."

Solange squeezed Elena's arm reassuringly. "Maman promised to be civil, Elena. She's put all that behind her."

"That's what Georges told me," Elena said, a worried expression in her eyes. "But I'll believe it when I see it."

She and Solange joined Georges and Rupert on the deck.

In the Town Car on the way to the dinner party, Marie and Theophilus were in the middle of a heated argument. "Three weeks is plenty of time to get to know one another," Theophilus said. "I don't care what anyone else thinks. Their opinions are irrelevant. Only yours and mine matter."

"Well, it's my opinion that you're rushing things."

"You're only saying that because you're scared."

"I'm not scared!"

"You're scared crapless, is what you are," bellowed Theophilus.

"James, stop the car," Marie ordered in her most imperious voice.

James slowed the car.

"James, don't you dare stop this car," Theophilus countermanded Marie's order.

James put his foot on the accelerator.

"James, if you don't stop this car, I'm going to yell my head off."

"What do you think you've been doing for the past ten minutes?" Theophilus asked.

Marie cut him in two with her eyes. "Marry you? I'd rather slug you."

"Well, go right ahead."

Marie went to slap him, but he caught her wrist, pulled her roughly against him, and kissed her hard on the lips. Marie struggled for a hot second, and then gave in. Theophilus kissed her with passion and with slow deliberation.

"Aw, damn," said James, looking at them via the rearview mirror. "Y'all ain't gettin' busy back there, are you?"

Not a word from the couple in the backseat. He drove on.

He, for one, was relieved when they arrived on Solange's street and he pulled behind a late-model SUV in her driveway. "We're here. Are you going inside, or should I just step outside for a few minutes?"

Theophilus raised his head first. "Don't be impertinent, old man." He smiled. "We're going inside."

"After I fix my lipstick," Marie said. "And you wipe your mouth. You look like a clown."

James got out of the car to get the door for them. Alone in the car with Marie now, Theophilus took the opportunity to ask, "Have you told them about us?"

"No," said Marie gently.

"Why not?" Theophilus asked, his voice soft. "I've told Samantha."

Marie looked startled. "What did you tell her?"

"That I'm in love with you, damn it!"

Marie looked deeply into his eyes. "I love you, too. But

you're right. I'm afraid to gamble on love. I've lost so many times."

James bent and peered inside the car, wondering what was taking them so long.

"Please take a short walk, James," Theophilus told him.

James immediately left them, going to stand in front of the Town Car, where he was out of earshot. The smell of barbecue was wafting on the evening breezes. He decided to go around back and see what Solange and Rupert had on the grill. He hadn't had dinner himself. Not that he would invite himself to dinner, but if they wanted to give him a plate to go, he wouldn't refuse. No telling how long Mr. Gault and Ms. DuPree would be in the backseat. He wished they'd go ahead and get married and get it over with. If there were ever two people who were suited for each other, it was those two!

They reminded him of his own parents, who had loved each other and fought with each other for more than forty years now.

In the Town Car, Theophilus pulled Marie into his arms. "Everything we do in life is a gamble. Think of me as a sure bet. I am loyal to the core, Marie. I have loved only three women in my lifetime. Maryam, Francesca, and you. Death separated me from both Maryam and Francesca. It would take death to separate me from you, too. My own, because I couldn't bear for you to go before me. I'm scared, too. But I'd rather have you in my life than to be without you. Marry me, Marie."

Marie's eyes glistened with tears. "I can't. I can't marry you, Theo."

Theophilus kissed her quickly three times. "I'll ask you again tomorrow."

He'd done that every day for the past two weeks. Always,

her answer was no. Always, he'd reply, "I'll ask you again tomorrow."

They sat for a while longer, and then he got out of the car, reached back for her, and helped her out. They walked to the house arm in arm.

The moment Solange met them at the door, she knew her mother had been crying. She hugged both of them, then said to Theophilus, "Please go on outside, Theophilus. We'll be right behind you."

In Theophilus's absence, she hissed, "What's going on? Have you two been arguing? Your eyes are puffy. Your eyes always get puffy when you've been crying."

Marie's hand went to her face. "I only had a hand mirror. I thought my face was fine."

"Well, it's not. Has he been horrible to you?"

Solange liked Theophilus, but she knew he could be a ruthless businessman. Maybe he could be equally vicious in a relationship. Perhaps Samantha didn't know her father at all. Her parents might have shielded her from the ugliness in their relationship.

Marie smiled at her well-meaning daughter. "No, sweetheart. Theophilus is—" She couldn't finish her sentence because she was crying again.

"Maman!" Solange exclaimed, putting her arms around her. She looked in the direction Theophilus had gone. She had a good mind to tell him off! Her mother was sobbing uncontrollably. Solange had no choice but to console her, but as soon as she had calmed down, Solange was going to give Theophilus Gault a piece of her mind.

Solange rocked her mother gently in her arms. "Go on, get it all out. Then we're going back there and get him straight once and for all."

Marie sniffed, then went into her purse, which she still had on her arm, for tissues, and wiped her nose. She peered up at her belligerent daughter. "It was stress, baby, that's all. Theophilus hasn't been anything but a gentleman."

Solange put her arm about her mother's shoulders and directed her toward the back of the house. "Stress? Work related?"

"No, it's due to my insecurity where Theophilus is concerned. He wants to take our relationship at a faster pace, and I'm afraid to."

"You mean he's pressuring you for sex?"

Marie shook her head in the negative. "On the contrary. He's pressuring me to marry him."

They paused in the kitchen. The door that led out to the deck was only a few feet away. Solange could see Rupert out there laughing at something his father had said to him, while he kept an eye on the food on the grill.

Solange faced her mother. "You've been keeping your relationship a secret. Why? I've already told you Rupert and I couldn't be happier about how you and Theophilus feel about each other."

"Baby, this is your time," her mother said, in that reasonable way she had. "A wedding, a marriage, is a sacred occasion. This is a time when you should be in the spotlight. My relationship with Theo shouldn't overshadow it. Whatever's happening with me and Theo can wait until you and Rupert are off on your honeymoon."

Solange laughed. She grabbed her mother by the shoulders and turned her around to face her. "Maman, listen to me. We could have a double wedding, for all I care! But don't postpone your happiness for me! Do you know how pleased I am that you and Theophilus are in love? I mean, I had an inkling that you two would hit it off, but this! I'm too happy for words." She hugged her again. "You deserve everything that big, generous man can bestow on you. Let him love you, Maman. Love him back. Men like him don't come along every day."

Marie looked stunned. Her daughter had believed her lie hook, line, and sinker! She felt so guilty, there was no recourse but to confess to everything. "Oh, baby, I feel like such a fraud! Here you are gushing over me like I'm already a bride, and I'm lying to you. Lying because I'm a coward."

Solange was confused. "What are you talking about?"

"That's not the reason I won't accept Theo's marriage proposal. I won't accept because I'm afraid we'll end up just like all the rest of my relationships have ended in the past. On the rocks!"

Shaking her head and frowning, Solange put her hands on her hips and said, "Oh, no. You're not getting away with being chicken, Maman. Not the woman who always told me to go for it. Not the woman whose motto was Feel the Fear and Do it Anyway! You've conquered every area of your life. Look at the two of us. Two years ago, we barely communicated with each other. We were so estranged that I didn't even know the basics about your life before you came to this country. Now, I know everything about your struggles to get here. No, Maman. You've always been a fighter. Don't tell me you're not going to fight for love because I won't hear of it! I'm not going to let you give up without a fight."

She began pulling her mother toward the deck.

Marie held back. "Please don't do anything to embarrass me, Solange. Not in front of Elena."

"Elena?" Solange asked. "Elena is the least of your problems."

She stopped in front of the door and regarded her mother. "Maman, do you love Theophilus Gault?"

Marie clamped her mouth shut and gazed up at Solange defiantly. "Who is the mother here: I, or you?"

"Oh, cut that out," Solange said, unconvinced. "Answer the question."

"I will not be intimidated by my own daughter."

"Maman, don't make me ask everyone to come in here so I can tell them what's going on," Solange threatened.

"Yes!" Marie cried. "I love him!"

"Now, was that so hard to say?"

"No, it wasn't," Marie replied with a smile.

"I'm glad to hear that," Theophilus said from behind them. In fact, everyone who had been on the deck was standing there with the deck door open, looking at Marie and Solange.

Rupert went to Solange's side. "We thought you two were getting ready to throw punches. Thought you might need some backup, babe." He smiled at Marie. "Since you were up against Muscles Marie here."

Theophilus went and placed his arm about Marie's shoulders. "There's no need to be embarrassed, darling. We're among family and friends."

Georges, holding Elena by the hand, stepped forward. "It's your turn, Marie."

Marie looked into Elena's eyes. Elena did not lower her gaze this time. "If anyone deserves to be happy, it's you," Elena said sincerely.

Marie knew then that she had truly forgiven Georges and Elena for what they'd done all those years ago because, in that instance, she didn't feel any animosity toward Elena, not a drop of vitriol. No acid-laced words popped into her mind about the younger woman. Elena was simply her ex-husband's wife—not the target that she heaped the blame on for her failed marriage. She had told Solange that she was long past all of that. But it wasn't the truth. Now, though, she was certain she was over it.

"Thank you, Elena," she graciously said.

"Well, I'll get out of everybody's hair," a masculine voice said. Everyone turned to find James standing next to the grill with a disposable plate loaded with grilled shrimp and chicken in his hand. "Thanks for the eats, Rupert, Solange."

"Why don't you join us, James?" Solange offered.

"Thanks, Solange, but I thought I'd go check on my parents this afternoon while you all enjoy your meal." He met Theophilus's gaze. "When do you want me back, sir?"

"Take the night off, old man. We'll take a cab home tonight."

James grinned. "Thank you, Mr. Gault!" He turned to leave before Theophilus could change his mind. "Have a great evening, folks!"

"Nice guy," Georges said when James had left. Then he looked at his daughter and asked, "Those shrimp James had on his plate looked good. I don't know about the rest of you, but I'm ready to get down."

Elena playfully elbowed him. "Where are your manners?"

"I left them at home, along with my dress shoes. Solange said to come as I am, and what I am is a hungry man."

Everyone laughed, and Solange and Rupert asked their guests to go on out and have seats at the patio table that was already set; they would be out with the food shortly.

Alone in the kitchen, Solange smiled up at her fiance. "Can you believe those two, falling in love right under our noses?"

"You DuPree women are irresistible," Rupert told her, and kissed the tip of her nose. Solange walked into his embrace. "It is going to be kind of strange, though.

We're going to be husband and wife and stepbrother and stepsister."

"Isn't incest legal in Florida?" Rupert joked.

Solange stepped back and punched him on the arm. "No more southern incest jokes, Giles!"

Eleven

The name "Miami" was derived from an unknown Native American tongue, and means "sweet water." There is very little physical evidence left of the first people, the Tequesta, who made the area their home.

That didn't stop Solange from taking her first-year archaeology students on a dig at a site outside of the city limits one Saturday morning in late May. The site was reputed to have been a Seminole Indian village about a hundred years ago. Permission to dig there had to be given by the present-day Seminole tribe. Anything found there had to be reported to them as well. Such were the legalities that modern day practitioners of archaeology had to abide by.

So, armed with her license to dig, Solange led an expedition into the jungles of northern Miami. They arrived early: fourteen students, two graduate assistants, and one professor, and began unloading their cars. Solange had advised everyone to dress in shorts, short-sleeve shirts, and sturdy boots, to bring along a wide-brimmed hat to guard against heatstroke, and not to forget kneepads. Digging on your hands and knees was murder.

Solange had spent the two previous days surveying the site. She'd already laid out the site grid, dividing the site into squares, or units. She walked along the surveyed site, assigning students in pairs of two to each unit.

In class the day before, she'd gone over what the students would be required to do at the site the following morning: remove the sod and topsoil, meticulously dig with their trowels only in their grids, transfer the dirt they dug up to a screen to be sifted so that no artifacts would be missed, and take notes or photographs of every artifact they found. Simple.

Solange's job, and that of her graduate assistants, would be to look over the shoulders of the students and make sure they were doing their work to the best of their abilities.

All was going well. They'd been at it since six that morning. It was nearing eleven o'clock. The students were engrossed in their work, and appeared to be enjoying themselves as well. Most of them were engaged in lively conversation with their partners while they worked.

Solange was standing near a couple of students, watching as they sifted dirt through a screen. Usually they found broken pieces of pottery, bones, coins, and small household utensils carved out of wood. But this time, one of the students found an arrowhead.

The student, an eighteen-year-old African-American girl, yelled as if she'd dug up a huge gold nugget. "Dr. DuPree, look! It's an arrowhead, isn't it?" Her dark eyes sparkled with delight. Solange leaned over to take a closer look. She smiled at the girl. "It's in great condition, too. No visible cracks. Excellent, Serena."

Solange moved on to the next duo, a girl and a boy, both looking enviously at the student who'd actually found something. They had, so far, dug up nothing but rocks.

The girl drew her eyes away from her fortunate classmate to look at Solange. "Dr. DuPree, have you noticed that guy standing in the bushes over there?"

Solange's first thought was that Jason Thorne, or one

of his team, had let himself be seen by the students. But she had to be certain. She looked in the direction the girl was pointing. Palmettos ringed the clearing where they were working. Mangrove, banyan, and Dade County pine trees created a dense wood that could serve as the hiding place for man or beast. In the case of Moustapha Aziz, Solange thought, he was both a man and a beast. "I don't see him," she told the girl. "What did he look like?"

"You know that actor who costarred in the last Lara Croft movie?" she asked.

"I'm not familiar with Lara Croft," Solange said. Sometimes she felt ancient compared to her students.

"Okay, then, he was also in that movie about the slave ship that a bunch of Africans took over and tried to sail back to Africa? *Amistad!* That's the name of the movie. I can't think of the name of the actor."

"You mean Djimon Hounsou?" Solange asked. "He was also in *Gladiator.*"

"That's him!" the girl said excitedly. "Anyway, that's who the man I saw looked like, Djimon Hounsou."

Solange felt the ice cold fingers of fear creep down her spine. No one on Thorne's team could remotely be mistaken for Djimon Hounsou. The blacks on his team were not nearly as dark skinned. Their African blood had been diluted.

"Was he tall or short? Thin or heavy?"

"Very tall, and built like Arnold." She gave a fair rendition of Arnold Schwarzenegger's accent. She looked at her partner, who nodded his agreement.

"Excuse me," Solange said, turning away. She unclipped the cell phone from her belt, flipped it open, and dialed the number Thorne had given her. It rang on his end twice before he answered. "Solange? What's wrong?"

"Where are your people right now?" she asked as calmly as she could manage.

"Parked a couple of blocks down the road from your group. Two men are on foot, watching you from the south end of the area you surveyed yesterday."

Solange looked all around her. "Two of my students say they saw a very large man who could pass for actor Djimon Hounsou. Does Moustapha Aziz look anything like him?"

"I suppose they do look somewhat alike," Thorne admitted. "What direction?"

"The north end," Solange told him with a sigh.

"We'll check it out, Solange. Stay put, and I'll call you back."

Solange hung up and returned to her students. No sooner had she walked back over to the group than a Hispanic boy walked up to her and said, "Dr. DuPree, I'm worried about Leslie. She said she was going into the woods to, you know, use the bathroom out there, but that was more than half an hour ago."

"Oh, Lord, didn't I tell you all not to go into the woods alone?"

The boy looked sheepish. "I reminded her about that, but she said there was no way she was going to have me close by while she went to the bathroom."

"What direction did she go in?" Solange asked.

"North," the boy said.

Panicked now that she knew one of her students might be in Moustapha Aziz's clutches, Solange began running in that direction. The boy looked after her for a moment, then started yelling for the other students to gather around him.

Solange rang Thorne when she reached the edge of the woods. "One of my students is missing in the north woods," she said. "Please get some of your people over here right away. I'm going in after her."

"Solange, no!" Thorne ordered her. "Stay put, do you hear me? We'll handle it."

"That girl's my responsibility," Solange told him, and hung up. She clipped the phone to her belt and, holding a huge palmetto branch aside, entered the north woods.

The woods of that part of south Florida were home to critters like squirrels, rabbits, opossums, and deer. There have even been black bears spotted in the woods.

But Solange wasn't afraid of any of them. She feared reptiles more than anything else, rattlesnakes and coral snakes being the most dangerous of the species. Of course, there was also Moustapha Aziz to keep her eyes peeled for. If there was ever a time for an alligator to eat somebody, this is it, she thought grimly.

She thought it wasn't a good idea to call out Leslie Gayle's name as she searched for her. If Aziz was still out here, it would give him a fix on her location. But time was also of the essence. If Leslie had simply fallen and hurt herself, but could speak, the sooner she found her, the better.

So, she called to her. "Leslie! Leslie! If you can hear me, please answer me!"

Her footsteps made crunching sounds on the fallen leaves and pine needles on the ground. The temperature was in the high eighties, without much of a breeze. And mosquitoes were out in droves. When she went on digs she always carried a tube of insect repellent that could be smeared over the arms and any other exposed skin. It was in solid form, and resembled a tube of antiperspirant. She dug it out of her pocket and spread a bit more over her arms, neck, and face. It smelled like eucalyptus oil.

She had been out there around twenty minutes when she heard a sound like a small wounded animal. It was low and muffled. She paused in her footsteps a moment to listen closely. There it was again. Keening. The sound of either a hurt animal or a terrified animal. It was coming from behind her.

Solange turned around, and when she did, she came face to face with Moustapha Aziz. She tried to turn and run, but she wasn't quick enough. He grabbed her by her hair and yanked her backward. Blinding pain shot through the back of Solange's head and neck. She struggled anyway. He grabbed her around the waist and pulled her firmly against his chest, imprisoning both her arms at her sides. Solange tried to kick him. He leaned down close to her ear. "I can snap your neck like a twig, and I will if you don't stop struggling."

He placed his stubble-covered chin on the side of her neck. The feel of it made her skin crawl. "There, there, little pet," he said after she'd stopped trying to kick him. "I'm not going to hurt you. I want you to deliver a message to Giles for me. Tell him he has failed to protect you twice. If he slips up a third time, I will not leave you alive.

"Tell him I'm not going to kill him. Dead men don't suffer. He has to be alive to mourn your death. He took my woman from me. I'm going to take his from him. Now, go, little pet. The girl you seek is gagged and tied to a tree not six feet away."

He pushed her away from him and calmly turned and walked, in no particular hurry, in the opposite direction. Solange watched him go. This time, she wasn't nearly as afraid as she'd been when he'd grabbed her on the dance floor of Cristal's. This time she was mad. It had finally been driven home to her that no one could protect her except her! Aziz had made it clear his objective wasn't to kill Rupert. He was going to use her to hurt Rupert. He meant to kill her. And he was probably planning a very painful death for her.

All of this because he blamed Rupert for sending him to

prison, which broke up his marriage to Ashante. He was totally insane. He was not taking into account that he'd been a murderous dictator. It was as if that had nothing to do with the breakup of his marriage. Ashante was probably supremely relieved when he was dragged off to prison. She'd probably taken her first calm breath in years!

"Leslie!"

That muffled noise again.

"Keep it up, Leslie. I'm coming for you."

Solange followed the sound to the girl. Leslie seemed to be hugging a pine tree.

Solange bent down. Something had been shoved into her mouth. Solange noticed Leslie's boots were on the ground near the base of the tree.

She gently reached into Leslie's mouth and removed one of the girl's socks from her mouth. Thank God it was made of thin material. Otherwise it might have choked her.

"Is he gone?" Leslie asked, her eyes darting back and forth.

"He's gone," Solange told her.

She walked around the tree and found the girl's wrists had been bound together with her second sock. It took only a few seconds to loosen the knot.

This done, she helped Leslie to her feet. "Are you all right? Can you walk?"

"My legs feel weak with fear, but I don't think he hurt me. He scared me something awful, but he didn't hit me or anything," Leslie said. She was a dark-eyed brunette. Very fair skinned. She appeared even paler now. "He kept talking crazy, Dr. DuPree. He said your fiance created him. 'I wasn't a monster until he created me,' he kept saying over and over again. Reminded me of Frankenstein. Remember when the monster killed the bride of Victor Frankenstein? Killed her while she was in her wedding dress. I'll never forget that. I was seven the first time I saw it and it really scared me." She looked at Solange with spooked eyes. "I'm rambling because I'm still shook up. But that's what he reminded me of, Frankenstein's monster."

Solange pulled Leslie into her arms and held her until she stopped shaking.

Thorne and two of his men caught them like that five minutes later.

"Come on, ladies. We've got paramedics in the clearing waiting to examine Miss Gayle and take her to the hospital, if need be."

"Who're you?" Leslie asked.

"Miami-Dade police," Thorne lied. He flashed a bogus badge so fast you would have had to have been a speed reader to catch a word on it.

Leslie was obviously coming out of her shock because she smiled at him. "By way of Britain?"

"You noticed my accent, huh?" Thorne asked, being the charmer he could be.

"It's hard not to notice," Leslie said.

Solange tuned out the rest of their conversation. She was remembering something Aziz had told her. "If he slips up a third time, I will not leave you alive." Strike three, you're out. Her hourglass was just about empty.

That night, as she and Rupert lay in bed, Solange told him, "I want you to train me." Rupert turned over and faced her.

"You're already proficient with a firearm. You're getting so good at it that I think you're going to reach sharpshooter status soon."

"That's not enough," she said. "He grabbed me twice, and I couldn't get out of his grip. I want to be able to do something to get away from him. I want to incapacitate the creep!"

"You're only five-four and a hundred and thirty pounds, sweetness. You would have to be a martial-arts expert to be able to incapacitate a man of Aziz's size and strength, and I don't have time to train you. You will simply have to stay out of his reach."

"What?"

"Stay aware of his position in reference to yours. This second time, you were face to face with him. If you had been aware of how fast he moves compared to how fast you can move, he would not have been able to grab you like that. You're much smaller than he is. Hence you have the capability to be much faster than he is."

"Show me," Solange said.

"All right," Rupert said, sitting up in bed. He got out of the bed and waited until she climbed down using the footstool.

He was wearing navy blue pajama bottoms, while she wore the top.

"Okay," he said, as he circled her. "I want you to watch me move. I want you to observe everything about me. I might look as if I'm going right, but feint to the left. You've got to be able to anticipate in which direction I'll go. I'm going to try to grab you. And I'm not going to hold back. This is for real. If I were Aziz, and I got my hands on you I could hurt you, so take this seriously. Okay?"

Solange was bouncing from side to side on the balls of her feet. "Okay, got it. Sort of like that game we used to play in the neighborhood. Hot Momma was what we called it. A boy would try to catch a girl, and if he caught her, he got to kiss her. I was pretty good at not getting caught. Funny, I'd forgotten all about that game until now."

Rupert suddenly pounced in her direction like a jungle cat, but Solange dodged him.

She pranced around the room in a victory dance, laughing gleefully. "You didn't really try to catch me, did you? You're going easy on me."

Rupert eyed her from across the room, chewed on his bottom lip a few moments, and began walking toward her. "No, I really did try to grab you, but you avoided me. That was very good indeed. Of course, you're not frightened of me, like you were with Aziz. Perhaps fear has something to do with how swiftly you react."

"You could be right," Solange said. "But now that I'm aware, maybe I'll be able to think more clearly and not panic when he comes after me again. I believe preparing for him will help a lot." She smiled at him. "Let's go to bed, sweetie. We can practice some more tomorrow."

She turned her back on him.

That was when Rupert let out a war whoop and launched himself at her. When Solange looked back and saw his face, contorted in rage, she screamed, leapt onto the bed, rolled onto the opposite side of it, and leapt off again.

Rupert roared with laughter. "Girl, when you want to, you can move pretty fast. You scampered across that bed like a bunny."

"Is that the face you show your enemy just before beating him within an inch of his life?" Solange asked, breathing hard. "Because it's a wonder they don't die of fright before you can lay a finger on them. Damn, baby, you were snarling like a big cat. Your lips all curled back from your teeth! I thought you were going to bite me."

"Scared you?" Rupert asked.

"Cleared the bed without a footstool, didn't I?" Solange said proudly.

* * *

Solange started taking her gun with her everywhere. By handgun standards, it was small—a Smith and Wesson 9-millimeter pistol. She was always aware of the weight of it, along with the extra fifteen-round clip, in her bag. A little finagling on the agency's part and, now, the handguns she and Rupert carried were registered, and they both had licenses to carry them. The agency was good at solving small problems.

Solange tried not to be resentful of the fact that they hadn't found Aziz yet, especially with their wedding day rapidly approaching. It was already the middle of June; the wedding date was only two weeks away.

Practically all of the seventy guests had responded, saying they were coming, among them, Toni Shaw Waters, her husband Charles Edward Waters, their daughters Briane and Georgette, and their husbands, Clayton and Dominic. Gaea had phoned to say she, Micah, and Mikey would be there with bells on. Gaea was to be the matron of honor, and Samantha was the one and only bridesmaid. Rupert's best friend from his university days until now, Aaron Mafani Musonge of Douala, Cameroon, was going to stand up for him as his best man. That summed up the wedding party.

It was Sunday, and Desta was restless. Solange and Rupert tried to assure her that when Aziz was caught, she would be on the first plane out of Addis Ababa. However, no amount of reassurances were good enough for Desta. "I feel like I'm alone again, you've changed your mind about adopting me, and this is a ploy to let me down easy," she said in a sad voice.

Solange was sitting on the couch in the living room, Rupert next to her. She met Rupert's eyes as she said,

"Baby, that's not true. We love you. If it were safe, you would be here by now."

"I don't care. I should be there with my family," Desta said. "Families go through things like this together. I'm tough. I'm not afraid of him."

"I know you're not afraid of him, Des. You're not afraid of anything. I'm the one who's scared. You're safe there. If you came here, we would try our best to protect you. But we're not perfect. Something could happen."

"Shouldn't I be the one to decide whether or not I want to take that risk?" Desta reasoned.

"No. We're your parents. We decide on the best course where your safety is concerned." Solange was firm. "Don't argue with me. It's only a matter of time now, Des. Be patient a while longer."

"The other children here say I'm never going to America. They say I'll always be here, just like the other older children that nobody wants to adopt." She began sobbing.

Tears were rolling down Solange's cheeks.

Rupert reached for the receiver. She gave it to him.

"Desta," he said. "I'll tell you how sure we are that this case is going to be wrapped up before the wedding. We're going to send you your plane ticket and money for traveling expenses ahead of time. So, the moment we get the word we can phone you and ask Mr. Manawi to put you on a plane."

Desta screamed in his ear. "I get to come on my own?"

"Yes, you do. You're a mature young lady. We're positive you can handle it."

Solange's eyes stretched in horror. She tried to take the receiver back, but Rupert held it out of her reach. "Now stop that crying and start planning your trip. Remember, we expect you to be extra careful. Don't talk to strangers. Pay close attention to your surroundings so you won't miss any connections, and be polite to airline personnel. Got that?"

"Got it!" Desta said excitedly, her crying jag forgotten. "I love you, Rupert. Tell Solange I love her, too!"

"I will, sweetheart. Good-bye," said Rupert gently.

He hung up the phone and turned to face the music. Solange was shaking her head in amazement. "What happened to our agreement that we will decide together what's best for Desta?"

"I'm sorry," Rupert said in his defense. "But crying females unnerve me. I had to offer a solution, and offer a solution fast! Think about it, Solange. Desta is not helpless. You're coddling her too much already, and she's not here yet. What kind of woman do we want to rear? Someone who relies on others all the time? No, we want her to be confident and independent. You've recently come to that realization yourself. A woman needs to be able to take care of herself."

"And to engender that kind of behavior in Desta, we have to allow her to do things on her own from time to time," Solange said, agreeing with him. "Okay. You're right. But that doesn't mean I'm not going to worry myself gray over this!"

Rupert laughed and pulled her into his arms. "We're both going to worry until she gets here. But she will get here. I have the utmost confidence in her."

"Me, too," Solange said. "I have confidence in her. It's the rest of the world I tend to worry about."

"You know what your problem is?" Rupert asked, smiling at her.

"No. What's my problem?"

"You miss house hunting. There must be hundreds of houses for sale that we haven't seen yet."

Solange groaned. In the past three weeks, they'd been all over Coral Gables looking at houses. Older houses and model homes. They had read up on the city itself, learning tidbits like "Coral Gables is the Corporate Capital of the Americas. Over 150 multinational corporations use it as their Latin American headquarters. The population is nearly 43,000 people of different cultural backgrounds, all coexisting in a city known for its fine neighborhoods, historical landmarks, and exceptionally high quality of life."

To Solange it sounded like a place the *Stepford Wives* movies could have been set in. Too perfect for her. She knew her mother lived there, but her mother thrived on perfection. She, on the other hand, rather liked her neighborhood, with its bungalows and various other houses of dubious architectural origins. She liked her neighbors, especially Peter Wychowski, and didn't like the idea of moving on up, to borrow a phrase from *The Jeffersons.*

"Oh, I beg of you, kind sir, please don't make me go house hunting today!" she pleaded rather dramatically.

"Sunday is the perfect day to check out model homes," Rupert said. "Traffic won't be as congested. Not as many potential buyers out. Realtors are less aggressive on Sundays."

"You know what we haven't done in a long time on a Sunday?" Solange suggested. "Taken a walk around the neighborhood. I bet Mr. Wychowski has the old chessboard set up hoping you'll venture out and he'll be able to convince you to play a game."

"You'd have to sit and watch," Rupert said. "How boring is that? When we could both be looking at houses?"

"I'd like nothing better than to watch you and Mr. Wychowski play chess. It's so intellectually stimulating. And you look so sexy when you frown in concentration."

"You really hate house hunting, don't you?"

"With a passion!"

Rupert laughed shortly. "Okay. I'll go put on my walking shoes."

"Great," Solange said happily, rocking back on her Adidas.

After they left the house, Rupert suggested, "Why don't we take the long way around? If we go past Peter's at the outset, and he has the chessboard out, I might be too tempted. And there goes your walk."

"You're right," Solange said, trying not to laugh at Rupert's comment about being too tempted by a chessboard. She found the game unbelievably boring. But then, she wasn't a war strategist. Both Rupert and Mr. Wychowski were former soldiers.

The game of chess was, after all, based on war maneuvers. One king and his army trying to capture the other king. Counting coup. Rupert and Mr. Wychowski got great satisfaction out of trouncing each other.

As they walked, they talked.

"I still think we ought to tell the immediate family about what's happening," Solange said. "What if Aziz crashes the wedding and tries to kill one of us? An innocent person could get hurt."

"All telling them would do is panic them," Rupert said. "It's best they don't know. Theophilus, for one, would want to bring his own security staff in. Speaking of security staff, he's really pressuring me to take that chief of security job. I'm going to have to turn him down, though. If I want to work in security, I'll start my own firm. Right now, I'm enjoying being with you too much to seriously think of anything that's going to take me away from you. But eventually I won't want to continue being idle."

"Theophilus isn't courting you just for a chief of security job, Rupert," Solange told him. "Think about it. You're his only son. He wants to get you interested in the business so you'll take on more responsibilities."

"I have given that some thought," Rupert admitted. "Perhaps I ought to have a talk with Theophilus, and let him know that although I appreciate his wanting to bring me into the family business, I would prefer to be on my own. On the other hand, maybe he's just being a father and he's worried that I'm out of a job."

"Doesn't want you to starve, and take me down with you," Solange joked.

"Exactly," Rupert said. "I'll have to explain to him that we're set financially."

"We've just got a homicidal maniac to deal with," Solange put in.

"And together we will vanquish him," Rupert returned with a smile in her direction.

"Kick his butt."

"Demolish him."

"Make him wish he'd never been born."

"Make him say uncle."

"Send him running home to mommy."

Solange suddenly stopped in front of a large Victorian house painted white with black shutters: the Kingston house. She'd always loved the multileveled house. There was a front porch with a latticework partition shading the south side of it.

On half an acre, the yard was deep in both the front and the back. White wicker chairs invited visitors to sit and enjoy the afternoon breezes on the verandah. There was even a widow's walk on the roof.

"It's for sale!" Solange said, already strolling up the sidewalk leading to the front porch. "I love this house."

Rupert eyed the for sale sign dubiously. The house was old. It definitely wasn't truly of the Victorian era, either. It was a copy. None of the houses in this neighborhood dated back to that time. Though the house was charming, he was determined to buy his bride a new house, not a hand-me-down. There was beveled glass in the ornate double front doors. Mrs. Alyce Kingston must have seen them coming because she swung open the doors as soon as Solange stepped onto the porch.

"Hello, Solange, how are you?"

Mrs. Kingston was seventy, around five-six, slender, and attired in a pair of slacks and a short-sleeve tunic, both in cotton. The slacks were burnished gold and the tunic was pale yellow. Her short, white hair was thick and wavy. She wore it combed away from her lovely heart-shaped face. Solange didn't know Mrs. Kingston's ethnic origins. She'd never asked. But her skin was a consistent golden-brown color, and Solange had never known her to sun herself. She reminded Solange of Lena Horne.

Her husband, Davis, had died three years ago. He had been a native Floridian with a marked southern accent, lively blue eyes, and a lust for living. He'd died in a boating accident.

"I'm well, Mrs. Kingston, and you?"

Alyce stepped forward and touched her cheek to Solange's. "Splendid. Won't you and Mr. Giles come in?"

Solange was surprised Mrs. Kingston knew Rupert's name, because though she and Mrs. Kingston had known one another for nearly ten years, she had never had an occasion to introduce her to Rupert.

Alyce laughed shortly when she saw the expression on Solange's face. "Peter and I share a meal together once a week. He told me about Mr. Giles."

"Please," said Rupert stepping forward and offering her his hand. "Call me Rupert."

"I will, if you'll call me Alyce."

"Done."

Alyce cocked an eye at Solange. "That one never has been able to drop the Mrs. Kingston."

"It's her southern upbringing," Rupert told her.

"Oh, I see," said Alyce.

She looked down at her bare feet. "Please forgive me. I rarely wear shoes in the house. Dates back to when I was a child and my mother always told us to leave our shoes in the foyer closet to prevent bringing sand inside the house."

"Oh, would you like us to take off our shoes?" Solange asked, the toe of her right Adidas already at the heel of her left.

"If you're here to see the house, which I hope you are, yes, please do take them off."

Solange and Rupert bent and removed their shoes. Alyce told them they could leave them underneath the foyer table.

She took them on a tour of the house.

To the left of the foyer was her office. The walls were painted eggshell white and the linen/cotton upholstered sofa and chair were in pale blue and white stripes. The sun coming through the windows suffused the room with warm light. "I'm writing my memoirs. That sounds so pretentious. But I really have led an interesting life, so I'm writing it down for my daughter and her children. Constance, that's my daughter, knows so little about her family. I recently told her that I'm black and that really threw her for a loop."

She enjoyed the fact that both Solange and Rupert were trying, and failing, to conceal that her statement had shocked them. "You're both lovely children. I'm past seventy now, and the one luxury I've afforded myself upon turning this illustrious age is to be as candid as I wish to be. Davis and I didn't advertise that ours was a mixed marriage because when we got married in the fifties, mixed marriages were frowned upon, and sometimes cause for imprisonment in this country, and especially in this part of the country. I'm originally from San Francisco. That's where Davis and I met."

She led them to her living room. The floors in the house were light oak throughout. In the room, the furnishings sat upon a sisal carpet. The sofa, love seat, and two chairs were all covered in linen and cotton fabric in a mixture of stripes and solids.

Alyce walked over to the fireplace. She touched a beautiful blue-lacquered vase. "Davis's ashes. He wanted me to pour them into the Atlantic Ocean, but I refused. He's going home to San Francisco with me. After all, he usually chose wherever we went when he was alive. I'm choosing the destinations now."

They went from the living room to the dining room. The entire east wall was made up of four windows that stretched from the ceiling to the floor. A door opened onto the large back porch, from which you could see the beautifully landscaped yard beyond.

In this room, as in the others, light colors on the walls and on the furnishings created a sense of an abundance of space. "I love to cook. Boy, the dinner parties we've had in this room. Once, back in the fifties, Fidel Castro came to dinner. He has an eye for the ladies. He flirted outrageously with me all evening. Davis almost came to blows with him. Fidel apologized, but then told him that if he wanted to protect his sheep, he ought not to invite the wolf to dinner. That was at the time when Davis was in politics. Thank God he left that notion behind in the sixties when this country was really in turmoil. Not that it hasn't been in turmoil ever since! This neighborhood was very different back then, Solange. It was considered like the neighborhoods where the overpaid athletes reside now. Gated communities of the newly rich. Davis made his money in real estate speculating. Believe me, back in the day, this state was a buyer's market, and it still is in some respects. The greedy prospered at the expense of the working man. If real estate speculators wanted property where poor men lived, guess whose property taxes suddenly went sky high? So, Davis is not going to rest at the bottom of the Atlantic Ocean. I'm taking him to San Francisco and I'm going to sit him on the mantle of the fireplace in my family's home.

"Now, my folks were not born with silver spoons in their mouths. Daddy was a physician. The first black heart surgeon in San Francisco. Momma was a nurse. When they died, they left the Pacific Heights house to my sister, Lara. There are only two of us left, and Lara wants me to come live with her. She was widowed five years ago. So, I'm selling this house, and I'm San Francisco–bound. You children look like you'd be happy here. I'll let you have it for a song. Well, for below market value, anyway!"

She looked at them with laughter dancing in her eyes while she patiently waited for their reaction to her proposal.

Twelve

"Sorry, sweetheart, but I'm on Rupert's side. I'd love to have you all living in Coral Gables, not too far from me. Desta could come to my house after school. I'm adjusting my work schedule so I'll be home every day by three. I'm delegating more now since I actually have a personal life," Marie said.

She, Solange, and Dani were having lunch at Lily's, a powwow two weeks before the wedding to make sure everything was on schedule.

"Are you talking about Alyce Kingston?" Dani asked, her delicately sculptured brows rising. She took a sip of her wine while she awaited Solange's response.

"Yeah. She lives in my neighborhood."

"I know that house," Dani said. "I once did an anniversary party for Alyce and Davis. Lovely couple. So much in love after nearly fifty years of marriage." She gave a sad sigh, and cast her eyes in Marie's direction. "I'm on Solange's side. That house is divine. Big, airy rooms, hardwood floors, a kitchen a professional chef would dice someone up for. Five bedrooms upstairs. A guest suite. A pool, and a pool house. Now they knew how to live! Poor Alyce. I heard that Davis had passed away. The house must be too much for her to handle alone. A house that size requires someone with energy to spare to maintain it." She leaned toward Solange, and said in low conspiratorial tones, "Did you know they were a mixed couple? Got married in the fifties, right under Jim Crow's nose."

"How do you know?" asked Solange. Dani was an inveterate gossip. She seemed to know just about everybody in Miami, and if she didn't know them personally, she certainly knew someone who did.

"Sweetie, please. Those lips. I'm willing to bet Angelina Jolie has black blood in her, too. And Alyce has some junk in her trunk for a slim gal. Jennifer Lopez notwithstanding, junk in the trunk is usually the province of women of color." She looked at Marie for corroboration. "Am I right?"

"You're right," Marie confirmed.

"Come on now, ladies," Solange said, trying to inject some reality into the conversation. "Courtesy of South Beach plastic surgeons, anyone can have junk in their trunks nowadays."

"Ooh, child," said Dani. "Are you hooked on *Nip/Tuck,* too?"

"Hooked might be too strong a word," Solange said. "I watch it to catch glimpses of the actor who portrays the greedy one."

"Christian, the bad boy," Dani said. "He is yummy with those hooded eyes of his."

"Both of you are sitting here salivating over an actor when you have real men in your lives," Marie complained. She turned her head to observe Dani. "Speaking of which, you haven't said a word about Sidney today. What's going on?"

Dani took another sip of her wine to fortify herself. "I'm thinking of telling him I can't see him anymore."

"Why?" Solange asked. She hated to admit it, but she'd become morbidly curious to find out how Dani's relationship with Sidney would turn out. Dani was playing a dangerous game in Solange's opinion. What if Sidney turned violent when he learned he'd been dating a man instead of a woman? Gay-bashing was not unheard of. Dani could get hurt.

"It's as you said, I'm getting emotionally involved with him. That's the barometer for getting out while I can. I have not even let him kiss me because I haven't been able to tell him who I really am. He's beginning to wonder why I won't kiss him. Last night he told me he believes I think he's unattractive, which is far from the truth. I think he's absolutely gorgeous. But I can't bear to tell him who I am, to see that look come into his eyes."

"Dani, it's obvious you really care for Sidney," Marie said. "I'll go with you when you tell him. We'll meet at a restaurant, and I'll sit at the next table."

"We'll both be there," Solange offered. "Give us the time and the place, and we'll be seated when you walk in."

"You would do that for me?" asked Dani, amazed they would offer to support her after knowing her for only two months.

"We've got your back," Marie said.

Dani was so eager to get it over with that she set up the time of confession for noon the next day. She dressed with care, choosing a navy blue double-breasted pantsuit with a shell underneath. She wore conservative three-inch-heel navy blue pumps with it.

She arrived ten minutes early, was shown to her table and, as soon as she sat down, she spotted Solange and Marie, three tables away, looking at menus.

Dani fluttered the fingers of her right hand at them. They briefly waved back, then returned to their menus. They were supposed to be her silent, invisible support.

Dani ordered a tall glass of iced tea while she waited. And waited. And waited.

After half an hour, she was steaming mad. No one stood her up! She went into her purse to get her cell phone. After digging it out, she dialed Sidney's number. He'd better be in the car on the way here, she thought testily. She got his voice mail.

In the meantime, Solange looked up from her menu and saw a tall, dark-skinned man entering the dining room. Her breath caught in her throat as his eyes met hers from across the room. Moustapha Aziz. His gaze left hers and settled on Marie. He smiled and then changed course. Instead of coming to her table, as Solange had thought he would upon seeing her, he turned and left the dining room.

Solange looked desperately around for one of the agents. Joanne Harris was supposed to be somewhere in the restaurant. After Aziz's back had disappeared, she saw Joanne coming from the direction Aziz had gone in. She would have walked right past the wanted man. It was apparent, though, that she hadn't seen him.

Solange felt conflicted. On one hand, she had to continue to conceal the fact that her life was in danger from her mother, who was right next to her. On the other, Aziz was here, and if Joanne Harris hurried, she might be able to catch him before he got away. She glanced at her mother, who was examining her face in a compact.

"Excuse, me, Maman. I'm going to the ladies' room."

Marie closed the compact, and looked up at Solange. "Okay, sweetie. I'll order dessert for you if the waiter comes before you return."

"Okay, thanks. Order the apple tart for me, please," Solange said.

She turned and walked swiftly away. She came within five feet of Joanne Harris's table. "Follow me," she said loud enough to be heard by Joanne as she passed.

Joanne had been tracking her progress across the room,

so she knew when she saw Solange coming toward her that something was wrong. Solange kept walking, but as she turned the corner she saw that Joanne had gotten up and was following her.

Joanne caught up with her near the phone booths in the back. "What's the matter?"

"Didn't you see him?" Solange asked, incredulous. "He was leaving the dining room as you were coming back in. You had to have seen him."

Joanne looked at the entrance to the dining room. There was an exit door nearby.

"He must have gone out that door while I was coming out of the restroom," Joanne guessed. "Stay here, I'll go see if he's still in the parking lot." She ran toward the exit, her hand going inside her jacket to retrieve her cell phone to call for backup.

After Solange saw Joanne go through the side exit, she turned back toward the dining room entrance and saw Dani. Dani had a look of consternation on her beautiful face.

"I tell you, I'm confused," Dani said as she approached Solange. "I told him I had something important to tell him, and he seemed very receptive. I got the feeling he thought I was getting ready to let down my guard with him. Why wouldn't he show up?" She frowned. "Goodness, I hope he hasn't been in an accident! Here I am worried about my pride and he could be somewhere fighting for his life."

Solange smiled and went to place her arm about the shorter woman's shoulders.

"Dani, he probably got held up at work, and hasn't been able to phone you yet. Don't go getting yourself upset when there could be any number of reasons, besides injury and death, why he didn't keep his date with you. Are you going to wait a while longer?"

Dani sniffed. "No, I refuse to be the martyr. Let him phone me and grovel."

"Then would you mind giving Maman a lift? Rupert just phoned and wants me to meet him at the marina. Something about a yacht he's thinking of chartering for our honeymoon."

Dani brightened. "A yacht! Now, that man has his thinking cap on twenty-four-seven! Go, on, girl. Go to that Henry Simmons lookalike, and test that yacht for stability, if you know what I mean. If the boat's a rockin', don't come a knockin'."

Solange laughed. "Dani, you're too much. And you watch way too much television."

They went back into the dining room and got things straight with Marie, who was amenable to Dani driving her home. Solange took time to pay the check before going in search of Joanne Harris.

Since Joanne had told her to stay near the exit, she returned to that spot and waited.

While she waited, her mind kept going back to Dani's predicament—Anything to take her mind off seeing Moustapha Aziz again, which had been startling, but not nearly as scary as their encounter in the woods, probably due to the fact that they were in a restaurant full of people.

Her heart went out to Dani, who always seemed to lose in love. It couldn't be easy to carry on a relationship with a man when you were a woman living in a man's body.

Shame on Sidney for standing her up after Dani had raved about him to her! She could still hear Dani's enthusiastic description of him: "He towers over me. I like them tall. His skin is such a rich chocolate, it's bittersweet. Big hands, big feet. You know what that means!" Solange had pretended she didn't, and let Dani explain

herself. Solange had ended up laughing so hard she'd
been in tears by the time she'd heard Dani's theory of
being able to tell how well-endowed a man was by the
size of his hands and feet.

"He has a French accent," Dani had continued when
she got back around to describing Sidney. "Says he's
Haitian. But, I swear, I've never seen a Haitian man that
tall before. Truth be told, he looks African to me. My
own personal Mandingo warrior!"

Remembering their conversation as she stood next to
the exit now, Solange suddenly had a terrifying thought:
What if Moustapha Aziz and Sidney were one and the
same?

When he'd shown up at the restaurant, maybe he'd
been as surprised to see her as she'd been to see him.
Perhaps he was keeping his date with Dani. Of course,
he couldn't stay around and let Dani see him because
with Solange, who could identify him, present, the gig
would be up! However, if Solange was the only person to
recognize him, how could she put two and two together
and come up with his having an alter ego? She could
voice her suspicions, but she wouldn't be very convincing. She'd only succeed in alienating Dani, who would
be upset with Solange for fingering her new boyfriend as
a murdering ex-dictator.

Solange could not tell Dani she suspected Moustapha
Aziz and Sidney were the same man. However, she would
definitely tell Rupert, Thorne, and the others.

Joanne Harris returned with sweat rolling down her
face. "Somebody sped out of the parking lot in a late-
model Mercedes. The guys followed him in the van. Can
you give me a lift back to your place?"

"Sure," said Solange. "It'll give me time to tell you
what I think I've come up with on the case."

Joanne looked skeptical. "I guess we can use all the help we can get."

"You can say that again," Solange said with a humorous glint in her eyes.

"Okay, okay," said Joanne, smiling. "No agent bashing allowed. We're trying our best. Believe me, no one suspected Aziz could be this slippery. I suppose his last encounter with your fiancé brought out the worst in him."

"He's definitely motivated," Solange agreed.

Once they were on their way across town, Solange told Joanne how she'd come to the conclusion that Aziz and Sidney were the same person. Joanne listened, not interrupting. Then, she scrunched up her nose and said, "I suppose that would be a way to get into the wedding through the back door, so to speak—come as the wedding planner's guest. Sharp thinking on his part. We'll stake-out Ms. Chevalier's place to see if he shows up."

"You don't think you should talk to Dani and get a description of Sidney? Maybe show her a photo of Aziz?"

"No," Joanne said. She was busy removing her jacket. She wore a shoulder holster with an automatic weapon in it. Her long, dark, curly hair was in a ponytail. "We don't know how involved Ms. Chevalier is with him. Who knows how she'll react if it is Aziz? He could have some type of psychological hold on her. I've known women like her, someone who got involved with a felon on the run, who fell in love with the guy. Once they went to prison, they visited them on a regular basis. One woman even married a guy in prison. No, it's best to watch her place and pick him up if he shows."

"Wow," said Solange.

"Yeah," Joanne told her. "I've seen some weird things since I've been with the agency."

"How long have you been with them?"

"About ten years. I was there when your fiancé was at top form. He had a reputation among the other operatives."

"Oh, what was it?"

"He was known as the MacGyver of agents."

"Why?"

"You've never seen that TV show about the guy who can create anything out of anything?"

"No, sorry," said Solange.

"Well, Giles was good at using anything in his environment to subdue the enemy. He knew how to make bombs out of a few household products. Made your average furniture into lethal weapons. He once staked a man with a chair leg. I'm still amazed the guy lived. We called him Van Helsing for a long time after that."

"After the character who was Dracula's nemesis in the book," Solange supplied.

Joanne smiled at her, impressed. "Right. Anyway, Giles was a damn good agent. A lot of us were shocked when he left."

"And upset with him?" Solange asked.

"No," Joanne denied. "Why should we be upset with him? He has the right to choose his own course in life."

"Thorne told him the agents on this case didn't care whether he lived or died," Solange told her, quoting what Rupert had told her about a conversation with Thorne.

"Thorne is the only one I know of who has any animosity toward Giles, and I think it's because they were partners for so long, and Thorne felt abandoned when he left. They made a good team."

Solange smiled. "You mean Thorne's feelings were hurt?"

"I'm saying that Thorne, macho agent that he is, wasn't able to deal with his feelings about Giles when he left, so he convinced himself he hated him. Hate is much more masculine than admitting you missed a fellow agent whom you considered to be your friend. We're supposed to remain somewhat detached in this business. Forming attachments is frowned upon because, really, you never know when your partner is going to get blown away. I don't ascribe to that way of thinking. But then I've always been a maverick. I think for myself."

"That's allowed?"

"Generally, no," Joanne replied. "But I don't care. Now, personal question for you. How did you and Giles meet?"

"He was investigating the theft of fertility statues from around the world, and I happened to be in possession of one of the statues that was on the list that the culprit was trying to gather. I got caught up in the game and wound up in Addis Ababa where the case unfolded. He caught the bad guy and asked me to stay in the country for a couple of weeks to see if we had anything in common. I accepted, and the rest is history."

"You stayed in a foreign country with a perfect stranger for two weeks?"

"There was something about him that I trusted right off the bat."

"Plus, you were horny as hell, right?"

"That, too," Solange said, laughing. "Joanne Harris, you're all right."

Joanne eyed her with a mixture of amusement and respect. "So're you."

That night, Dani curled up on her couch in the living room and tuned the TV to *NYPD Blue*. She'd microwaved low-salt popcorn and grabbed a can of Diet Coke from the fridge. Within minutes she was engrossed in the episode, especially when Henry Simmons came on the screen.

Henry was undressing for a shower scene when the phone rang.

Dani picked up the remote control and clicked "record" before picking up the receiver, her eyes still on the screen. "Yeah? And this had better be good. I'm watching *NYPD Blue*."

"Danielle."

She recognized Sidney's voice right away.

"You stood me up!" she cried. "I waited over an hour for you." A lie contrived to make him squirm.

"I'm sorry, Danielle. My sister phoned me with horrible news. Our father is dying."

His announcement took a bite out of Dani's indignation. Both her parents were still living, but she was certainly dead to them. She knew how it felt to be separated from your parents. "You poor baby," she sympathized. "Where are you now?"

"I'm in Port-au-Prince, still at the airport. I'll have to find a car to take me to Sans Souci. I don't even know if my cell phone will work there, but I'll get to a phone to call you in a couple of days. Again, I'm sorry I couldn't be there today, Danielle. My sister says he's failing fast. I'm trying to get there before he expires."

"I understand," Dani told him, her tone soft. "I'm so sorry about your father. I'll be praying for your family."

"That's sweet of you. But then, you're the sweetest woman I've ever met," Sidney told her. "I have to go now, Danielle. Good night."

"Good night, Sidney. Take good care of yourself."

"You, too, my sweet one."

I love you, Dani thought, as she replaced the receiver on its base. Outside, in the surveillance van, Thorne removed his headset. "That didn't sound like Aziz to me."

Joanne removed hers, too, and met his eyes. "I've never

met the man, but you're right. It didn't sound like the tape I've heard of his voice."

"He could be disguising his voice."

"Or that could be someone else, and not Aziz at all," Joanne said.

"We'll know tomorrow after we do a voice comparison test." Since they were alone, Thorne took the opportunity to bend forward and place a kiss on Joanne's mouth.

Although she was enjoying the kiss, Joanne turned her head and broke it off. "You're a great kisser, Thorne. But no amount of kisses is going to convince me to get naked with you. Not until you have that talk with Giles."

"This is blackmail," Thorne said, his blue eyes narrowing.

Joanne kissed him again. "Call it incentive. It's been so long since I've slept with anyone, Justice is starting to look good to me."

Michael Justice was the electronics genius on their team. He was short, myopic, and wore suspenders every day, even though he also wore a belt. Now, there is a man who means to keep his pants up, Joanne thought.

Thorne leaned in and they kissed hungrily. Joanne was breathless when they parted. Thorne's eyes were actually dreamy looking. She smiled at him. "It would be a crying shame if we never got together."

Thorne groaned.

"You know, that yacht idea sounds good," Rupert said as they were standing at the kitchen sink doing the dinner dishes. He smiled encouragingly, both dimples showing.

Solange didn't return his smile. "Don't give me those puppy-dog eyes," she said. "You're not getting me in the middle of the ocean. I told you, I don't go in the ocean."

"I thought you meant you don't swim in the ocean," he said innocently enough.

"Swim, cruise, sail, fly over if I can help it," Solange clarified. "All of the above. You're not going to change my mind, Giles, so stop trying."

"I was just thinking that that's the only thing you're afraid of. If you could conquer that fear, you'd probably feel as if you could accomplish anything."

"I already feel as if I can accomplish anything," Solange said. "Except that!"

"You went on a boat when we were in Ethiopia," Rupert reminded her.

"Yeah, and we were on the river. A rather small river at that. I could see the bottom. I can't see the bottom of the ocean. It just goes on, and on, and on. Forever!"

"If you're afraid I can't handle a yacht, I assure you, I can. My Dad and I used to go sailing quite often. I know everything there is to know about a good-sized boat."

"Well, great, Rupert. I'm glad to hear that. But I still won't be going on a boat with you. Not while I'm breathing. When I'm dead, you can do whatever you wish with my body. Until then, forget it!"

"Will you stop yelling at me?"

"Will you stop bullying me about going into the ocean?" she countered, dark eyes flashing fire. "Just leave me alone about it."

"Okay! If I had known you'd get this upset, I never would have brought it up."

"If you had nearly died, you would know how I feel," Solange said, throwing the dish towel onto the counter and storming out of the kitchen. "You're such a damned Superman that you think we've all got to be perfect, meet your standards of excellence. Well, I'm a human being, Rupert. I'm supposed to have fears and foibles. That's how we're made."

She had hoped that she would be able to leave him in the kitchen, but he followed her down the hallway all the way back to the master bedroom. She felt off-kilter whenever she was reminded of her near drowning. She supposed everyone did when they were faced with their mortality.

"At least let me apologize," Rupert said evenly from behind her.

Solange turned. Her face was flushed, and her chest was heaving. A layer of perspiration had appeared on her upper lip. Her lips were slightly opened.

She knew she'd gotten defensive because Rupert was right. Fear of drowning in the ocean was her biggest fear. She had thought that swimming as often as she could in the pool proved that she really wasn't afraid of the water. In reality, it was only a Band-Aid, something to assuage her subconscious that she wasn't afraid of dying. Because that's what it came down to. She was afraid to die. But, wasn't everybody? Of course not all of us had stared death in its ugly face and lived to tell the tale, like she had. Death was laughing at her because it had had the final word. It would win. It was inevitable that death would someday come to claim its winnings. In the meantime, she stayed out of the ocean!

"Don't apologize, Rupert. You've been apologizing too often lately. In this instance, you have nothing to apologize for. I know you want me to be the best I can be. I wish the same thing for you. But you're not going to fix this. It's been with me for nearly twenty years. On the day I died—"

"You died?"

"I was gone for nearly ten minutes, according to my parents. How I came out of it without brain damage, I'll never know. But my death was not something sweet and spiritual like those accounts from people who claim they've gone into the light. My experience was scary. I felt these cold, dead hands pulling me down to the ocean's bottom. I couldn't see any light at all. Nothing but darkness. And those hands, trying to pull me apart. Hands on my wrists, on my ankles, on my throat, cutting off my breath. I was in hell!"

"You were not in hell, baby, you were experiencing oxygen deprivation," Rupert said. "You were not dead, either. That happens when your brain isn't getting enough oxygen. Nightmarish images arise. Your brain fooled you into believing it was really happening. I know because I've gone without oxygen myself. I nearly suffocated once, locked in a freezer."

He didn't tell her that before he'd been shoved into the freezer, he'd been beaten and shot. She didn't need to know that. Nor that the only reason he'd been found in time was because the freezer had been left in an alley next to a Dumpster, and the city garbage workers who'd emptied the Dumpster had decided to check out the condition of the freezer before hauling it off. Sanitation workers were notorious for finding usable items in the things people threw away. So, they'd opened the locked door of the freezer with a crowbar, and Rupert had fallen out, unconscious. Rupert had personally given each of the three men a monetary reward, plus a night on the town with their wives.

"Are you saying that my fear is irrational?" Solange asked quietly, her eyes on his face. She had begun removing her jeans, her hand on the top button, unfastening it.

"No, you have a reason to be afraid. You almost drowned. All I'm saying is, you shouldn't connect anything spiritual to your experience. It was all a physical reaction to being oxygen deprived. That's all. You were not in hell. And you are not going to hell when you die.

With all the goodness you have in your heart, do you really think God wants you in hell?"

"So, you think that's what I'm really afraid of, dying again and going to hell?"

"Baby, you didn't die that day. So, don't tack on the word, 'again'," Rupert said. "But, yeah, that's what I think you're really afraid of."

He looked down as she pulled her shirt out of her waistband, and unzipped the jeans, revealing her flat belly. He could just see the top of the waistband of the aquamarine panties she was wearing.

"Aren't you?"

"Afraid of death?" he asked, his eyes still on her belly. "No. I'm more afraid of not having lived enough before I die. I'm afraid of regret."

"What would you regret if you died suddenly?" she asked as she moved closer.

Rupert took a step or two toward her, as well. "Not having a child with you," he answered, not having to think about it. Solange practically flew into his arms. "Oh, I wish you hadn't said that," she said as she kissed his chin. Rupert took her face between his hands and kissed her mouth.

He peered down at her. "Why not?"

She smiled, though her eyes were sad. "Because it's the one thing I may not be able to give you."

"You might be pregnant right now. You haven't had a period in over two months."

"That's not unusual for someone with my condition."

"Your former condition. You're healed."

"That remains to be seen. Until my belly starts growing, I won't get my hopes up."

"Have faith, sweetness," said Rupert with a gentle smile.

He kissed both her cheeks, the tip of her nose, and her forehead. Tipped her head back, and kissed her throat.

Kissed that space behind her ear. While she relished the feel of his mouth on her skin. Breathed in the male scent of him. Endeavored to live in the moment, forget about the past, and not worry about the future.

Finally his mouth came down on hers. His lips were so soft, so gentle that she sighed into the kiss and closed her eyes as if she were falling into a cloud. She floated higher.

Fear forgotten. Buoyant with her own bravery.

His hands were busy pulling her jeans down as she wriggled, trying to help, but not helping because the movement of her hips only made him all the more urgent. He fumbled when he was impatient.

Solange laughed against his mouth. He broke off the kiss, looked down at her.

"What?"

"For all your sophistication, sometimes you're like a horny teenager when it comes to getting me out of my clothes. I think it's sweet."

He frowned. "Sweet? I'll show you sweet."

He picked her up, carried her across the room to the bed and placed her, bottom first, on it, then he bent and removed those troublesome jeans. He was out of his own jeans and T-shirt in record time.

Solange was pulling her T-shirt over her head when she felt his hands on her ankles.

He dragged her to the edge of the bed, grabbed the T-shirt, snatched it off, and threw it to the floor with the rest of their clothing.

Then he lifted her off the elevated bed, and set her back down. "Hands over your head, please."

Solange raised her arms.

Rupert quickly undid the clasps on her front-hooking bra and tossed it aside. "Spread your legs."

Solange did as she was told.

He removed her panties. They went the way of the

bra. He stood in front of her in a pair of black Jockey
briefs. Going to her, he encircled her in his arms and
pressed his crotch to her buttocks. Ran his hands over
both her breasts, teasing the nipples while his tongue
tasted the tender spot on the side of her neck.

Her nipples grew hard against the palm of his hand.
His hands went lower to the warm, soft flesh between
her thighs. Solange relaxed, surrendering to his sensual
manipulations. Though he hadn't removed the briefs,
she felt his distended penis on her buttocks, at the space
where her thighs met. She bent at the waist, and Rupert
instantly grew harder, his penis straining to be loosed
from its contraints. Solange was throbbing between her
legs.

She felt his hands moving up her thighs again. This
time, he didn't stop at the vee where her thighs met.
He gently parted the lips of her vagina with his forefinger, felt that she was slick with wetness, and delved
deeper. "You feel good," he murmured, his warm breath
on the back of her neck.

A delicious thrill of excitement shot through Solange,
beginning in her center and radiating out to encompass
all of her.

He continued to press his member against her bottom
while he gently brought her to her first orgasm. Never
rushed, he seemed to sense how tenderly to touch her.
When she wanted it rougher. When to pull away and let
her get her bearings. Sometimes she liked to prolong
the sensations, to be teased and enticed, to be tor-
mented with the promise of release but when it was
within reach, to be denied it. Until, finally, she could not
wait any longer.

Rupert had to close his eyes to keep from exploding inside his briefs. Her soft cries, filled with passion, aroused
him, made him want to bend her over further and take

her from behind. He was using two fingers now. One on either side of her labia. It flowered under his patient caresses. He felt her quiver. Felt more lubrication on his fingers. Heard her panting now. That was when he pulled the waistband of his briefs down below his fully erect shaft and entered her from behind. They both moaned.

She, because his upwardly pointing penis was brushing against her clitoris and, he because entering her felt so good to him, he could not help broadcasting the fact.

She was hot, and tight, and slick all at once.

It took all his willpower to pull out and coax her onto her back on the bed. He wanted to see her face when she came again. The good thing about having a bed that sat so high off the floor was that Rupert could easily stand and thrust deeply between her legs. He stood now, pumping her, holding onto either sides of her hips, raising her behind off the bed as he gave her everything he had. Solange's feet were resting on his collarbones as he pulled her closer, closer until he came. Warmth spread inside of her. Rupert felt her thigh muscles spasm. He pulled out of her, and gathered her into his arms. "I'm going to give you a massage after our shower."

Then, he picked her up and carried her into the bathroom.

Thirteen

Desta was too excited to be nervous. She breezed right through the reservations desk at the airport. Couldn't remember handing anyone her ticket but she was, miraculously, aboard the wide-bodied airplane and sitting in an aisle seat. Mr. Manawi had wished her a safe trip. She did recall that part. She'd given him an impulsive hug. Mr. Manawi had seemed embarrassed by her show of gratitude. But he'd hugged her firmly and set her away from him. "Don't forget us," he'd said.

Forget them? Never. Desta loved them all. They'd shown her that not all orphanages were poorly run. She had felt safe and happy in their care.

"Young lady, you're in my seat," a British man of about thirty told her. He looked down at her with such disdain that Desta's hackles immediately rose. She had been a street kid, after all. Nobody pushed around a street kid. However, she had promised Solange and Rupert she would behave herself. She couldn't break that vow. So, she peered up at the man who had long dark hair tucked behind his ears, gray eyes, and a rather large nose, and said in her best British accent, "Do forgive me." She got up and moved to the next seat.

He sat his carry-on bag in the aisle seat. Desta pretended she was fascinated by something out the window when, in reality, she was paying attention to him. He groaned as he grasped the carry-on bag and stored it in the overhead compartment.

Desta wondered what he had in his bag that was so heavy. He didn't appear particularly weak. He was around five-eleven, and a hundred and sixty pounds. Trim, but not emaciated. He was dressed like a tourist, in her estimation. Khaki shorts, short-sleeve denim shirt, ankle boots, and socks. She hadn't missed the camera bag, either.

After stowing his bag, he sat down. Bit his bottom lip awhile. Twiddled his thumbs. Slapped the tops of his thighs with his hands. She thought he must be very eager to get under way.

An attractive flight attendant came to stand next to their seats. She addressed her comments to Desta: "I'm told this is your first flight, Miss Roba. If you need anything at all, please feel free to call on me. Enjoy your trip."

"Thank you, I will," Desta said, smiling up at her. She glanced at the name on the flight attendant's badge: Felicity Elliot.

Felicity nodded to the British guy as she prepared to leave. "Welcome back, Mr. Varner."

"Thank you, Felicity," Mr. Varner said.

Felicity smiled at each of them again before departing.

Desta sat back in her seat, smiling. Now, she knew his name.

The two of them were silent for several minutes. Then, Varner said, "I can see you're not the talkative type."

"I'm not supposed to speak to strangers."

"Good advice. However since Felicity was kind enough to call our names, we now know each other. Or, at least, our names. My name is Varner and you are Miss Roba. How do you do, Miss Roba?"

He held out his right hand. Desta gave it a firm shake.

"Very well, thank you, Mr. Varner."

They laughed.

"I'm sorry I was rather sour when I asked you to vacate my seat," he said. "But I woke up this morning realizing that I had to go back home, and I don't want to go back home."

"Why not?" Desta asked before decorum dictated she not ask such a personal question.

"Because I love your country," Mr. Varner replied. "I think it's the most beautiful place on earth. I think, perhaps, I am part Ethiopian."

Desta squinted at his white face. There was no indication whatsoever that he had a drop of Ethiopian blood in him. Perhaps he was Ethiopian in spirit, which suited most Ethiopians fine. They accepted honorary Ethiopians.

She smiled at him. "Yes, I believe you are."

Johnathan Varner immediately fell in love with her.

"I'm going to miss you," Rupert said.

"I'll be a twenty-minute drive away," Solange said. They were spooning in bed after making love. "And it'll only be for a week. We can go without sex for a week. It won't kill us."

"Might make me pretty sick, though," Rupert joked.

Solange laughed. "I've spoiled you."

"Yes, you have." He kissed the nape of her neck.

Rupert tweaked her nipple between his forefinger and his thumb.

"Ouch," said Solange.

"I wasn't squeezing hard."

"I know, but my breasts have been sore for a few days now. You don't think I should get a checkup, do you?"

"Of course you should get a checkup!" said Rupert.

"And the sooner, the better. Call your gynecologist first thing in the morning." He sat up, forcing her to sit up too, since he was holding her in his arms. Reaching over, he switched on the lamp sitting atop his nightstand. "Let me take a look."

They were both nude. Rupert turned toward her and reached out to gently place his hands on her breasts. He peered closely. He even lifted them to look underneath them.

"You don't have any bruises."

Solange met his eyes. "If you're finished feeling me up, I'd like to tell you about something I read in a brochure that I picked up in Darrell's office the last time I was there."

Rupert continued touching her breasts. "Can't you talk while I feel?"

"It's one of the early symptoms of pregnancy. Sore breasts."

Rupert grinned. "I knew it! You're pregnant. You probably conceived the moment I got back from Mauritania."

"Wait until I have a pregnancy test before you start assuming I'm pregnant."

Rupert kissed her mouth briefly and climbed out of the bed. He did a little dance at the foot of the bed. "You're having my baby! Our boy, or girl!"

"It'll be our second girl, if it's a girl," Solange put in.

She knelt on the bed. "Are you sure you're ready to be a father to two children?"

"Ready or not, here they come," Rupert said. But she could tell by the joy in his gorgeous eyes that he was more than ready. He came to her and pulled her into his arms. "Oh, baby, I'm looking forward to being a daddy. I'll gladly change diapers and do two A.M. feedings. I'll be soccer dad, and chauffeur dad, and PTA dad."

Solange had to pull him down onto the bed and kiss him to shut him up, he was so excited by the prospect of becoming a father.

The next morning, she phoned Darrell Van Ness's office and got one of his nurses, Christine Williams. Solange had been coming into Darrell's office for years, and Chris had been with Darrell since he opened his doors. She recognized Solange's voice.

"Dr. DuPree, good morning. What can I do for you?"

"Hi, Chris." Solange recognized her voice, too. "I haven't had a period in two months, and my breasts are sore. Do you think I should come in to see Darrell?"

"Of course you should!" Chris said, mirroring Rupert's sentiments of the night before. "Be here by noon. We'll work you in."

"Thank you, Chris. I'll see you then."

Solange hung up the phone and accepted the cup of tea Rupert was holding out to her. They were in the kitchen, standing in front of the window. Rupert stood behind her with his arms about her waist. "Big day," Solange said, leaning into his embrace.

"I could find out I'm pregnant, and Desta gets in at ten tonight."

Rupert was silent, too full to speak at the moment. Everything he'd ever wanted was within his reach. In a little over a week, he and Solange would be married. But Aziz was still out there somewhere.

"Baby, this idea of yours to stay at your mother's until the wedding just to set an example for Desta doesn't make any sense under the circumstances."

"Thorne said three agents would be guarding Maman's house at all times," Solange reminded him. "We'll be safe."

"I would prefer to be in the house," Rupert said. "We don't have to sleep together. Besides, Desta probably already knows we sleep together. She's smart. Kids are aware of more than we give them credit for."

"You're right, kids know everything nowadays. But I would feel better if we didn't stay in the same house once she gets here. Not until we're married. It's only for a week!"

Rupert let go of her, and they faced one another. "I'm nervous, Solange. The closer it gets to the wedding, the more I'm convinced that Aziz is getting ready to strike."

"That's just it, we don't know when he's going to strike. We can't keep arranging our lives around him. If he comes, he comes."

Rupert smiled at her. "Okay, you win. I guess I'll camp out with the agents who will be on surveillance because I'm not going to be far from you."

"Thanks, baby. Plus, time at Maman's will give her and Desta a chance to get acquainted. After all, she's going to be staying with Maman while we honeymoon."

"Okay, okay," Rupert said. "I still don't feel good about it, but we'll try to make it work."

"I'm coming home," Sidney said. "I'll get in next Saturday."

Dani sighed on her end. "That's the twenty-sixth. I have a wedding that day. I'll have my hands full all day long."

"You mean I won't be able to be with you when I return?" Sidney asked, sounding very disappointed. "It's been so long, Dani. I dreamed about being with you again the whole time I've been away. My father is gone. My mother is gone. All I have left are two sisters and a brother in my immediate family. Many cousins, aunts and uncles. But right now, it's you I want to be with. You have been my salvation, Dani.

"In more ways than one. I will explain when I see you again. So, that's going to have to be on Sunday? Okay, but please make it Sunday morning. I don't think I can wait much longer than that."

"Come to the wedding," Dani said, proud of herself for coming up with a solution. "I will be busier than a one-armed paper hanger, but I will make time to be with you. I promise."

"Oh, I couldn't, Dani. I don't even know the people who are getting married."

"They're good people, darling. They will welcome you. Wear a nice suit. I want to dance with you at the reception. Now, here's the address and the time . . ."

"Relax, Solange. You're tense," Darrell said as he ran the cold sonogram attachment over Solange's belly. Darrell's eyes remained on the screen of the monitor. Solange was watching it, too. But from her angle, everything was indistinguishable. All she saw were dark images on the screen.

"See anything?" she asked Darrell.

Darrell suddenly grinned from ear to ear. "I see a little tadpole, yeah."

"Oh, God, Darrell. Are you sure?"

"I'm positive," Darrell assured her. "It definitely wasn't there the last time I looked."

"I thought if I was pregnant, it would be too early to see anything!" Solange gushed.

She wanted to sit up, but she didn't dare move and make Darrell lose his spot.

"Hold still," cautioned Darrell. "I'm taking your picture. Well, your baby's first snapshot." He continued to smile happily. "I see you and Rupert didn't waste any time. You two got busy, and I mean busy!"

Solange was laughing and crying at the same time.

Darrell looked over at Yolanda, his nurse, and said, "Yolanda, go get that big gentleman in the waiting room and bring him back here."

Yolanda hurried off.

She returned a couple of minutes later with Rupert in tow. Rupert went straight to Solange and clasped her hand in his. "Baby, are you okay? Yolanda told me to come quickly." He looked at Darrell. "What's going on, man?"

Darrell pointed at the monitor. "Take a gander at your son, or daughter, my man!"

Rupert peered closely at the monitor. Darrell pointed at the small dark mass that was his and Solange's child. "Congratulations, you're a father!" Darrell said.

Tears came to Rupert's eyes. He bent and repeatedly kissed Solange on the mouth.

"I'm so blessed. Thank you, sweetness. Thank you for making me a father, twice!"

Darrell began putting the equipment away. "You can sit up now, Solange."

Rupert helped Solange to a sitting position, and pulled her into his arms. "How do you feel?"

"I feel fine." She smiled wonderingly. "I feel great!"

Rupert offered Darrell his hand. The two men shook. "Thanks, Doctor."

"Don't thank me, thank the Big Guy. He's the one who made this miracle happen, not me," said Darrell. "But I'm glad I'm here to witness it."

They let their hands fall to their sides. Rupert looked heavenward and cried, "Thank you, God!" Then he looked at Darrell again. "Can I take her home now? Any instructions? What can she eat? Can she continue swimming? She loves to swim."

"Calm down, Rupert," Darrell said. "Solange is healthy. I'm writing her a prescription for prenatal vitamins, but other than that, she should simply eat right, get plenty of rest, and exercise moderately. Swimming is okay for practically her entire pregnancy. I'll be advising her as she comes in for regular checkups. For now, you two should get out of here and go celebrate."

To Solange, he said, "I'll see you in about a month. Stop at the reception desk to pick up your prescription and make an appointment."

"Okay, thanks," Rupert answered for Solange. Then, he scooped her up into his arms and headed for the door.

"Oh, Rupert," Darrell said, almost as an afterthought. "Let her put some clothes on."

"Yeah, right, I forgot about that," Rupert said, and gently put Solange back down.

In the car on the way home, Rupert couldn't stop stealing glances at Solange as he drove. Had she gotten even more beautiful in the space of a few minutes, or was it his perception that had changed? Before this moment, he didn't think he could love her any deeper than he already loved her. But, somehow, he did.

Then, all of a sudden, he was struck by a feeling of guilt. He felt hypocritical for being so happy about this baby when he'd told her he would love her forever even if they could never have a child together. Had his words been empty platitudes?

No. They had not been just words. He had proved that over the months he had relentlessly courted her before she'd relented to marry him. No, his love was not a conditional love. He had adored her even when they'd believed this day would never come. They had transcended the physical and crossed over to the spiritual.

He smiled to himself. Funny, how loving her had made him a man of deep faith. Faith in God. Faith in the possiblity of an enduring life of love and giving with her and their children. A family man. He was a family man.

Solange turned and met his eyes. She'd been day-
dreaming. Thinking about her life more than two years
ago before this man came into her life. She had not been
especially unhappy. She would have described herself as
fairly content.

She was working in a field she loved, had been successful. She had good friends. A good relationship with her
father, if not her mother. She'd settled for limited happiness. With Rupert she felt as if there were no limits on
happiness. Happiness could be boundless. Happiness
could be piled upon happiness, and there'd still be room
for more. She wouldn't say that Rupert completed her, because she felt that a woman had to complete herself
before she could find happiness with any man. But Rupert
had certainly enhanced her life. He was the yang to her
yin. They were opposites that complemented each other.

"A penny for your thoughts?" Rupert said, breaking
into her reverie.

"I was thinking about how much you've brought to my
life."

"Me?" Rupert said. "Until I met you, I didn't even
think about becoming a husband and a father. And now,
I can think of nothing else. Right now, my darling, you
could ask me for anything, and I'd give it to you."

"Anything?" Solange said softly. She watched his
square-jawed face for some indication that he was not
wholly serious.

Rupert laughed shortly. "Yes, anything. Even the
Kingston house if that's what you were getting ready to
ask for."

"No. I had another thought about which house we
should buy. I thought we'd let Desta decide. She is, after
all, the other party who will be living in the house. If you
agree, we should not try to influence her to either of our
sides."

"Let a thirteen-year-old decide where we're going to live?" Rupert sounded skeptical.

"Look at it this way," Solange suggested. "We've had both houses tested for soundness. They're in great shape. In the case of the Kingston house, which is nearly fifty years old, there is no sign of termites. The plumbing's practically new, as is the roof, and the air and heating system. The upkeep on it has been exceptional. The grounds are gorgeous."

"Okay, okay," Rupert said, interrupting her. "I get you. No matter which house Desta chooses, we'll be in good shape. Okay, we'll let her make the final decision. But we can't tell her which house each of us prefers."

"Afraid I'll have the advantage?" Solange asked. "Because she adores you, you know. She thinks of you as the black James Bond, and she's quite fond of James Bond."

"Oh, Lord," said Rupert. "We're going to have to disabuse the poor child of that notion right away." He briefly glanced at her. "And, yes, I do believe she would vote on the side of her mother because her mother is so charming. I'm tempted to vote on her side as well."

"You devil, you," said Solange, and leaned over to kiss his cheek.

Rupert kept his attention on his driving. "Now, tell me what you want right now more than anything else, and your wish is my command."

"I want to tell Maman I'm pregnant," Solange said.

"Where is she?"

"At her office."

Rupert changed lanes. "No problem."

Marie's office was located in downtown Coral Gables in a multistory complex that housed businesses that offered services that ran the gamut—advertising, accounting, law firms, architectural firms. Hers was the only decorating business in the location, which she appreciated.

Solange and Rupert walked into the office—two fresh young people attired in casual clothing and wearing Ray Bans. Solange was in a white, sleeveless sheath, whose hem fell a couple of inches above her knees, and white sandals with two-inch heels. Rupert in his favorite pair of loose-fit jeans, a black polo shirt, and a pair of black Italian loafers, no socks.

The majority of the people employed in the showroom were women. Their eyes followed Rupert all the way to the receptionist's desk where they stopped to ask if Marie could see them.

The receptionist, a middle-aged, small but stout black woman named Rose, took one look at Solange and got out of her chair. "Solange! What a pleasant surprise. I haven't seen you in a long time." She leaned over the desk to give Solange a quick hug.

Her gaze moved to Rupert.

"Rose, this is my fiancé, Rupert Giles. Rupert, this is Rose Young. She's been with Maman for years."

Rupert smiled at her. "Hello, Ms. Young."

"Oh, honey, call me Rose."

"Rose, it is," said Rupert graciously. "If you'll call me Rupert."

"Be glad to," Rose said, smiling. Because her skin was a translucent pale golden brown, her blush was noticeable. She tried to hide her flushed expression by donning the mantle of professionalism. "You're probably wondering if your mother is busy or not," she said, her eyes back on Solange. "Actually, she's in a meeting with a client. But she should be finishing up soon. So, if you and Rupert would like to have a seat, I'd be glad to get you something to drink while you wait."

"Thank you, Rose," Solange said. She glanced up at Rupert. "Would you like something to drink while we wait?"

Rupert smiled at Rose. "Coffee would be nice. Thank you."

"Nothing for me, Rose. Thanks," said Solange.

She and Rupert walked over to the waiting area, which was in an alcove that afforded them some privacy. They were the only ones in the room. They sat on deep purple cotton-linen upholstered chairs. Rupert pulled his chair closer to hers. "I should have known you were pregnant," he said in low tones. Their faces were inches apart. "Your skin is glowing, and your breasts. Your breasts are, for lack of a better word, ripe."

Solange could see the brown striations in his golden eyes. "Ripe for the plucking?"

"I've always loved your breasts," he said, his tone intimate and sensual. "But, then, I love every inch of you."

"I love every inch of you, too," Solange returned huskily. She kissed his soft, luscious lips. She ran her right hand over his head as they kissed, while her left hand was on the bulging bicep in his right arm.

Rose came upon them in this state. She cleared her throat. "Here's your coffee, Mr . . . Rupert."

Solange and Rupert parted, Rupert looking as composed as ever. Solange's face burned with embarrassment. Rupert accepted the cup of coffee Rose was handing him.

On the saucer she'd included small containers of creamer and two packets of sugar, along with a teaspoon. "We're out of artificial sweetner," Rose said apologetically.

"Thank you, Rose," said Rupert, smiling warmly at her. "I prefer real sugar anyway." Blushing again, Rose regarded Solange. "Your mother told me to tell you she'll be done in about ten minutes." She smiled at her. "Congratulations on your upcoming marriage." Rupert was busy stirring creamer into his coffee.

Rose bent next to Solange's ear. "You're a lucky, lucky girl!" she said in a low voice. She straightened, smiled at

Solange again, took one last look at Rupert and left them, mumbling, "Doggone lucky!"

"Thank you, Rose," Solange called after her.

When she thought Rose was out of earshot, she told Rupert, "You have yet another name to add to your long list of female admirers."

"'A rose by any other name would smell as sweet,'" Rupert quoted Shakespeare, a mischievous glint in his eyes.

Solange just smiled and shook her head.

Marie came out to greet them perhaps fifteen minutes later. The consummate professional when at work, she wore a navy blue skirt suit, whose skirt hem fell just above her knees. The long-sleeve, short-waisted jacket was collarless, and the camisole underneath was baby blue. The color blue favorably complemented her skin tone and her black, silver-streaked hair.

She looked from Solange to Rupert. "You two got my receptionist so flustered the poor woman had to take a long break in order to go home and get her black cohosh. For those of us present who don't know what that is, it's an herb that has plant estrogens in it, and it helps control hot flashes in menopausal women." She narrowed her eyes at her soon-to-be son-in-law. "Check your charm at the door from now on."

"Yes, Maman," Rupert said, his brows furrowed.

Of course, when he called her that, Marie's icy facade melted. She went to him and kissed him on the cheek, which could only be accomplished with his cooperation since he was over a foot taller than she was. Marie smoothed her jacket. "To what do I owe the pleasure of your company?" she asked them, looking expectantly at Solange, whom she hadn't even remembered to kiss hello.

"Maybe you ought to sit down for this," Solange began.

"I don't have time to sit down, sweetheart," Marie

told her. "I have another client coming in at two, and it's almost two now."

"I insist that you sit down," Solange said.

"All right," Marie relented, going to sit on one of the purple chairs.

Solange and Rupert took seats across from her, and leaned toward her.

"About two months ago Darrell Van Ness told me it appeared that my infertility problem had cleared up," Solange said. She waited for that to sink in before continuing.

"What do you mean, 'cleared up'?"

"My ovaries spontaneously healed themselves."

"Just like that?"

"Darrell couldn't explain it. He calls it a miracle."

Marie's facial expression went from no-nonsense to intense interest. "Go on, what else did he tell you? If your ovaries are healed, does that mean you may be able to conceive a child? Come on, baby. Don't leave me in suspense."

"Apparently so," Solange said. "Because we've just returned from Darrell's office, and he says I'm pregnant."

Marie's mouth opened, her eyes grew large, then she threw up her hands and let out a bloodcurdling scream. "Oh, my baby! My baby's going to have a baby!"

She and Solange came out of their chairs simultaneously and hugged fiercely.

Marie held her daughter at arm's length to look into her dear face. "I'm so happy for you." She hugged her tightly again, and rocked her from side to side. "What a momentous day! Desta's coming home tonight, and now I'm told I'm going to become a grandmother again in about what? Seven months?"

Several of her employees had come running when they'd heard her screams. Five women and three men stood around them in a semicircle, waiting to be told what had made their usually composed boss scream like a banshee.

"We're having a baby," Marie told them.

To which everyone applauded, and heartily congratulated Solange, Rupert, and the very happy Marie.

Desta said good bye to Johnathan Varner in London. Then she was escorted to another carrier at Heathrow, where she later boarded a plane en route to New York City. This time she would not need to switch planes. She would remain on the plane while those who were going to New York disembarked. She had not slept the entire trip. As she sat down on the plane headed to New York, she felt a bit weary.

She did not want to miss anything, though, so she tried her best to stay alert. The lids of her dark brown eyes grew heavy in spite of her efforts. By the time her seatmate arrived, she was fast asleep next to the window with her head on her shoulder bag. Her seat mate, Mrs. Evangeline Chandler, an elderly woman who had been around the world twice, didn't have the heart to wake her and tell her the window seat had been assigned to her, so she took the aisle seat. When Desta woke, she'd passed through several time zones, and it was daylight again. Her stomach growled.

"I heard that," said Mrs. Chandler. Her brown eyes twinkled in her wrinkled face. "You must be ravenous. How long have you been traveling?"

Desta sat up. Her hair had come loose while she had slept. She usually wore it in a braid down her back. It was very dark brown, extremely wavy, and fell nearly to her waist. She had no control over it whatsoever. "Eight hours, I think," she said.

She held out her hand. "Hello, I'm Desta Roba from Addis Ababa."

Mrs. Chandler shook her hand. "Pleased to meet you, Desta. I'm Evangeline Chandler from Miami, Florida."

Desta perked right up. "Miami! That's where I'm going."

"All by yourself?" asked Mrs. Chandler.

"Yes, I'm going to be with my new mother and father."

"New mother and father?"

"I was adopted recently. My new name is Desta Roba DuPree-Giles."

"That's a mouthful," Mrs. Chandler said, laughing softly, mindful of the other passengers who were trying to catch a few winks. "About your growling stomach. You slept through dinner. Why don't I get up and see if I can find a flight attendant and convince her to get you something to eat? All I have in my bag is a rather old apple that I saved from lunch." She went in her bag anyway and brought out a Granny Smith apple. "You can nibble on that until I can get you something more substantial to put in your stomach."

"Thank you," said Desta, accepting the apple. As she watched Mrs. Chandler, a rather tall, slender woman wearing slacks and a sweatshirt, probably to guard against the chill of the airplane's air conditioning, she fleetingly thought of the fairy tale she had recently read, *Snow White*. In it an evil elderly woman, the witch, had given Snow White a juicy red apple. As soon as Snow White had bitten into it, she'd fallen into a death-like sleep. Desta bit into the apple, defying her overactive imagination. Mrs. Chandler wasn't a wicked witch, after all. She was simply a kind old woman who'd taken pity on a child.

Desta had finished eating the apple by the time Mrs. Chandler returned with a flight attendant who graciously

served Desta a hot meal of fried chicken, mashed pota-
toes, and peas, with a brownie for dessert. She gave her a
can of Pepsi to wash it all down with. Desta thanked her
profusely, and when she had gone, she smiled at Mrs.
Chandler, who had copped a brownie and a small carton
of milk for herself, and said, "Many thanks, Mrs. Chandler.
You're my guardian angel."

Mrs. Chandler grinned with chocolate-covered teeth.
"My pleasure, child. Eat up."

Desta dug into her food with vigor.

"Solange, will you sit down?" Marie said. She and
Theophilus were sitting next to each other in the waiting area of the American Airlines terminal at Miami
International Airport. Solange and Rupert had been sitting across from them, but now neither of them were
sitting; they were pacing. Parents. They were parents.
The impact of that new title seemed to have struck them
both the moment they arrived and had begun waiting
for Desta to step off the plane and walk down the long
aisle that led to this area. Solange had not been able to
decide what to wear tonight, knowing full well that it
wouldn't matter to Desta what she had on. Desta just
wanted her to be there to meet her. She'd settled on
jeans and a short-sleeve blouse. She knew Desta was
wearing jeans, and she wanted them to be matching. *Oh,
Lord, I hope I'm not going to be one of those mothers who's always trying to dress my daughter like a mini-me*, she thought
irritably.

Rupert was pacing out of sympathy for Solange. He
could have sat and worried about his incompetence as
a father. He knew he would make mistakes. All fathers
made mistakes. They would work things out together. He
had the utmost confidence in Desta. Solange, too. She

was going to be a wonderful mother. The two of them would help him along. Steadfast. That was probably his best quality. He was faithful.

He would always be there for them. He knew that. The rest would have to come later.

"If you think you're nervous now, wait until the baby comes," Marie informed them from her seat beside Theophilus. "Desta is thirteen. The baby is really going to depend on you for everything."

"They can handle it. They're young," Theophilus said. "I'm sure you remember when Solange was born. Did you worry for one minute that you wouldn't be able to handle taking care of her?"

"I didn't have time to worry," Marie said. "I was too busy changing diapers, feeding her, bathing her, rocking her to sleep, checking on her while she was sleeping to make sure she was still breathing. Back then, we were told to put them to bed on their stomachs. Now, we find out that babies should be put to bed on their backs to help prevent sudden infant death syndrome. Lord, having a baby is the most joyous thing in the world and the most nerve-wracking!"

"Amen," Theophilus concurred. "Once, when Samantha was about three months old, both Francesca and I were short on sleep. Francesca went and got Samantha out of her crib to breastfeed her. She was so exhausted, she fell asleep while she was feeding her. I woke up, found both of them asleep, took Samantha out of her arms, changed her, and put her back in her crib. I then went back to sleep. Francesca woke up a couple hours later, found the baby no longer in her arms, and panicked. Took me a while to calm her down."

"Sleep deprivation," Marie said sympathetically. She liked it when he talked about his late wife, Francesca. When he spoke of her, Marie could hear the tenderness in his voice. She was glad he had loved Francesca. A man who had truly loved his late wife, and who knew she would want him to be happy after her death, had the capacity to love another woman. It was the man who'd had a bad marriage who found it hard to accept love when it came into his life. And God help the poor woman who fell in love with him. She would have a hard time convincing him he was worthy of the love she was offering.

"The plane's here," Rupert said suddenly. He had been watching the arrival and departure board like a hawk, and had seen the arrival time the instant it had flashed across the board. All four of them got up and went to stand where Desta would see them as soon as she came into the terminal.

Solange was the first to spot her, walking beside a tall, elderly woman. Her heart began beating faster at the sight of Desta. It looked like she'd grown an inch since she'd seen her last. "There she is!" she cried.

"Where?" asked Marie.

"Right next to the tall, white-haired woman in the University of Miami sweatshirt," Solange said, pointing excitedly.

Finally, they were free to rush forward and hug her. Rupert was fastest, and reached her before the others. He picked her up in a bear hug, Desta giggling all the while. When he set her down, Solange hugged her and kissed both cheeks. "Hello, baby girl. Welcome home. Let me introduce you to your grandma. You already know your grandpa."

Marie couldn't wait. She stepped forward and hugged Desta so tightly poor Desta looked as if she might need rescuing. "Hello, darling."

"Grandma!" Desta exclaimed, tears in her eyes.

All of the females were crying now. The men sniffed and held onto their manly pride. After Theophilus had embraced his granddaughter, Desta took a step back to take all of them in. "Now, I want you all to meet a friend of mine."

She waved the white-haired woman over. "This is Mrs. Evangeline Chandler. We sat together all the way from New York City."

"Dr. Chandler," Solange said, recognizing the retired anthropology professor. "It's wonderful to see you again."

Fourteen

"It's beautiful, Grandma, thank you," Desta said when she saw her bedroom at Marie's house. Marie had avoided decorating the room in too girlish a manner. She'd given Desta a room in which a young woman would be comfortable. It was furnished with a full-size antique bed painted white and striated in blue, and matching nightstands and lamps with bright yellow shades. It had a large walk-in closet. A girl appreciated closet space. And her own bathroom. The walls were a soft eggshell white.

"Once you get settled in, we'll go looking for accessories that will personalize your space," her new grandma told her. She kissed Desta's forehead. "Good night, sweetie."

Alone with Solange, Desta looked around her. She had not stopped smiling since she'd gotten off the plane. Once they had gotten her to Marie's house, Solange had explained to her that this arrangement was temporary, just until she and Rupert returned from their honeymoon.

Now, she took her by the hand and led her over to the bed. "Sit down, sweetie. I want to talk with you about something important."

Desta sat down and regarded Solange with a serious expression. "What is it?"

Solange sat next to her on the bed and placed her shoulder bag on her lap. She reached inside it and withdrew an 8 × 11 inch–picture frame. Handing it to Desta, she said, "Do you remember my telling you about Mr. James Tan of the U.S. embassy in Addis Ababa? How he helped move your case along?"

Desta nodded. "Yes, I remember." She looked down at the photograph she was holding in her hands. It was of a good-looking Ethiopian couple in their twenties, and two children: a boy of around nine, and a little girl of around five.

"That's your father, Hailu, and your mother, Terunesh. The little boy is Tesfaye, and of course you recognize yourself," Solange said softly. "Mr. Tan found the photograph in the archives of an Addis Ababa newspaper. He called the publisher and asked them if they still had the original. They did, and he sent it to me to give to you. I put it in this frame so you can sit it on your nightstand or hang it on your wall, whichever you wish." Her voice caught at the end.

Tears rolled down Desta's cheeks. "I don't remember them," she said.

Solange put her arms around her. "It's okay, sweetie. You remember them with your heart, even if you can't remember them in your mind's eye. And now that you have a photograph of them, good memories will eventually return. Wait, you'll see."

Desta stood the photograph on her nightstand, then she turned into Solange's embrace and hugged her with all her might. "Thank you, Solange. Thank you for loving me."

"Oh, baby, that was easy to do," Solange told her.

They hugged a while longer, then Solange said, "I suppose you're tired?"

"A little," Desta admitted.

Solange rose. "Would you like me to help you unpack your things? You know, just the things you're going to need tonight. We can put away the rest of your things in the morning."

"No," Desta told her. "I put my pajamas and toothbrush right where I could find them in case I was too tired to think clearly. I'm just going to shower and go to bed."

Solange was disappointed Desta didn't need her assistance, but she put on a cheerful face and said good night. "All right then, I'll be right next door. If you wake up and need anything, just knock on my door. Unless you want me to sleep in here with you your first night. Things probably appear strange to you."

Desta smiled at her. "I'm fine, Solange. I'm with my family now. I'm going to be fine."

Solange came forward and impulsively hugged her again. "Okay, I promised myself that I wouldn't smother you. Good night."

"Good night," said Desta, yawning.

After Solange left, Desta got up and stood in the middle of the room, looking all around her. "I can't believe I'm finally here." Then, she took care of her needs, and went to bed and slept soundly. The firm mattress her grandma had on her bed was certainly more comfortable than the bed at the orphanage, and a hundred times better than the ground upon which she'd slept many times in the past. She slept like a baby.

"Giles, if I had known you would be joining us tonight, I would have invested in more air freshener," Joanne said jokingly. She, Giles, and Thorne were all in the van parked across the street from Marie DuPree's two-story home in Coral Gables. "Now I have two men stinking up my air."

"I'll have you know I bathe on a regular basis. I haven't had body odor since I was a recruit in boot camp."

"That's not what she means," Thorne told him. "You

see Harris, here, is in a snit because she hasn't been with a man in months. She's talking about our stinking up her air with testosterone."

"That was a little more than I needed to know, Thorne," Rupert said, narrowing his eyes at Thorne. "Whatever's going on between you and Harris is your business. I'm here because I don't want to be clear across town if Solange needs me."

"Yeah, yeah, we got that," Thorne put in with a smirk. "Super Giles to the rescue. As if we couldn't handle it."

"Well, you haven't been handling it," Rupert said, testily.

"Screw you, Giles!"

"Screw yourself, Thorne!"

"Now, boys, can't we behave like adults and stop picking fights?"

"Stay out of it, Harris," Thorne ordered.

"I don't have to stay out of anything," Harris said. "Why don't you just admit to Giles that you're jealous of what he has with Solange and get it off your chest, huh?"

"Jealous? Are you completely daft? I'm not jealous of a man who is going to be sleeping with the same woman for the rest of his life. Because that's Giles. He's like a faithful old dog. I'm a lone wolf. I can't be with one woman for the rest of my life. Jealous? I pity the fool."

Rupert laughed. "Don't waste your time pitying me. Solange is pregnant. We have everything we could hope for. Once Aziz has been dealt with, we can get on with our lives."

"Pregnant?" Thorne said, as though it were a dreaded disease.

"Oh, you didn't catch that bit of news with your listening devices?" Rupert guessed.

"I should have known," Thorne said. "You've been going at it like rabbits on Viagra."

"Don't need Viagra," Rupert said happily.

"I ought to knock that smug look off your face," Thorne said through clenched teeth.

"Go ahead," Rupert challenged.

Thorne hit him right in the mouth.

Rupert slugged him in the nose.

Harris quickly got up and opened the double back doors of the van. "Take it outside, you lugheads!"

Rupert grabbed Thorne by the collar and the waistband of his jeans, and tossed him outside. He leapt onto him from the van. They rolled on the blacktop, upsetting a huge green plastic trash can that the homeowner whose house they were in front of had sat by the curb.

Rupert got in a good one to Thorne's jaw, and while Thorne was shaking his head, trying to shake some awareness back into it, Rupert got to his feet. Thorne slowly rose too, and began dancing on the balls of his feet as if he were Mike Tyson: fists raised, legs apart in a fighter's stance for optimum balance. Rupert just stood in one place, waiting for Thorne to charge. He didn't have to wait long. Thorne ran toward him, growling like a savage beast. Teeth bared.

Rupert dropped him flat on his back with a perfect roundhouse kick to the head, at which point Joanne jumped onto Rupert's back and locked her arms around his neck. "All right, that's enough. You win, you big bully. You've proven that you can still kick butt."

Rupert shrugged her off of his back and glared at her. "I don't have time for these mind games. If Thorne has a problem, there are agency shrinks he can see. I only have one goal, and that's to make certain nothing happens to the people in that house!"

Thorne had roused and pulled himself to a sitting position on the pavement. Joanne went over and offered him a hand up. He refused her help and got to his feet on his own. Joanne suspected he was embarrassed.

She turned her back on him and went back into the van, leaving them outside facing one another. They moved around each other as if they were about to trade blows again.

"You left without even a good-bye," Thorne accused him.

Rupert was stunned. "What? Is that what this is all about? I left the agency without saying good-bye to you?"

"I thought we were friends."

"We were friends."

"Friends don't leave without saying good-bye."

"I figured since I left because I no longer could support the agency's views, you wouldn't want anything to do with me," Rupert told him frankly. "After all, you were still an operative."

"You were the only friend I had at the agency," Thorne said. He gingerly touched his bleeding nose.

Rupert knew how he felt. The truth was, Thorne had been the closest thing he had to a friend in the agency, too. But Rupert had felt he had to cut off everything associated with that way of life when he'd severed ties with them. That included Thorne. He had not, for one minute, assumed Thorne might think of him as anything other than a partner in espionage.

"Look, Jason," Rupert began. It was the first time he'd called him Jason since they'd met up again in London when all this had begun. "If I had thought that you and I could remain chums, knowing what we knew about each other, I would have stayed in touch. But the fact is, I figured not saying anything to you about my plans to leave, nor afterward, was best for the both of us. It was not my intention to make you feel as if the friendship we'd forged working together all those years had meant nothing to me because that's not true."

"Don't get mushy on me, Giles," Jason said. "I just

wanted you to know that I thought you were a bastard for leaving the way that you did, that's all. This isn't a reunion. I've got your back in this operation, just like I always did back in the day. You don't have to worry about me performing when the time comes because I'll do my job."

Rupert brushed sand off his jeans. "All right, then," he said, turning to go back to the van. Thorne followed him.

Joanne met them at the van door. "Have you boys kissed and made up?"

"Shut up, Harris," Thorne said with a laugh.

She stepped back and let them inside. Peering at Rupert's face she said, "Let's hope those bruises are healed before your wedding on Saturday."

Desta slept late the next morning, and when she got up she found her new parents and her grandma at the kitchen table eating breakfast. "Nobody woke me," she said as she went and sat down in the empty chair between Rupert and her grandma. Solange sprang up and went around the table to kiss her cheek. "Good morning, Des. Did you sleep well?"

"Oh, yes," said Desta. "I dreamed I was back in the orphanage. When I woke here, I still felt like I was dreaming. Then I came looking for you, and realized I was not dreaming. I'm really here."

Her grandma leaned over and kissed her cheek. "Yes, darling, and you're going to stay here. Now, eat up. We're going shopping today. We've got to get your dress for the wedding."

Desta was looking at Rupert. "Have you been in a fight?"

"Solange slugged me when I said she looked fat in those jeans," he joked. "Never tell a woman she looks fat in anything."

Solange looked at him as if she really might slug him.

* * *

The week leading up to the wedding was a busy one. Desta's head was in a spin. She was introduced to so many people, she had a hard time telling them apart. She immediately warmed to Peter Wychowski, and charmed the hyperactive Jimbo, who slowed down long enough to lay his head on her lap when she sat on the edge of Peter's porch while he and her parents chatted.

Then they took her to both houses, explaining that she was to choose which she liked best based on her own preferences. She was to think seriously of where she wanted to wake up every morning. After two days of thinking, she decided upon the Kingston house. When they asked her why she'd chosen that house, she told them, "It felt as if the spirits of those who'd lived there welcomed me. It feels like home. Besides, Peter and Jimbo are right down the street, and I like them very much."

Two days before the wedding was to take place, Gaea, Micah, and Micah Jr., who everyone called Mikey, arrived. They had booked a suite at the Biltmore, as had Toni Shaw Waters and her brood. The first night Gaea and her little family were in Miami, they all had dinner together at Marie's house.

After dinner, Gaea and Solange found a moment to stroll outside onto Marie's deck and sit down together. It was the only time they'd had the chance to talk. "I have to tell you, Pudge," Gaea said. "I've never seen you look so good. Whatever Rupert is doing, I hope he keeps doing it for the rest of your lives together. You're radiant."

"You just made a wish that I'd be pregnant for the rest of my life," Solange told her with a grin. Gaea jumped up and pulled Solange into her arms. They jumped up and down together the way they used to when they were girls. Tears were in Gaea's eyes when she looked down into Solange's tear-stained face. "You didn't call me!"

"And miss this reaction?" Solange said through her tears.

The day of the wedding arrived.

There had been no sign of Aziz since his appearance in Lily's on that fateful day when Dani had been stood up by Sidney. The voice comparison test had proved inconclusive. It might have been Aziz on the phone, and it might not have been.

As for the trace that the agency had put on the phone call, there was only one thing they knew for certain. The cell phone bill went to a Sidney Doucet. Therefore they were still uncertain as to Sidney Doucet's true identity.

The day of the wedding, Solange, Gaea, Desta, Samantha, and Marie moved into a suite at the Biltmore. All day long, there came knocks on the door as friends or family members arrived with congratulations.

The wedding was to begin at two in the afternoon.

At one-thirty, Solange asked everyone in the wedding party, who looked quite resplendent in their beautiful dresses, to give her some time alone. They filed out of the suite, each giving her a quick buss on the cheek as they left.

She then went to sit before the vanity and stare at her reflection in the mirror.

Her mother had been right about the shade of the dress bringing out the golden undertones in her brown skin. Her silky, black hair had never looked healthier. She wished she could muster up a smile. But the closer the hour of the wedding approached, the more she felt as if something awful was about to happen. She picked up the cell phone on the vanity top and dialed Thorne's number.

He picked up immediately. "No sign of him, Solange. Where are you? Aren't you supposed to be in the garden by now?"

"It's still early. I'm going down in about fifteen minutes."

Dani's heart leaped when she saw Sidney coming through the catering service area's double doors. She'd phoned him on her cell phone a few minutes ago to ask if he was on the way. He'd answered and told her he was and couldn't wait to see her. She'd then instructed him on how to get to the catering service area. Sidney looked so handsome in his camel-colored summer suit with a brown shirt underneath, and a brilliant gold-striped tie. Dani removed her headset. With it, she was in constant contact with her people who were working the wedding: her assistant, Nan, who was in the garden now, making certain guests were being seated properly; Gregory, who was in the huge kitchen, making sure the chef and his helpers would have the food ready by the time the reception was to begin. She would personally go get the bride in about ten minutes. For now, she gave Sidney her undivided attention.

They embraced, and she took him by the hand, leading him back out the door. "More privacy out here," she explained.

Sidney's dark eyes raked over her. "You look beautiful."

Indeed, Dani was as fresh as a tulip with dew on its petals in her white skirt suit. She gazed up at him with serious eyes. "Sidney, in your absence I came to realize how much you mean to me. And if there is any hope of a future for us, you've got to know something about me. Something I don't tell just anyone."

Sidney beamed. "There's something I should tell you, too, Danielle. Something I didn't have the courage to say to you before I went home and saw my family. I told them what was in my heart. Now I'm going to tell you, because I think I'm in love with you, and you have the right to know."

They were both so eager to disclose their secrets that they blurted them out simultaneously. Dani cried, "I was born Daniel, not Danielle. Sidney, I'm a man."

Sidney said, "Danielle, I've always been attracted to men. I've tried to fight it all my life. But until I met you, I'd never been attracted to a woman."

Somehow, each of them clearly heard what the other had said. Sidney shook his head in confusion. Dani removed the scarf from around her neck. "I'm in transition. I haven't been snipped yet."

Sidney understood then. Tears sat in his eyes. "I should have known I hadn't been miraculously cured of being gay. What was I thinking?"

Dani smiled at him. "I don't know what you were thinking, darling. But what you see is what you get. I'm a woman inside. I always have been. This is how I dress. I don't even own an item of men's clothing anymore. So, if you're attracted to men, then we may not be suited for each other."

Sidney smiled too. "No, Danielle. I think we're suited just fine. That is, if you can be convinced to give up the notion of that snipping you mentioned earlier."

"You mean you don't mind that I'm Danielle."

"No, not at all. I'm very attracted to you as Danielle." They embraced.

"Well," Dani told him. "If Alyce and Davis Kingston could fool people for nearly fifty years, I guess you and I can give it a go."

"Who are Alyce and Davis Kingston?" Sidney asked.

Dani didn't have the opportunity to answer because three men dressed in S.W.A.T fatigues descended on them and pushed Sidney roughly to the ground, securing his hands behind his back.

Solange was rounding the huge outdoor courtyard adjacent to the garden where the ceremony was to be held when she heard a sound from behind her. She turned and saw a waiter carrying a silver tray with a drink on it coming toward her. She continued walking. When the two of them were within four feet of each other, the waiter suddenly threw the tray with the drink on it into a nearby shrub. "We meet again, little pet."

He lurched forward, grabbing at her. Solange easily avoided him. His jaws clenched in rage. "What is this, rebellion? Your time is up. You will not become a bride today."

Solange screamed and ran.

Rupert heard her immediately. He had been standing under the gazebo with the minister. He bounded down the steps and ran in the direction he'd heard Solange scream. Thorne and Harris who were posing as guests, got up and ran after him.

Solange didn't know where she was going. She didn't know the layout of the grounds of the Biltmore. She could hear Aziz behind her—his heavy footfalls and labored breathing.

She didn't dare glance behind her for fear it would slow her down. She was nearing the large pool that was several hundred yards away from where the ceremony was to be held. She knew that much. She was running away from help, instead of toward it.

As Rupert ran, he withdrew his weapon from his shoulder holster. He rounded the corner of the building, and had a clear view of Aziz, dressed all in black, and the whiteness of Solange's wedding dress, like a bird in flight. He ran harder.

He could hear Thorne and Harris behind him.

Solange nearly tripped and fell into the pool as she raced around the edge of it.

Aziz's shoes, new leather, were slippery on the surface of the tiles. He also nearly fell into the water, and he had to slow down a bit to right himself.

Rupert came upon Aziz as he was struggling to stay on his feet. "Aziz, stop, or I'll shoot! Solange, get down!"

Aziz turned around, with a large handgun trained on Rupert.

Solange dove for a nearby flower bed.

Aziz's finger began squeezing the trigger, but before Rupert could get off a round, Thorne came out of nowhere and shot Aziz in the chest twice. He fell backward into the pool, floating on his back, his eyes looking but not seeing.

Rupert ran to gather Solange into his arms. "Oh, baby, are you all right?"

Solange burst into tears. "No, no, I'm a mess!"

Thorne looked back at Harris, who came up and hugged him from behind. "I'm tired of this job."

"What you need is a vacation," Harris said. "How does Jamaica sound?"

After Solange had calmed down sufficiently, the wedding commenced. Gaea walked down the aisle first, followed by Samantha. Desta stood beside her new father in the gazebo. She would stand next to him and Solange while they took their vows.

Georges walked Solange down the aisle and kissed her cheek before placing her hand in Rupert's. Solange took a moment to look out over the guests who had honored them with their presence.

Her friends Toni Shaw Waters and Charles Waters

were there sitting near their daughters, Georgette and Briane, and their husbands, Clayton and Dominic. Each of the young couples had brought their children with them. Georgette and Clay had twin girls, and Briane and Dominic had a son.

Micah was sitting down front with his and Gaea's son, Mikey. Jason and Joanne had returned to their seats and were smiling at her. Samantha's date, Chad Roberts, had eyes only for Samantha, who was in the gazebo with the rest of the wedding party.

Marie and Theophilus, Georges and Elena, and Benjamin and Helena Giles all had seats in the front. Solange saw Peter Wychowski and Alyce Kingston sitting together in the middle section. Lily and Adriano Calderon were sitting near them. Lily was blowing her kisses. And finally, Dani and Sidney were sitting in back, holding hands.

When the minister began the ceremony, Rupert interrupted him with, "Excuse me, father, but my best man phoned last night and said he'd broken his leg. I'm missing a best man." He looked into the audience. "Jason, would you mind filling in?"

Jason got up and joined them in the gazebo. Rupert slipped him the ring he'd been holding onto. "Thanks."

"No problem," said Thorne.

The minister continued with the ceremony.

Epilogue

"Mikey," Solange began.

"He likes to be called Mike now," Gaea told her best friend confidentially. They were sitting on lounge chairs poolside at Solange and Rupert's home. Gaea and her brood had come for a week's stay so that they could catch up with each other's lives and laze around in the sun. The two friends were watching their husbands and children splash in the pool while they chatted.

Solange was the mother of two now: Desta, fifteen, and sixteen-month-old Rupert Jr., who was clinging to his dad's neck in the pool. His dad was trying to coax him to let go. That wasn't going to happen anytime soon.

Solange grinned. "Oh, yeah, he's too old at six to be called Mikey anymore. Mike certainly does have an affinity for the water. He swims like a dolphin."

"I'll tell you a story about my Grandpa Cameron one of these days," Gaea said. "Everyone on that side of the family is particularly fond of the water."

"That's where you get it from," Solange said, looking at Gaea, who was fairly glowing in her seventh month of pregnancy. Solange's hands were clasped atop her own swollen belly. She was also seven months along. They'd placed friendly bets on who would give birth first.

Solange had let her hair grow during this pregnancy.

Now it was past her shoulders, lying in thick black braids that sparkled in the sunlight.

"Did you ever think, when we were girls growing up in Key West, that we'd ever be old, married women?" Solange asked Gaea.

Gaea reached over and clasped Solange's hand tightly in hers. "Never! Remember? We vowed to stay young forever, and never to let a boy come near us."

Solange suddenly felt cold, wet hands on her warm thigh. She looked down into the sweet, pudgy face of her son, who had managed to escape the clutches of his father, who was determined to teach him to swim. He peered up at her with those golden-hued eyes that were so much like his father's. "Mommy."

Solange reached for him and he came into her arms. Her heart melted whenever he called her Mommy. 'Ma' had been his first word. A few months later he was referring to her as Mommy. Only a parent can fully appreciate how the sound of a child's voice calling her name makes everything right with the world.

"Mom," said Desta from the other side of the pool. She was holding a cell phone in her right hand. "Grandma wants to know if she and Grandpa can take all of us kids to a matinee this afternoon while you old people enjoy some downtime. Her words, not mine." She was smiling mischievously as though she agreed with her grandmother's words, though.

"Do you think Mike would like to see the latest Disney film?" Solange asked Gaea.

"Yeah, Ma, I wanna go!" said Mike, who'd been listening in on the conversation.

"Fine with me," his mother said, one finger absentmindedly twirling a lock of her curly black hair.

"Tell her, yes, we'd love to get you rugrats out of our

hair for a few hours," Solange said. "But not to overload you with junk food."

"Aw, Mom," Desta moaned loudly. But she related the message just as her mother had instructed her.

Suddenly, Solange felt another pair of hands on her legs. These were big, strong and divinely familiar. She smiled down into the face of her honey, Rupert, who'd swum to the side of the pool to grab hold of her.

"Hello, beautiful," he said, his eyes possessively raking over her. "I can think of lots of ways to occupy our time with a whole child-free afternoon."

Solange blushed. "We've got guests," she said, cutting her eyes in Gaea's direction.

"They've got their own suite. Meet me in ours as soon as the grandparents come collect the kids."

Then he swam away, confident that she wasn't going to miss their rendezvous.

Shaking her head in mock consternation, Solange said, "See what I have to put up with?"

Gaea had heard the whole conversation. "At this rate," she said. "You'll give birth to number three before your fortieth birthday."

To which they burst out laughing.

Dear Reader,

Thank you for picking up one of my books. If you're a faithful reader, you know that *To Have and to Hold* is the sequel to my July 2002 book, *For Your Love*. Many of you wrote expressing a desire to see Rupert and Solange married. You also wanted to see Desta in a good home. *To Have and to Hold* is how I envisioned their wedding, and their lives. I hope you enjoyed it.

I certainly got a kick out of revisiting these characters.

This is farewell to Solange, Rupert, and Desta; and also to Toni Shaw-Waters and her family. I've had fun bringing them to life beginning with the novella, "To Love Again" in the *Love Letters* anthology. Then, bringing them back in *All the Right Reasons, A Second Chance at Love, For Your Love,* and finally in *To Have and to Hold.*

Feel free to drop me a line at Jani569432@aol.com, P.O. Box 811, Mascotte, FL 34753-0811, or leave me a message on my Web site at http://www.janicesims.com.

Thanks for staying with me for the entire ride.

Many blessings,
Janice Sims

ABOUT THE AUTHOR

Janice Sims is the author of ten novels. She has had stories in four anthologies. During her career, her work has been critically acclaimed, and she is deemed a favorite among readers.

She is the recipient of an Award of Excellence from Romance in Color for her 1999 novel, *For Keeps*. In 2000, she won the Novella of the Year Award from Romance in Color for "The Keys to My Heart," her contribution to the Arabesque Mother's Day anthology, *A Very Special Love*.

Romantic Times Book Club nominated her for their Career Achievement Award in 2000. She was nominated again in 2002.

She lives in Central Florida with her husband and daughter.

Enter the Arabesque 10th Anniversary Contest!

GRAND PRIZE: 1 Winner will receive:
- $10,000 Prize Package

FIRST PRIZE: 5 Winners will receive:
- Special 10th Anniversary limited edition gift
- 1 Year Arabesque Bookclub subscription

SECOND PRIZE: 10 Winners will receive:
- Special 10th Anniversary prize packs

ARABESQUE 10TH ANNIVERSARY CONTEST RULES:

- Contest open January 1–April 30, 2004.
- Mail-In Entries Only (postmarked by 4/30/04 and received by 5/7/04).
- On letter-size paper: Name your favorite Arabesque novel or author and why in 50 words or less.
- Include proof of purchase of an Arabesque novel (send ISBN).
- Include photograph/head shot (4x6 photo preferred, no larger than 5x7).
- Name, address, city, state, zip, daytime phone number and e-mail address.
- Contest entrants must be 21 years of age or older and live in the U.S.
- Only one entry allowed per person.
- Must be able to travel on dates specified: July 30-Aug 1, 2004.
- Send your entry to:

BET Books—10th Anniversary Contest
One BET Plaza
1235 W Street, NE
Washington, DC   20018